BRITISH ICE

OWEN D. POMERY

Published by Top Shelf Productions, PO Box 1282, Marietta, GA 30061-1282, USA. Top Shelf Productions is an imprint of IDW Publishing, a division of Idea and Design Works, LLC. Offices: 2765 Truxtun Road, San Diego, CA 92106. Top Shelf Productions®, the Top Shelf logo, Idea and Design Works®, and the IDW logo are registered trademarks of Idea and Design Works, LLC. All Rights Reserved. With the exception of small excerpts of artwork used for review purposes, none of the contents of this publication may be reprinted without the permission of IDW Publishing. IDW Publishing does not read or accept unsolicited submissions of ideas, stories or artwork.

Editor-in-Chief: Chris Staros.

Design assistance by Gilberto Lazcano.

Printed in Korea.

ISBN: 978-1-60309-460-3

23 22 21 20   4 3 2 1

Visit our online catalog at topshelfcomix.com.

BRITISH ICE

OWEN D. POMERY

TABLE OF CONTENTS

THE
BRITISH ARCTIC
TERRITORY

The British Arctic Territory consists of one main island with several smaller ones surrounding it, including inaccessible rocks and underwater formations. Its exact location cannot be disclosed due to an ongoing political dispute, but it is part of the Queen Elizabeth Islands, within the Arctic Circle.

Since its discovery in the early 1800s, it has remained British soil, maintaining its status despite Canada gaining its full independence in 1867. With a few exceptions, it has been almost constantly manned by a member of the British High Commission ever since. The remote outpost's endurance is due mainly to its inaccessibility, apparent lack of importance, and the fact that it is out of the public eye.

The centre of this colony was named by Captain J. Netherton; 'Reliance Island', after his ship. He also declared the entire area 'the gateway to the Arctic'. The indigenous people still call it 'Adle', which roughly translates as 'axe', due to its shape.

In the absence of facts, myth and legend have filled the gaps, with early British records and First Nations' accounts both describing the place, in their own ways, as 'cursed'.

PROLOGUE

ORIGINS

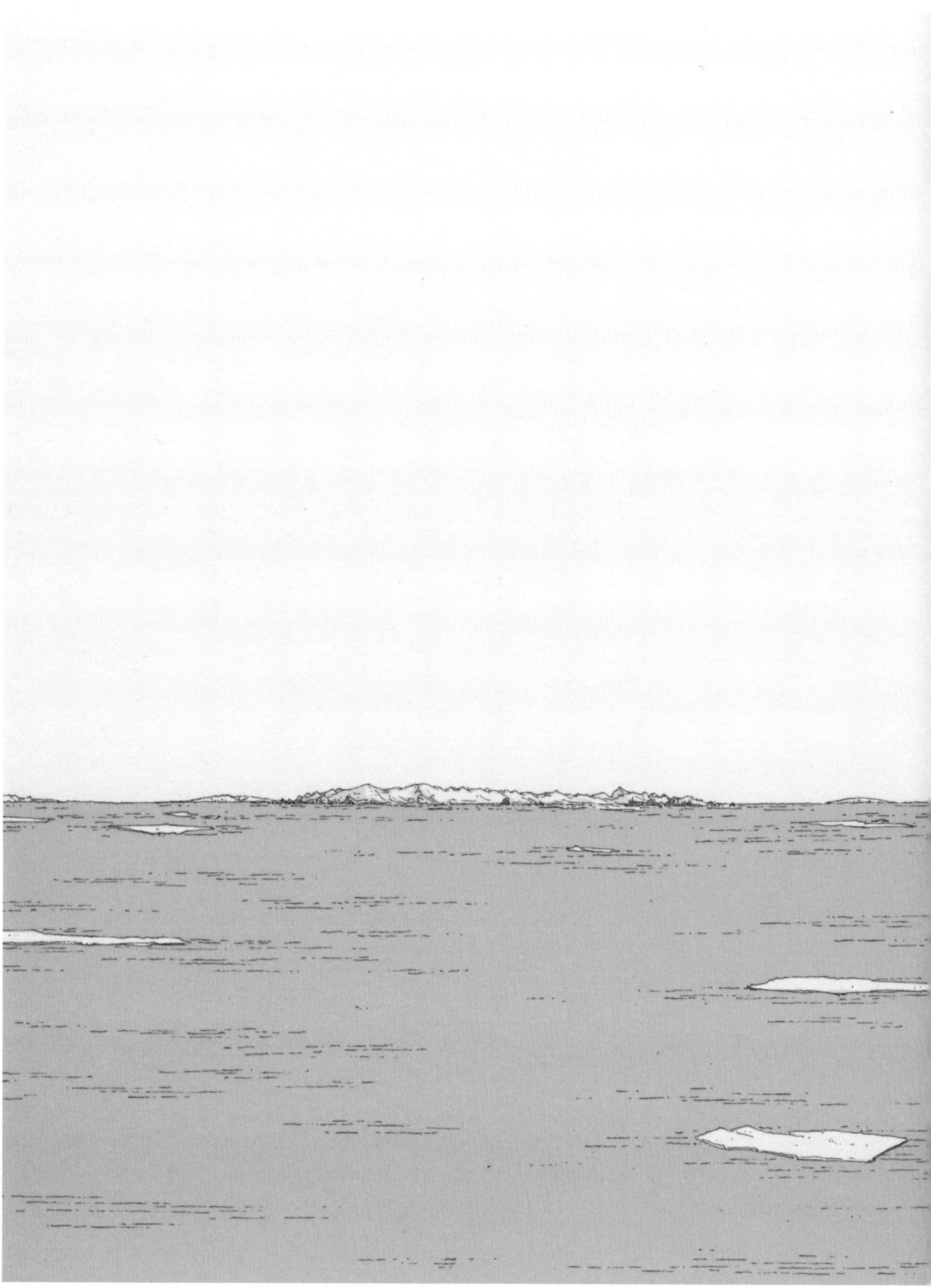

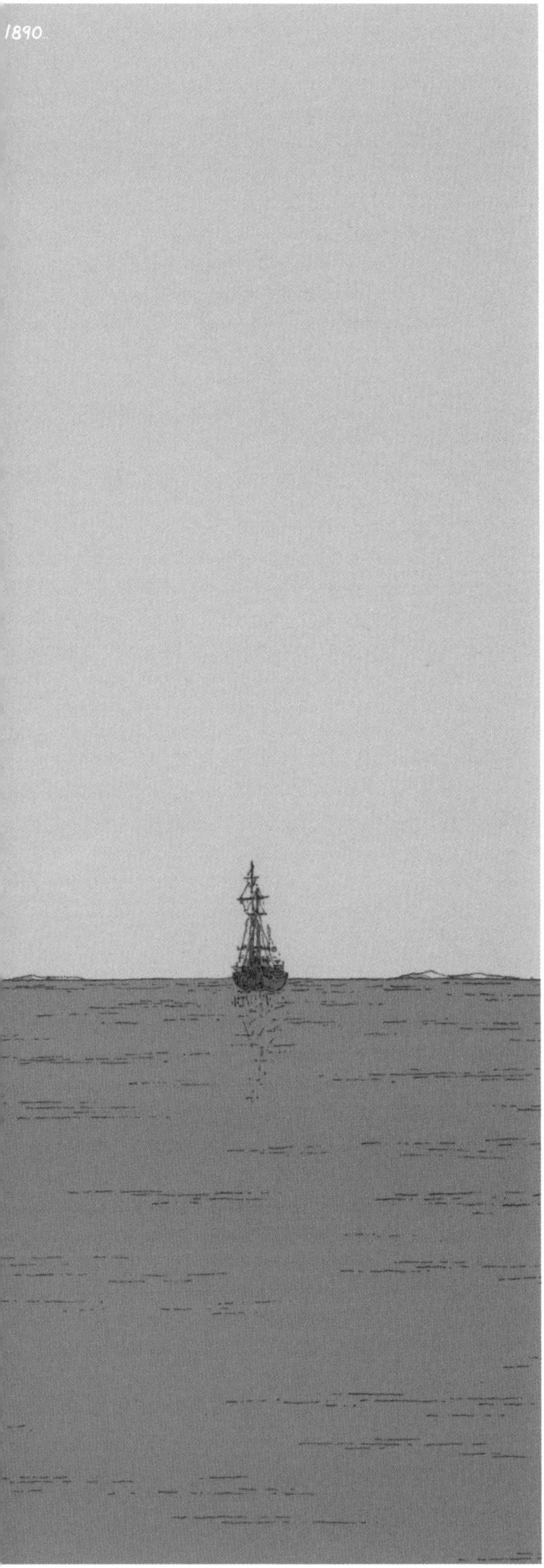
1890
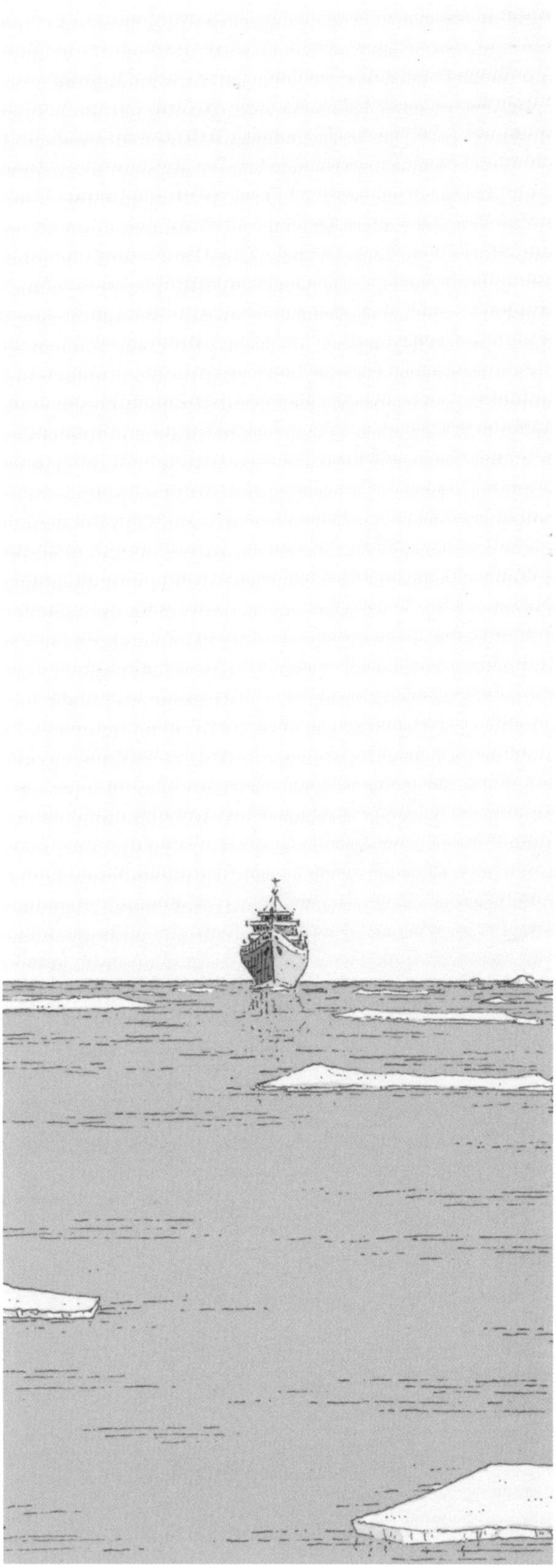

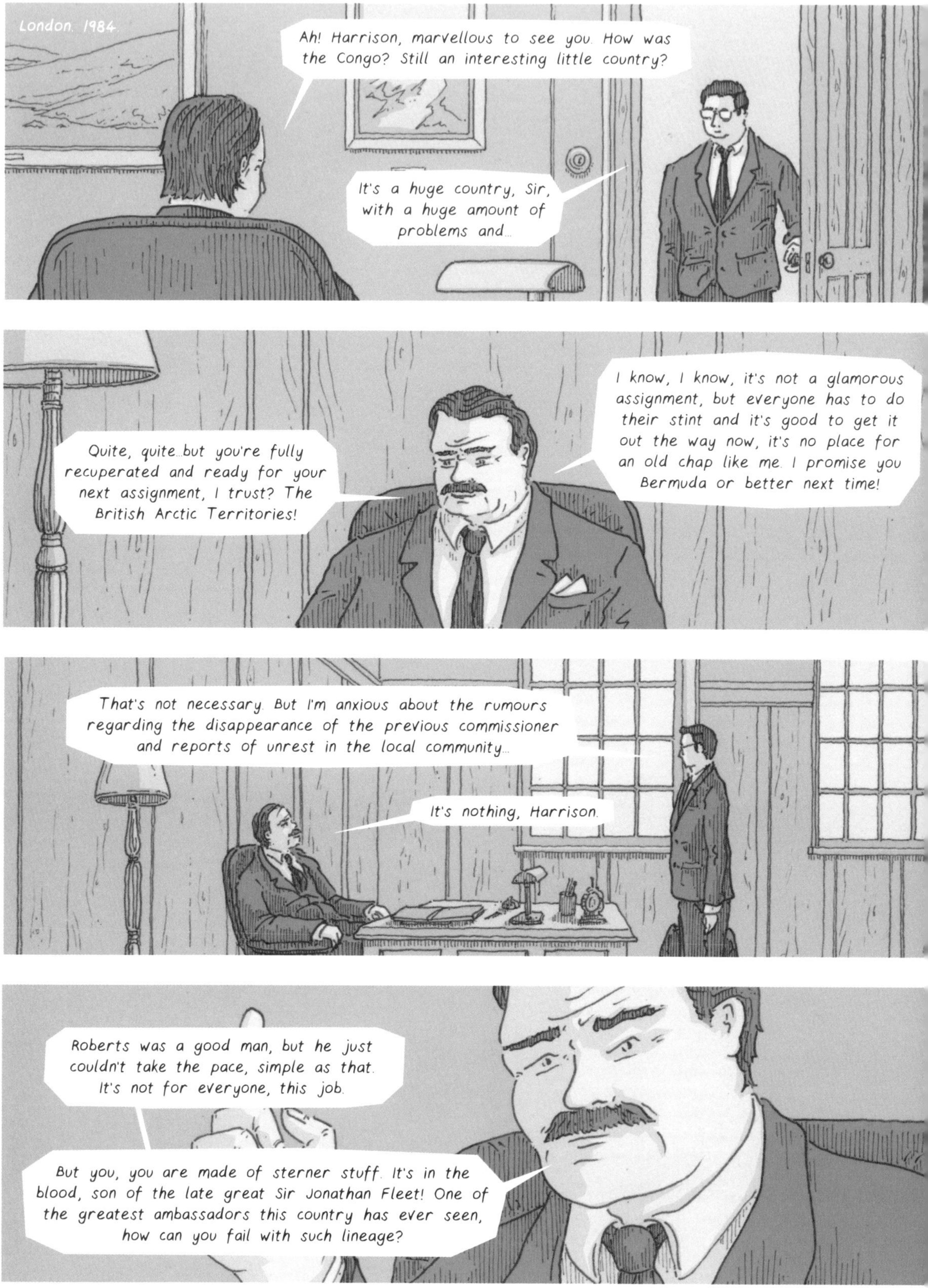
London. 1984.
Ah! Harrison, marvellous to see you. How was the Congo? Still an interesting little country?
It's a huge country, Sir, with a huge amount of problems and...
Quite, quite...but you're fully recuperated and ready for your next assignment, I trust? The British Arctic Territories!
I know, I know, it's not a glamorous assignment, but everyone has to do their stint and it's good to get it out the way now, it's no place for an old chap like me. I promise you Bermuda or better next time!
That's not necessary. But I'm anxious about the rumours regarding the disappearance of the previous commissioner and reports of unrest in the local community...
It's nothing, Harrison.
Roberts was a good man, but he just couldn't take the pace, simple as that. It's not for everyone, this job.
But you, you are made of sterner stuff. It's in the blood, son of the late great Sir Jonathan Fleet! One of the greatest ambassadors this country has ever seen, how can you fail with such lineage?

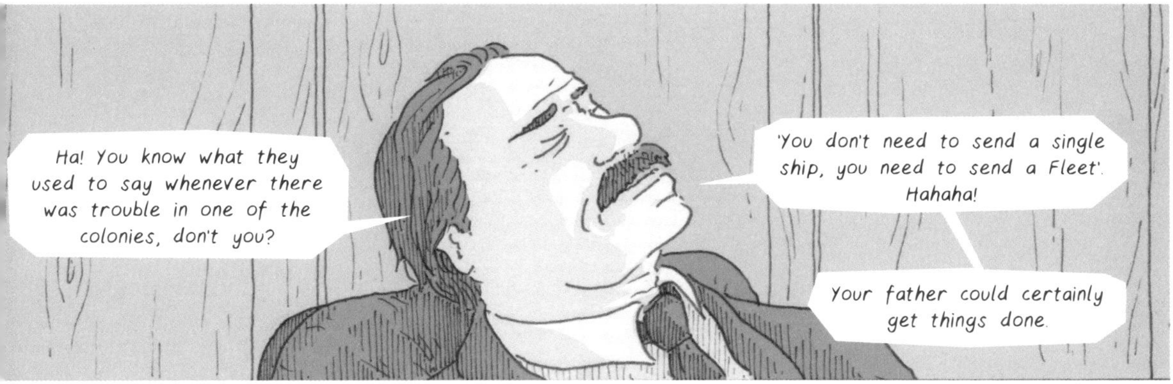
Ha! You know what they used to say whenever there was trouble in one of the colonies, don't you?
'You don't need to send a single ship, you need to send a Fleet'. Hahaha!
Your father could certainly get things done.

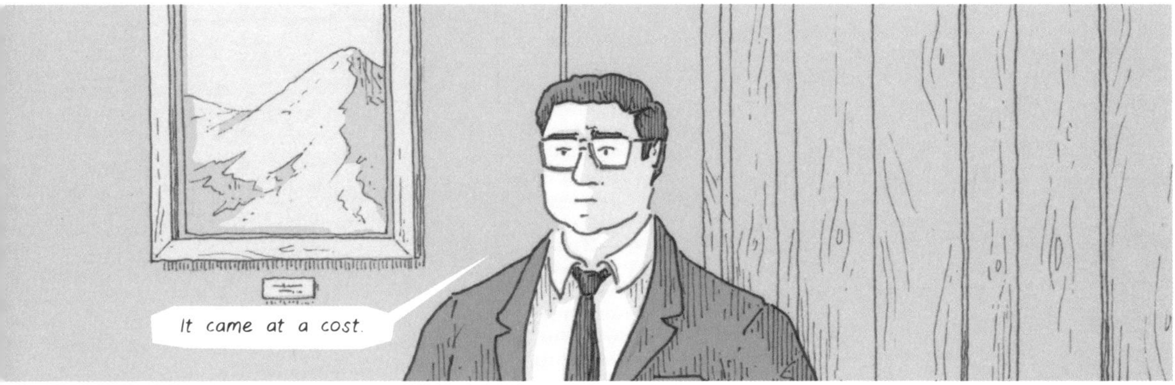
It came at a cost.

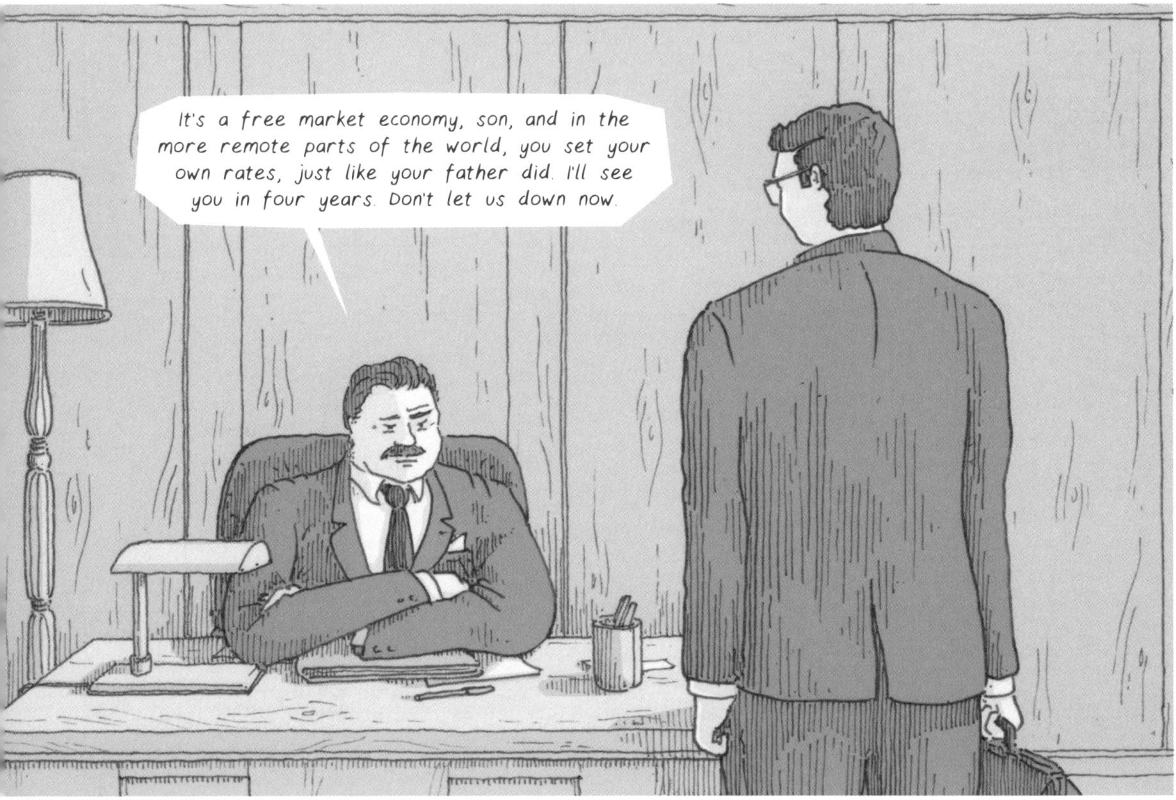
It's a free market economy, son, and in the more remote parts of the world, you set your own rates, just like your father did. I'll see you in four years. Don't let us down now.

PART I

FOUNDATIONS

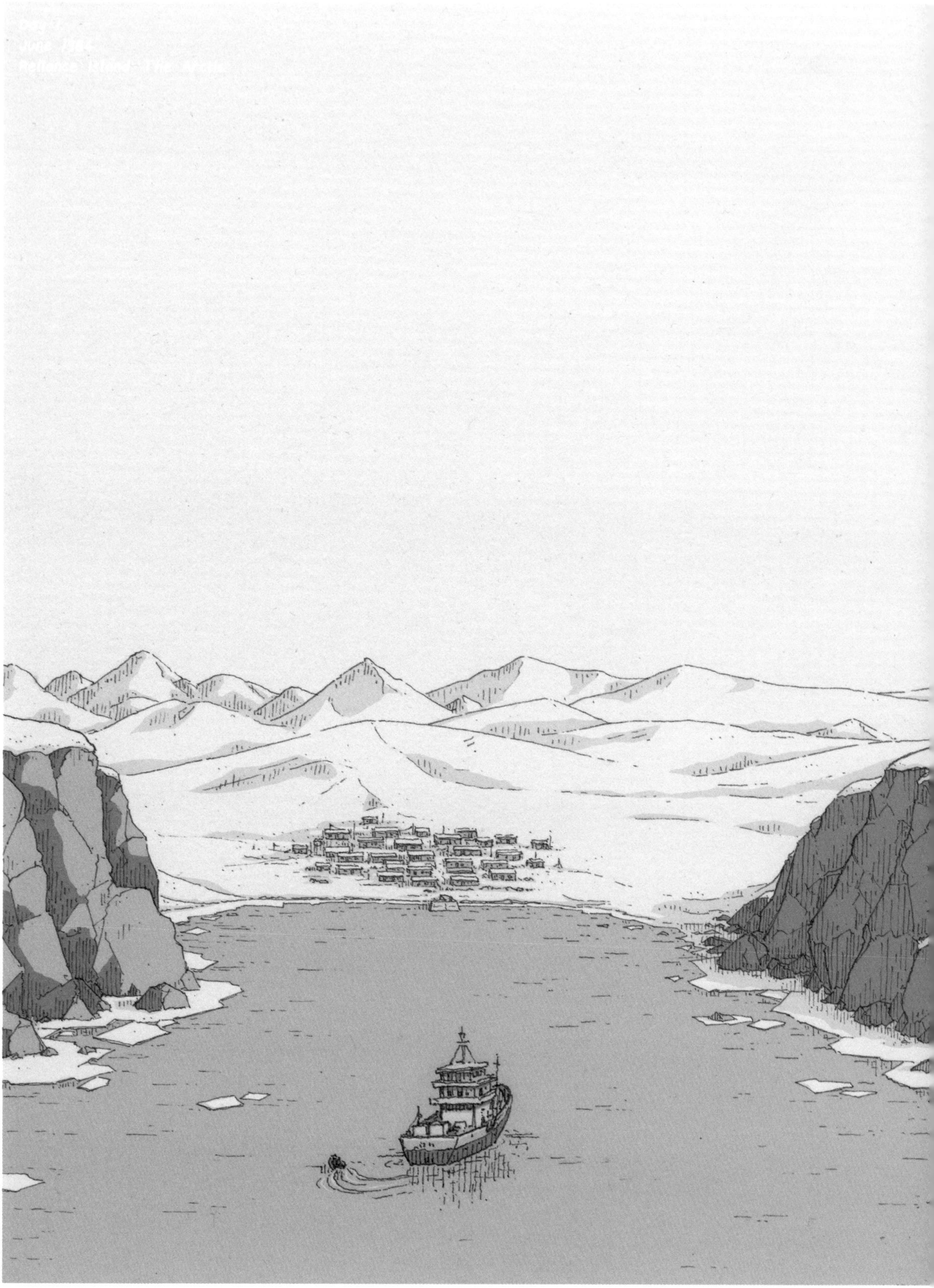

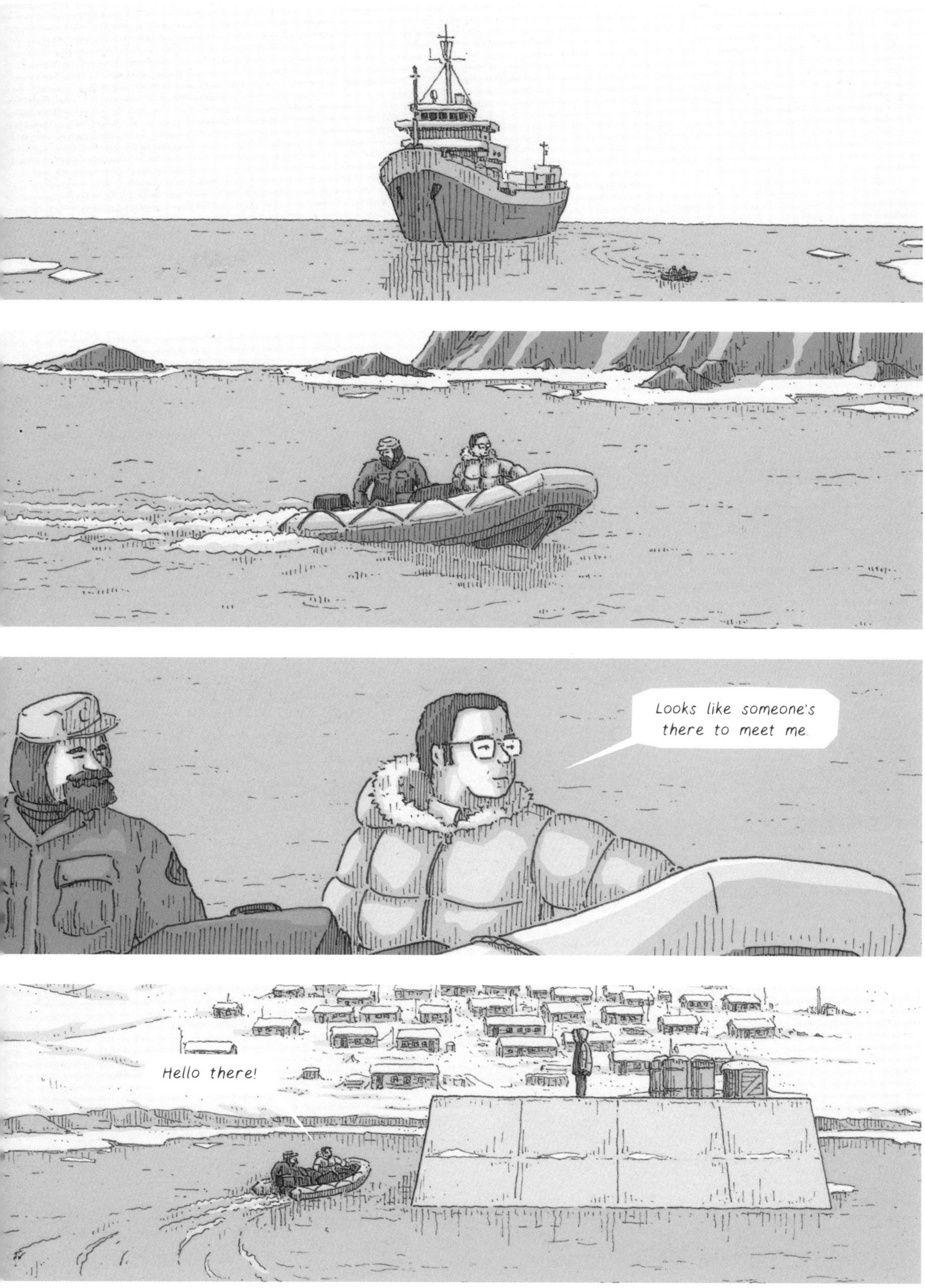
Looks like someone's there to meet me.
Hello there!

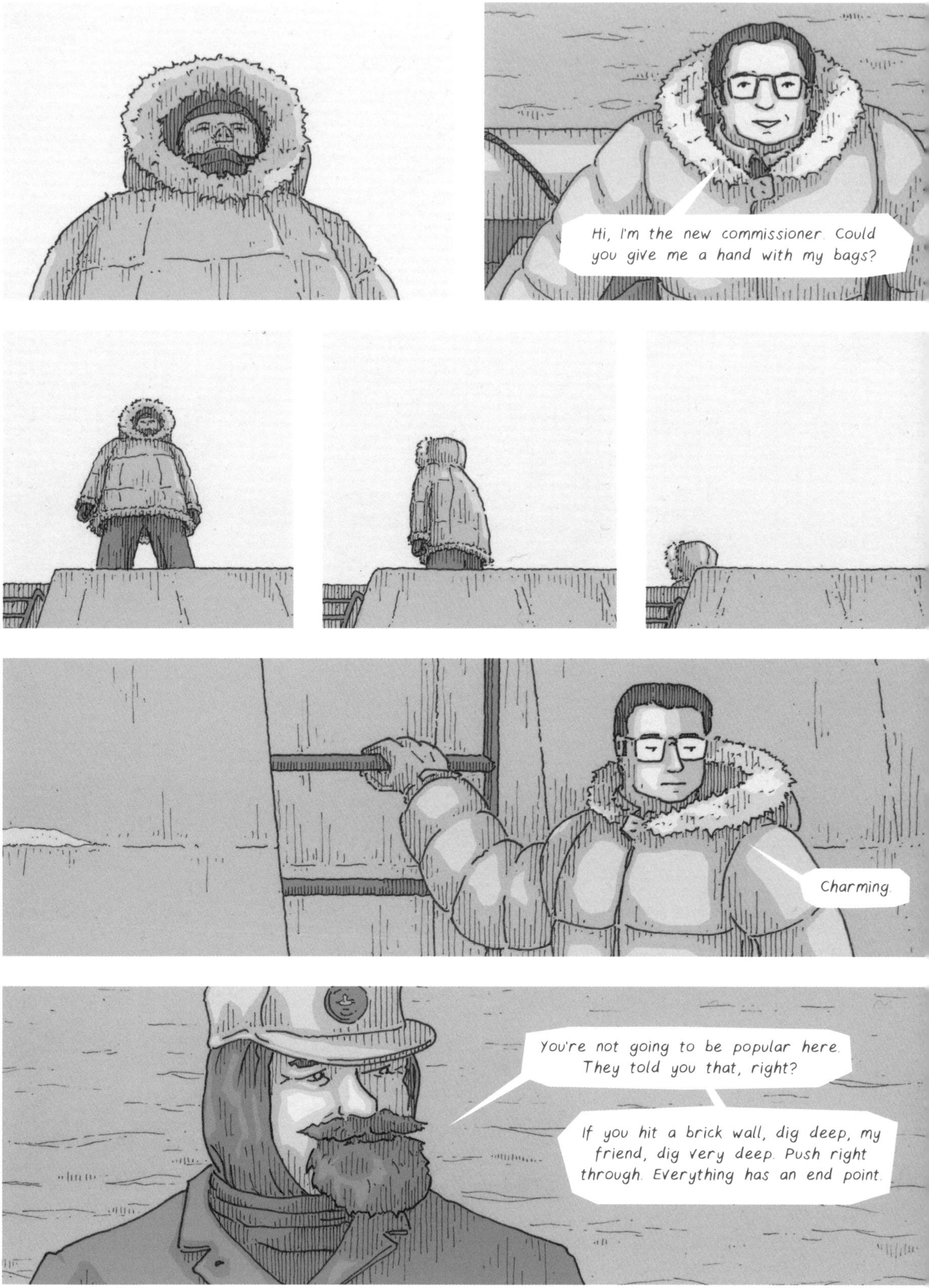
Hi, I'm the new commissioner. Could you give me a hand with my bags?
Charming.
You're not going to be popular here. They told you that, right?
If you hit a brick wall, dig deep, my friend, dig very deep. Push right through. Everything has an end point.

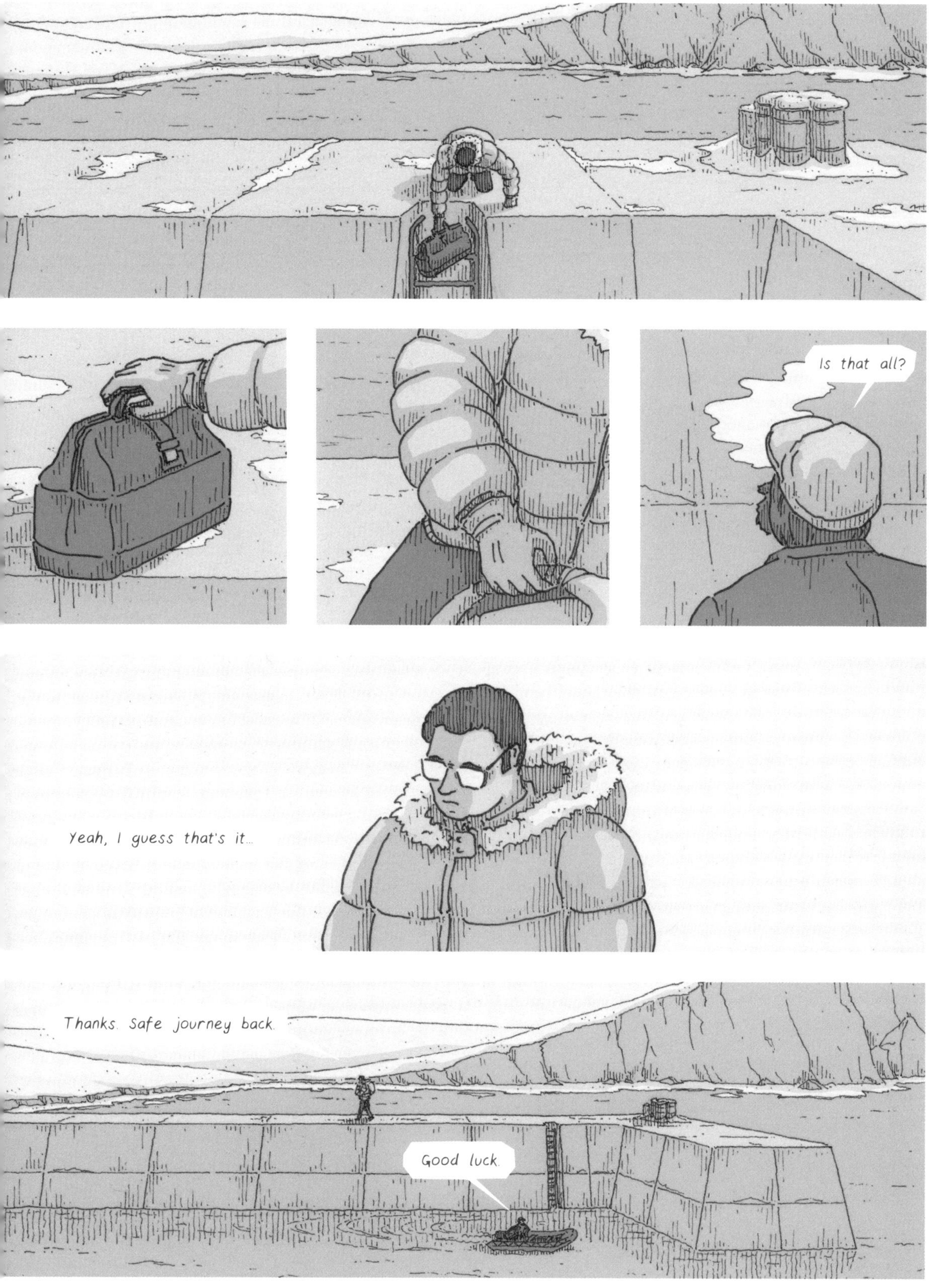
Is that all?
Yeah, I guess that's it...
Thanks. Safe journey back.
Good luck.

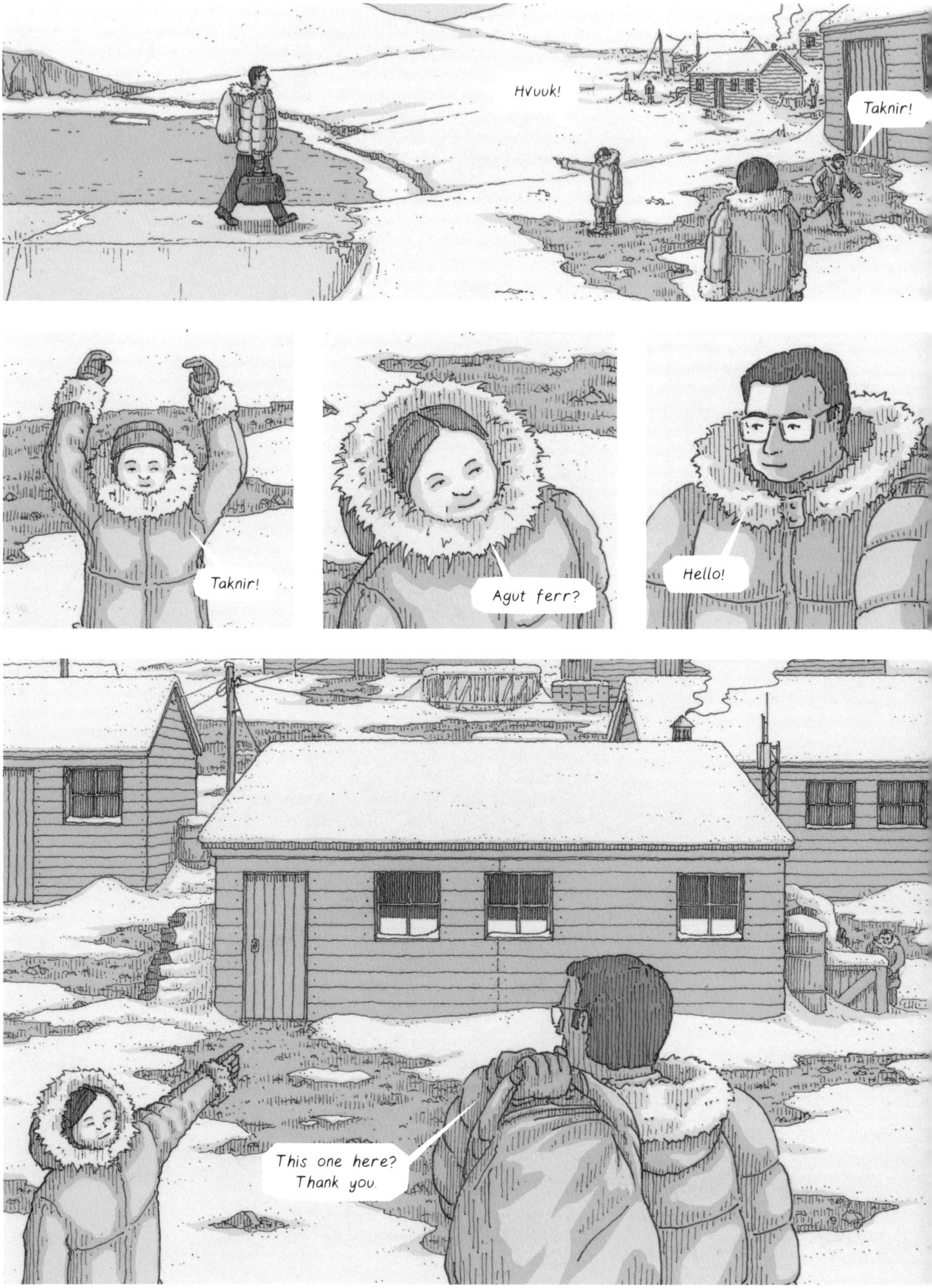
Hvuuk!
Taknir!
Taknir!
Agut ferr?
Hello!
This one here?
Thank you.

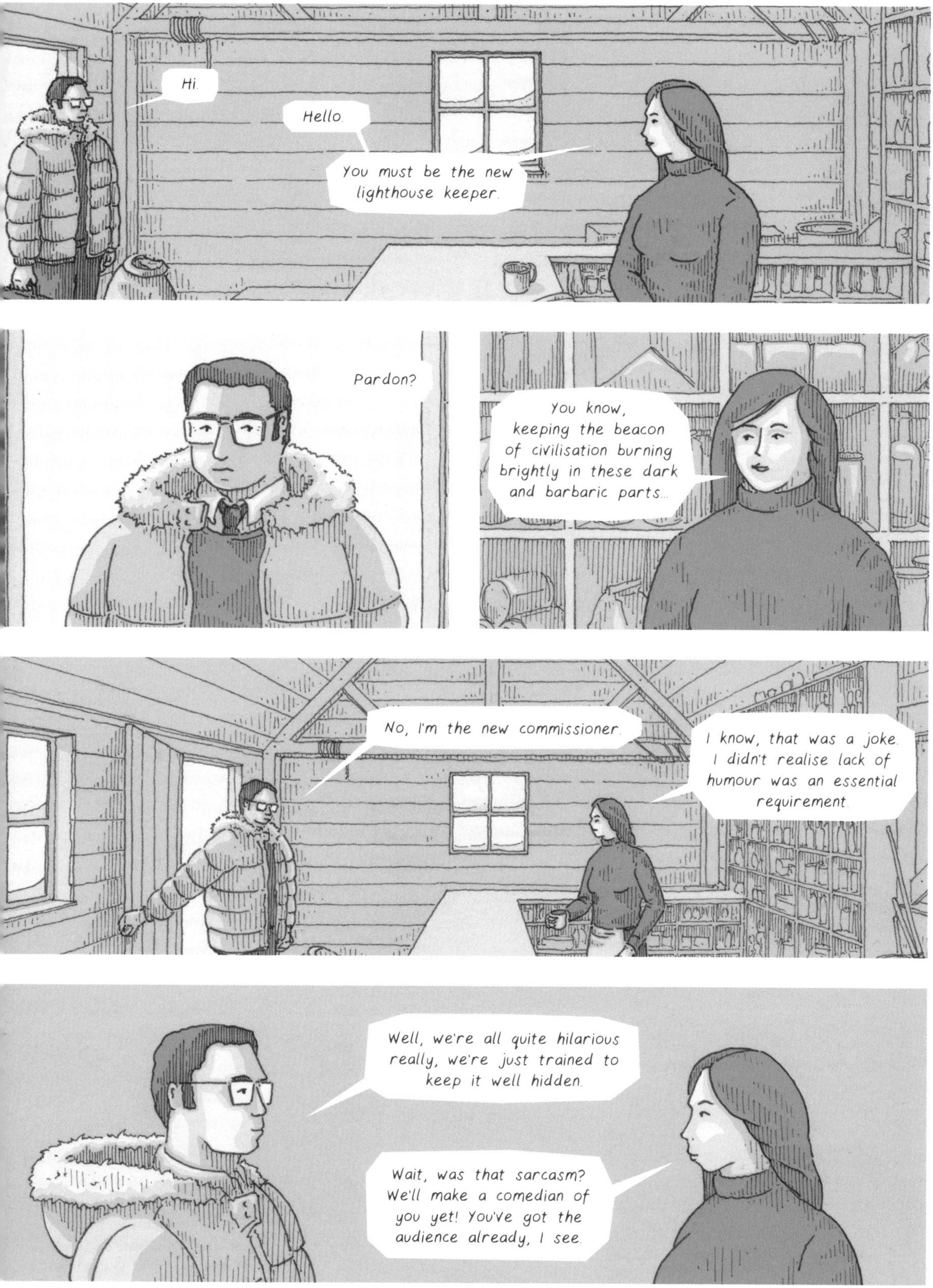
Hi.
Hello.
You must be the new lighthouse keeper.
Pardon?
You know, keeping the beacon of civilisation burning brightly in these dark and barbaric parts...
No, I'm the new commissioner.
I know, that was a joke. I didn't realise lack of humour was an essential requirement.
Well, we're all quite hilarious really, we're just trained to keep it well hidden.
Wait, was that sarcasm? We'll make a comedian of you yet! You've got the audience already, I see.

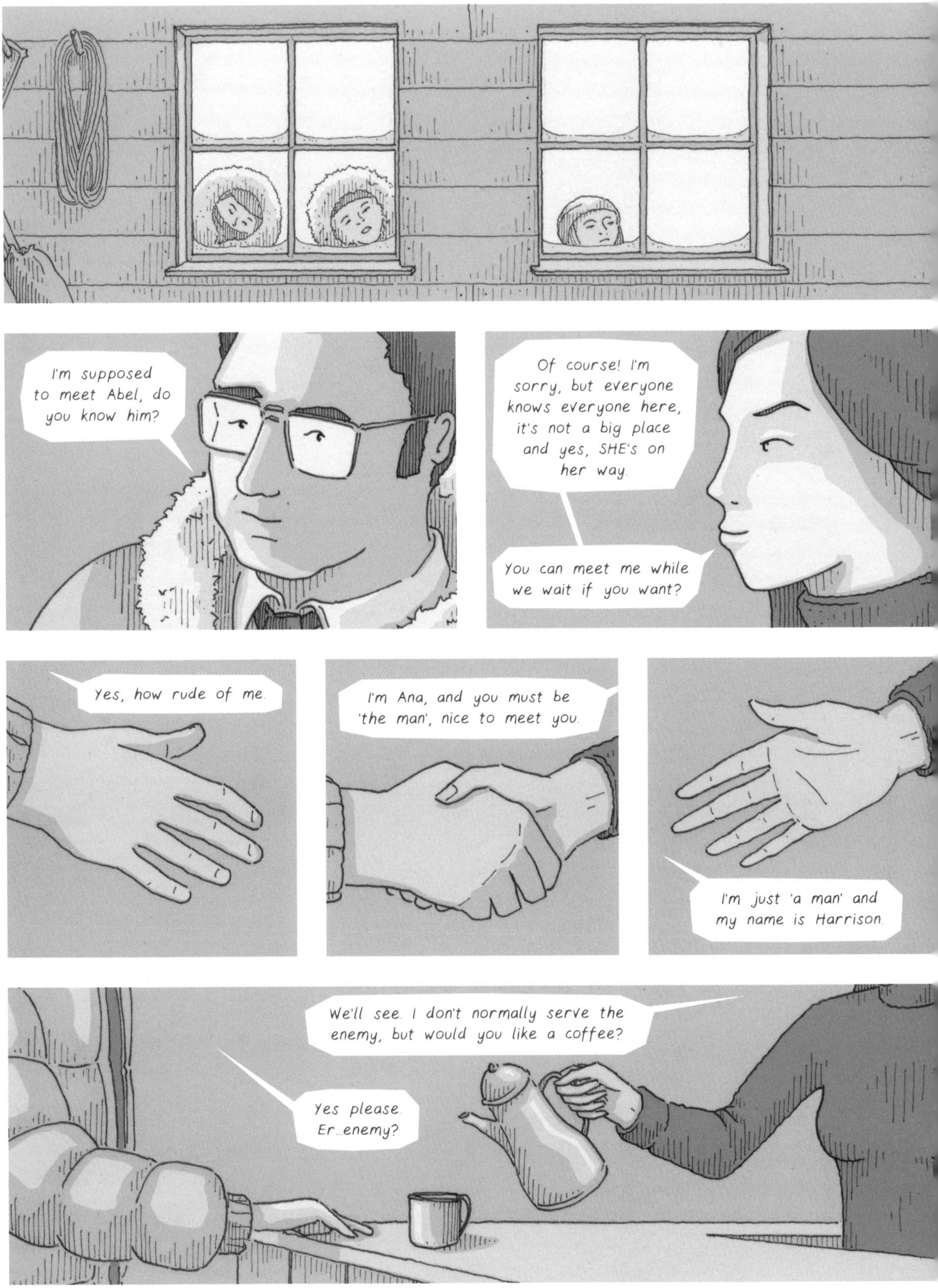
I'm supposed to meet Abel, do you know him?
Of course! I'm sorry, but everyone knows everyone here, it's not a big place and yes, SHE's on her way.
You can meet me while we wait if you want?
Yes, how rude of me.
I'm Ana, and you must be 'the man', nice to meet you.
I'm just 'a man' and my name is Harrison.
We'll see. I don't normally serve the enemy, but would you like a coffee?
Yes please. Er...enemy?

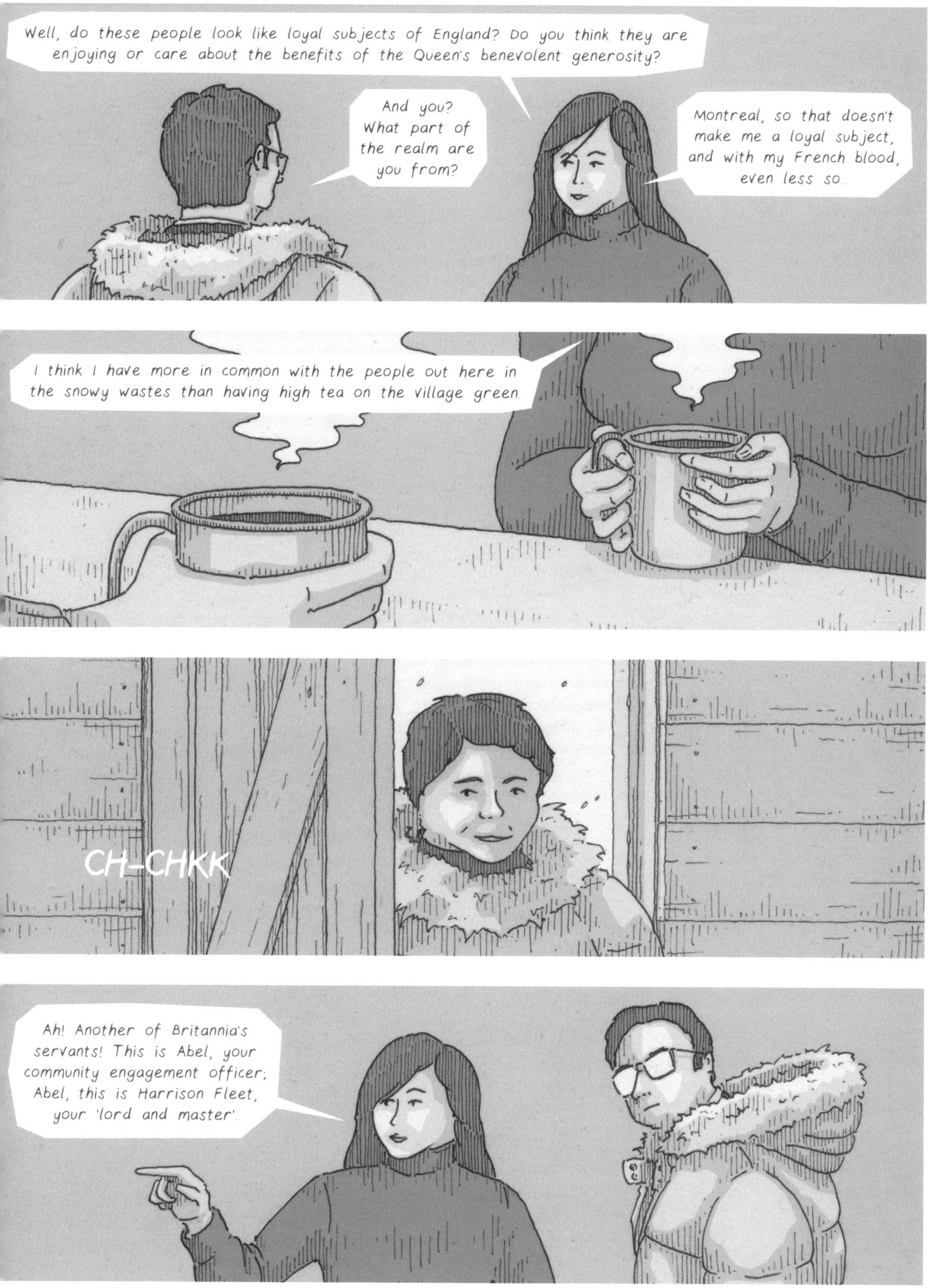
Well, do these people look like loyal subjects of England? Do you think they are enjoying or care about the benefits of the Queen's benevolent generosity?
And you? What part of the realm are you from?
Montreal, so that doesn't make me a loyal subject, and with my French blood, even less so...
I think I have more in common with the people out here in the snowy wastes than having high tea on the village green.
CH-CHKK
Ah! Another of Britannia's servants! This is Abel, your community engagement officer; Abel, this is Harrison Fleet, your 'lord and master'.

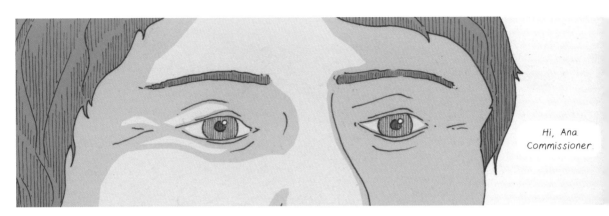

Hi, Ana. Commissioner.

Good to meet you. And just Harrison is fine.

Hi, Abe.

Let me take you to the house, there's a small flurry coming in from the sea.

Yeah, you should get moving.

See you soon. And if you need anything, I'll be here. Unless of course, I'm not.

Thanks. See you soon hopefully. Maybe for some tea on the village...er... white?

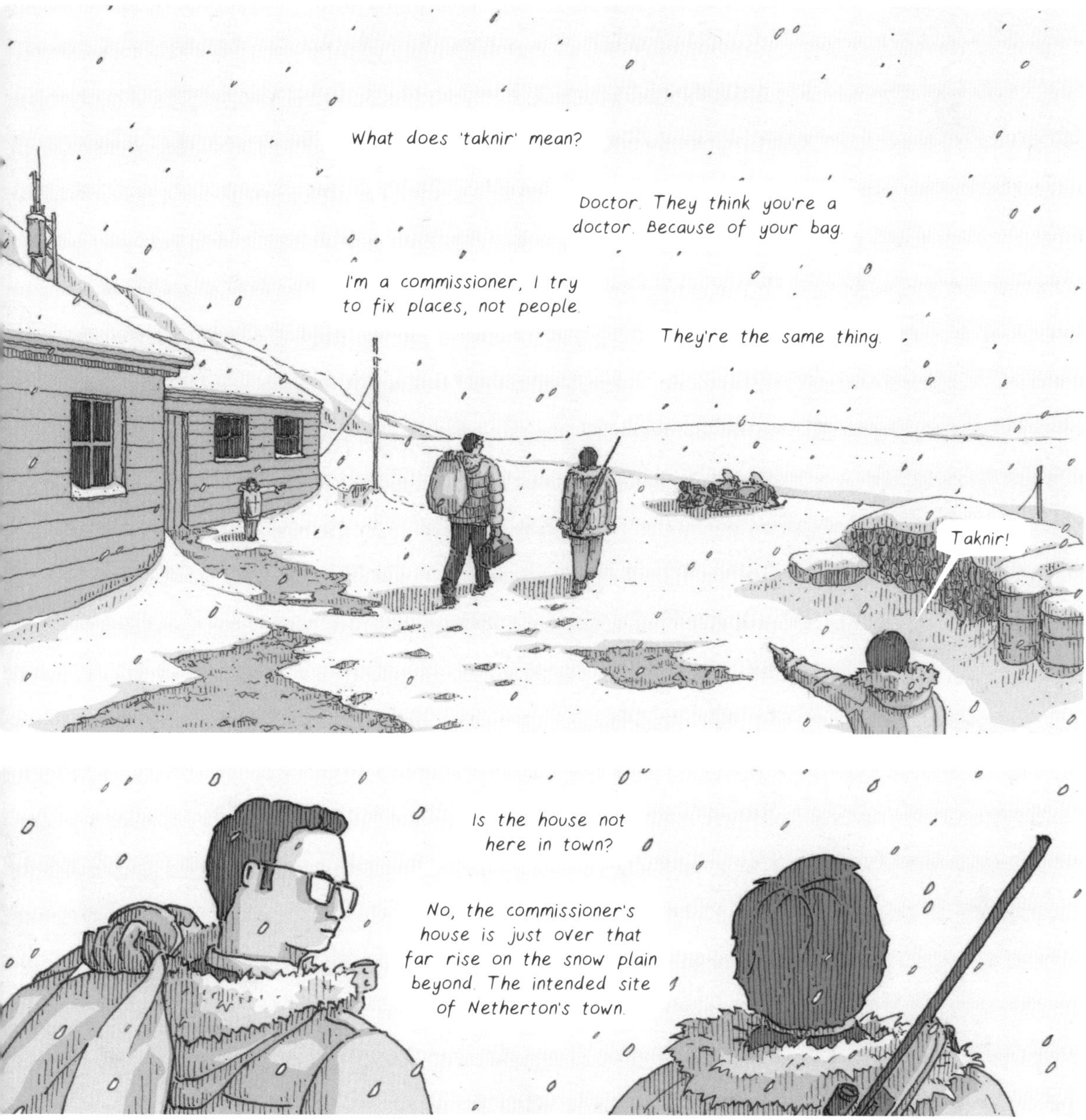
What does 'taknir' mean?
Doctor. They think you're a doctor. Because of your bag.
I'm a commissioner, I try to fix places, not people.
They're the same thing.
Taknir!
Is the house not here in town?
No, the commissioner's house is just over that far rise on the snow plain beyond. The intended site of Netherton's town.
None of this makes sense right now, Abel. But I have acquired a few files on the history before I left, so hopefully they will illuminate me.
Reading is only half of it. A lot of my people's history is oral, so it depends which version you want.

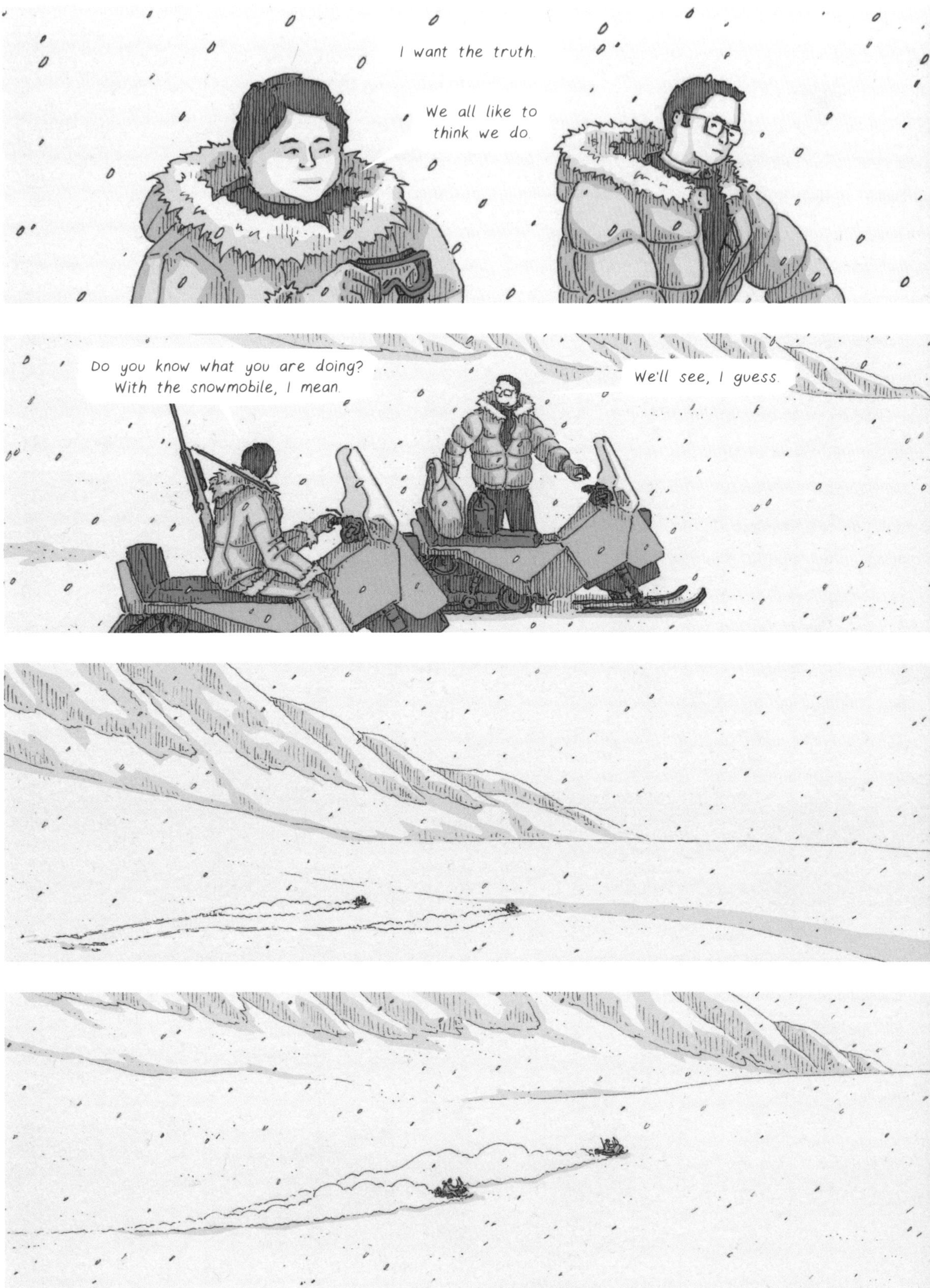
I want the truth.
We all like to think we do.
Do you know what you are doing? With the snowmobile, I mean.
We'll see, I guess.

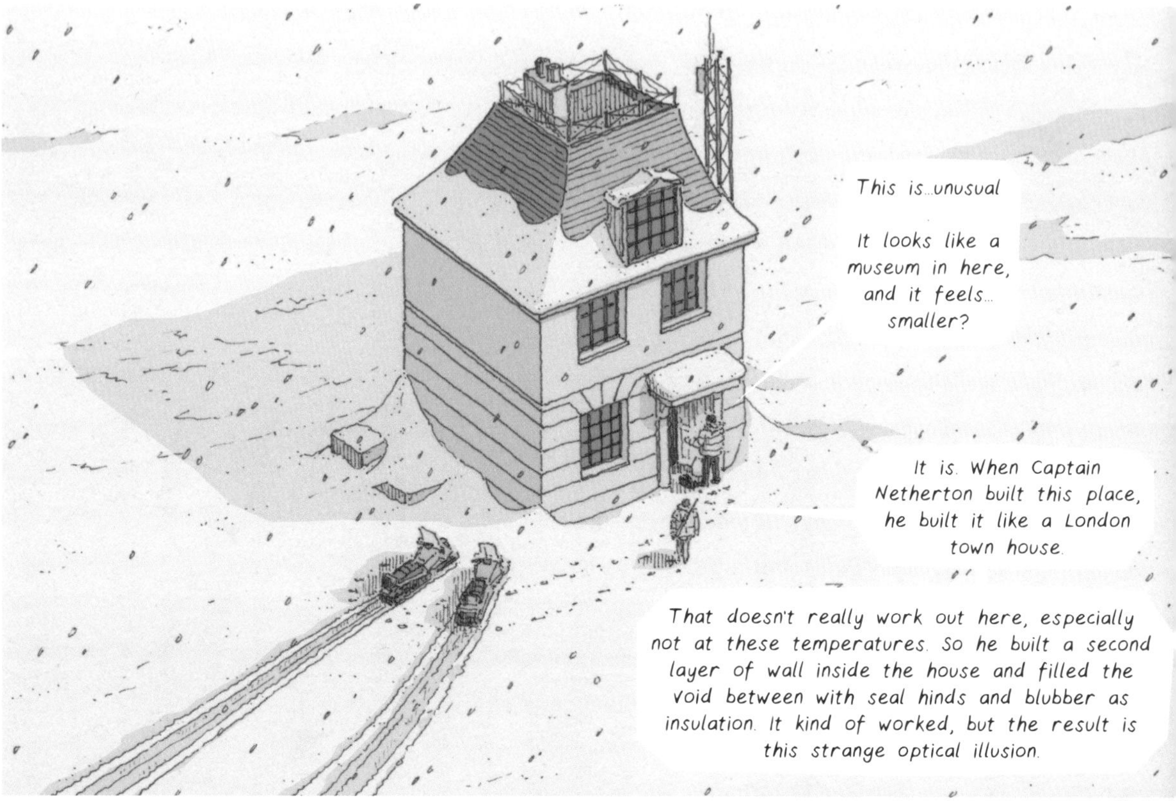
This is...unusual
It looks like a museum in here, and it feels... smaller?
It is. When Captain Netherton built this place, he built it like a London town house.
That doesn't really work out here, especially not at these temperatures. So he built a second layer of wall inside the house and filled the void between with seal hinds and blubber as insulation. It kind of worked, but the result is this strange optical illusion.

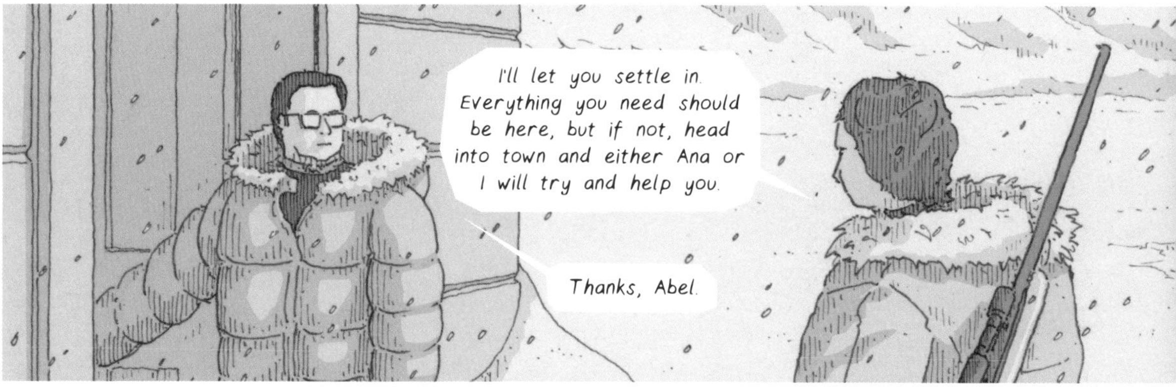
I'll let you settle in. Everything you need should be here, but if not, head into town and either Ana or I will try and help you.
Thanks, Abel.

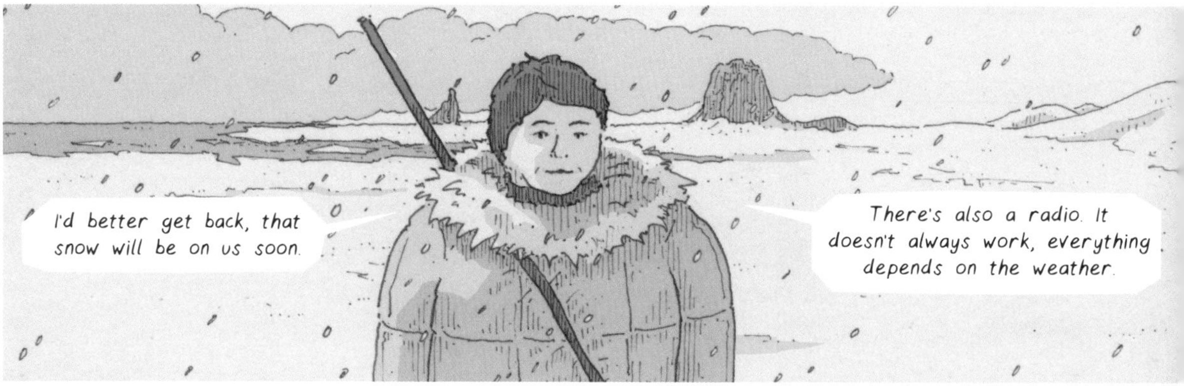
There's also a radio. It doesn't always work, everything depends on the weather.
I'd better get back, that snow will be on us soon.

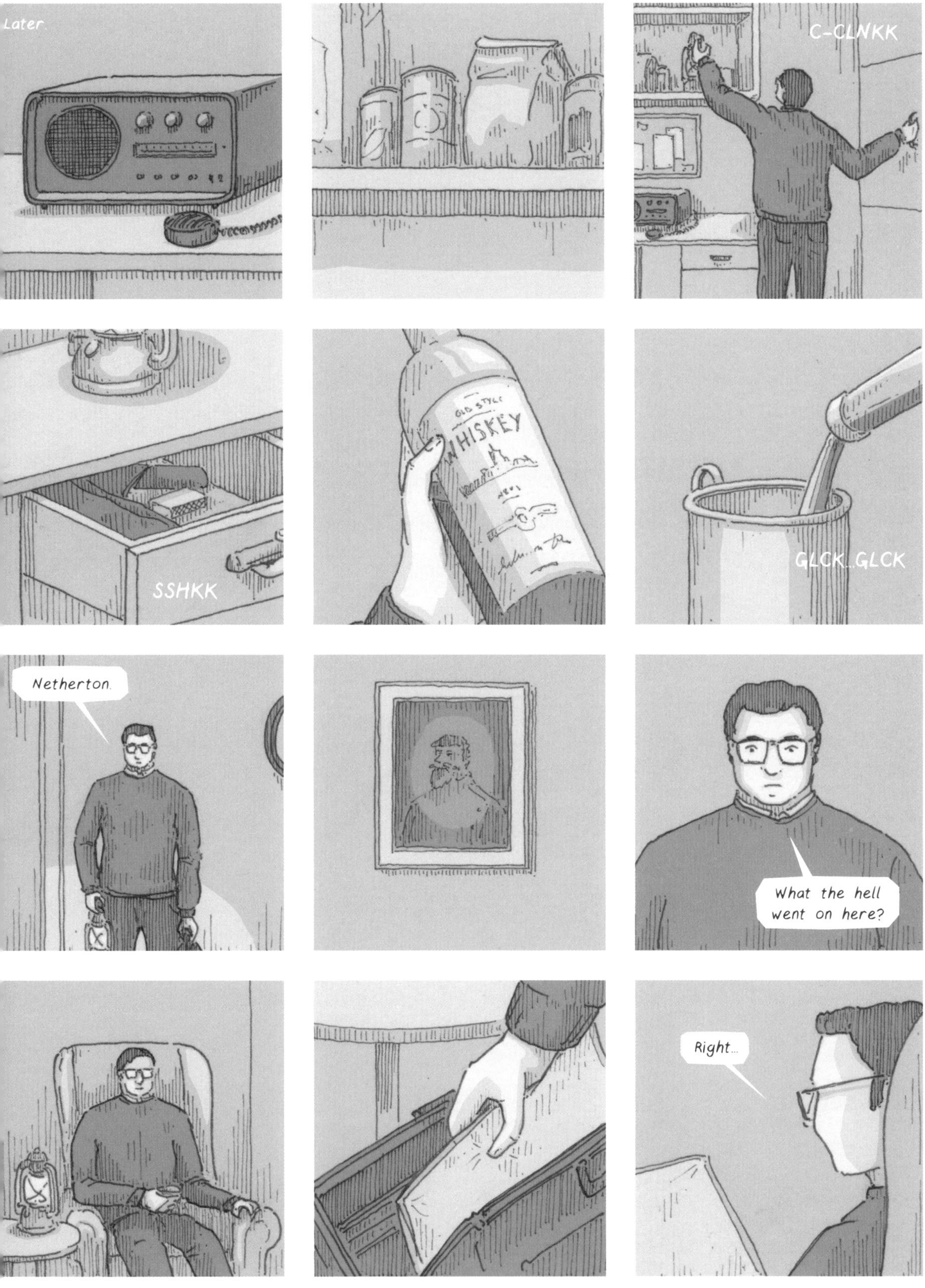
Later.
C-CLNKK
SSHKK
OLD STYLE
WHISKEY
GLCK...GLCK
Netherton.
What the hell went on here?
Right...

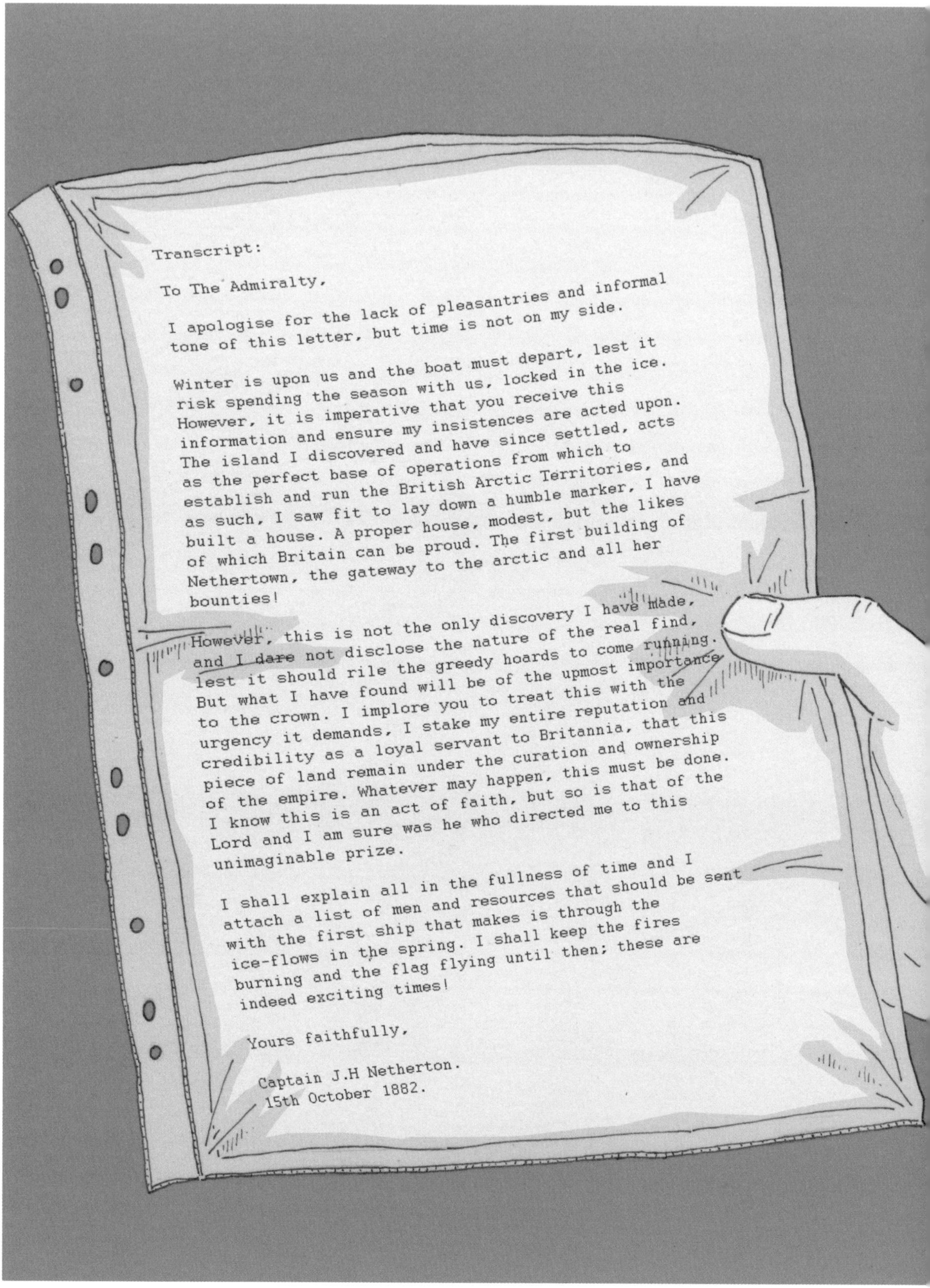
Transcript:

To The Admiralty,

I apologise for the lack of pleasantries and informal tone of this letter, but time is not on my side.

Winter is upon us and the boat must depart, lest it risk spending the season with us, locked in the ice. However, it is imperative that you receive this information and ensure my insistences are acted upon. The island I discovered and have since settled, acts as the perfect base of operations from which to establish and run the British Arctic Territories, and as such, I saw fit to lay down a humble marker, I have built a house. A proper house, modest, but the likes of which Britain can be proud. The first building of Nethertown, the gateway to the arctic and all her bounties!

However, this is not the only discovery I have made, and I dare not disclose the nature of the real find, lest it should rile the greedy hoards to come running. But what I have found will be of the upmost importance to the crown. I implore you to treat this with the urgency it demands, I stake my entire reputation and credibility as a loyal servant to Britannia, that this piece of land remain under the curation and ownership of the empire. Whatever may happen, this must be done. I know this is an act of faith, but so is that of the Lord and I am sure was he who directed me to this unimaginable prize.

I shall explain all in the fullness of time and I attach a list of men and resources that should be sent with the first ship that makes is through the ice-flows in the spring. I shall keep the fires burning and the flag flying until then; these are indeed exciting times!

Yours faithfully,

Captain J.H Netherton.
15th October 1882.

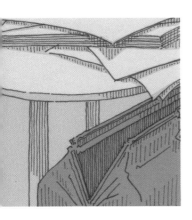

Later still.

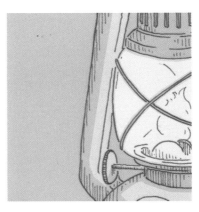

Wait...what is that? Drums?

D-DMM DMM DMM...D-DMM DMM DMM...D-DMM DMM

Jesus...

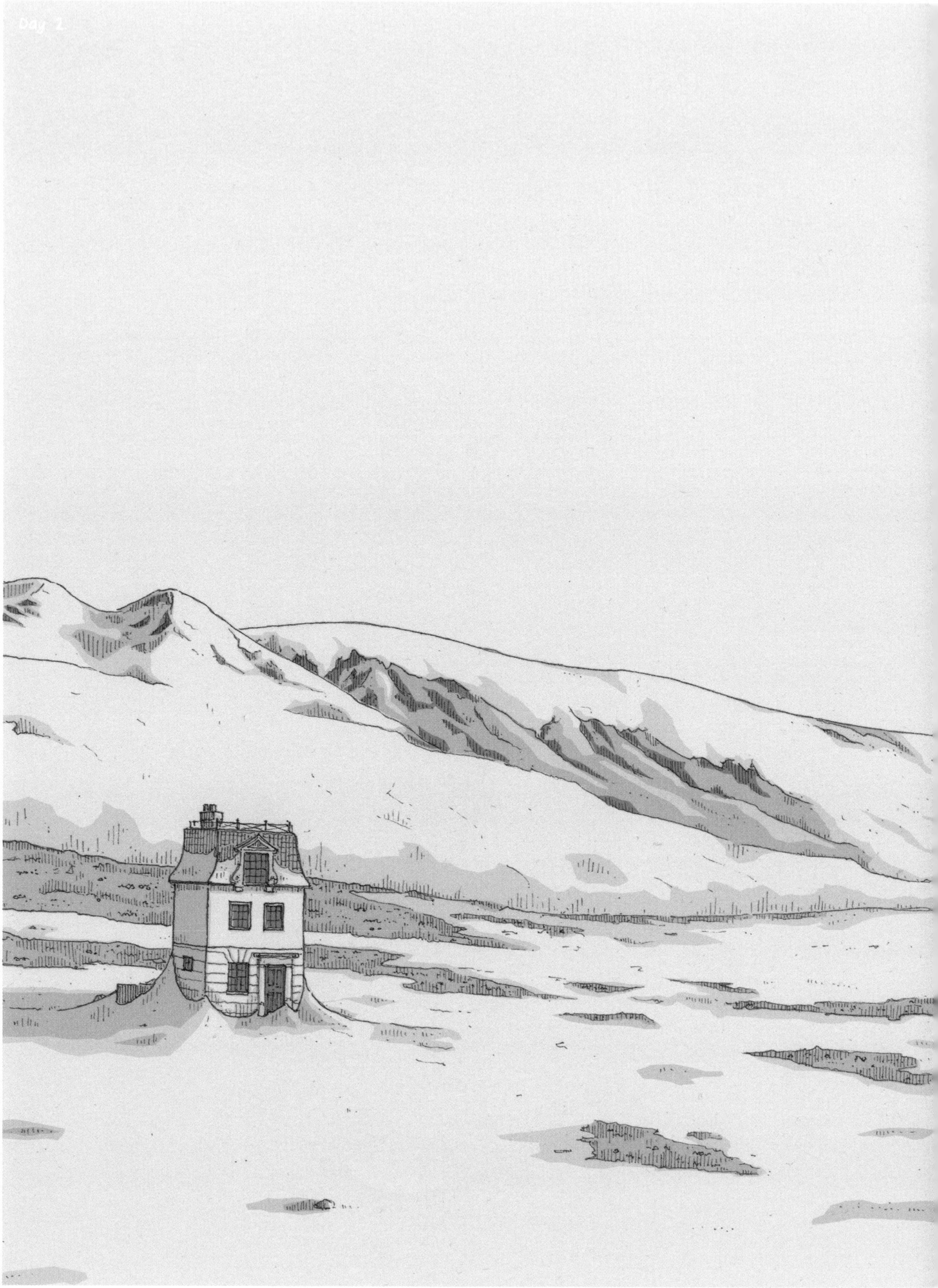
Day 1.

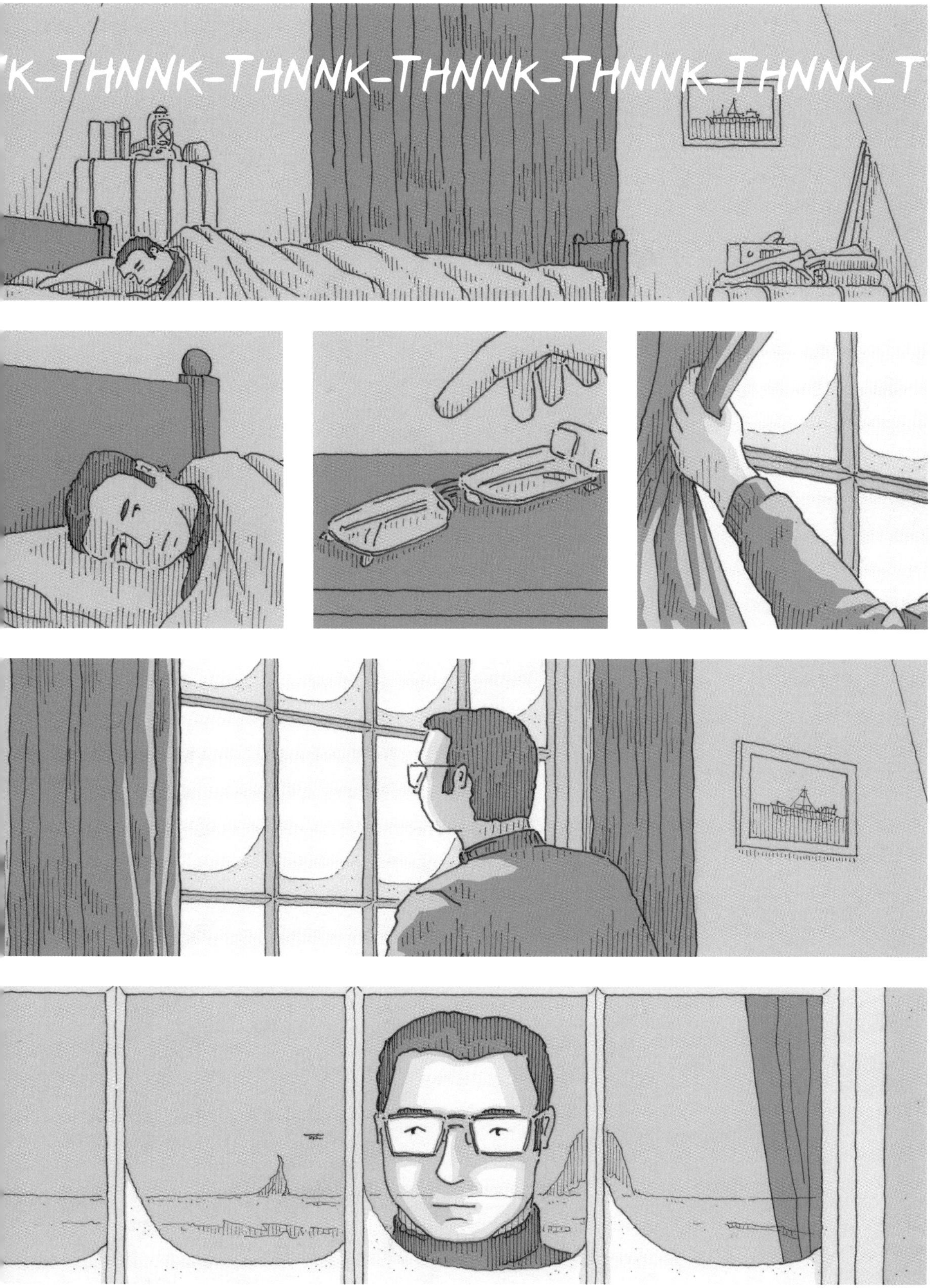
K-THNNK-THNNK-THNNK-THNNK-THNNK-T

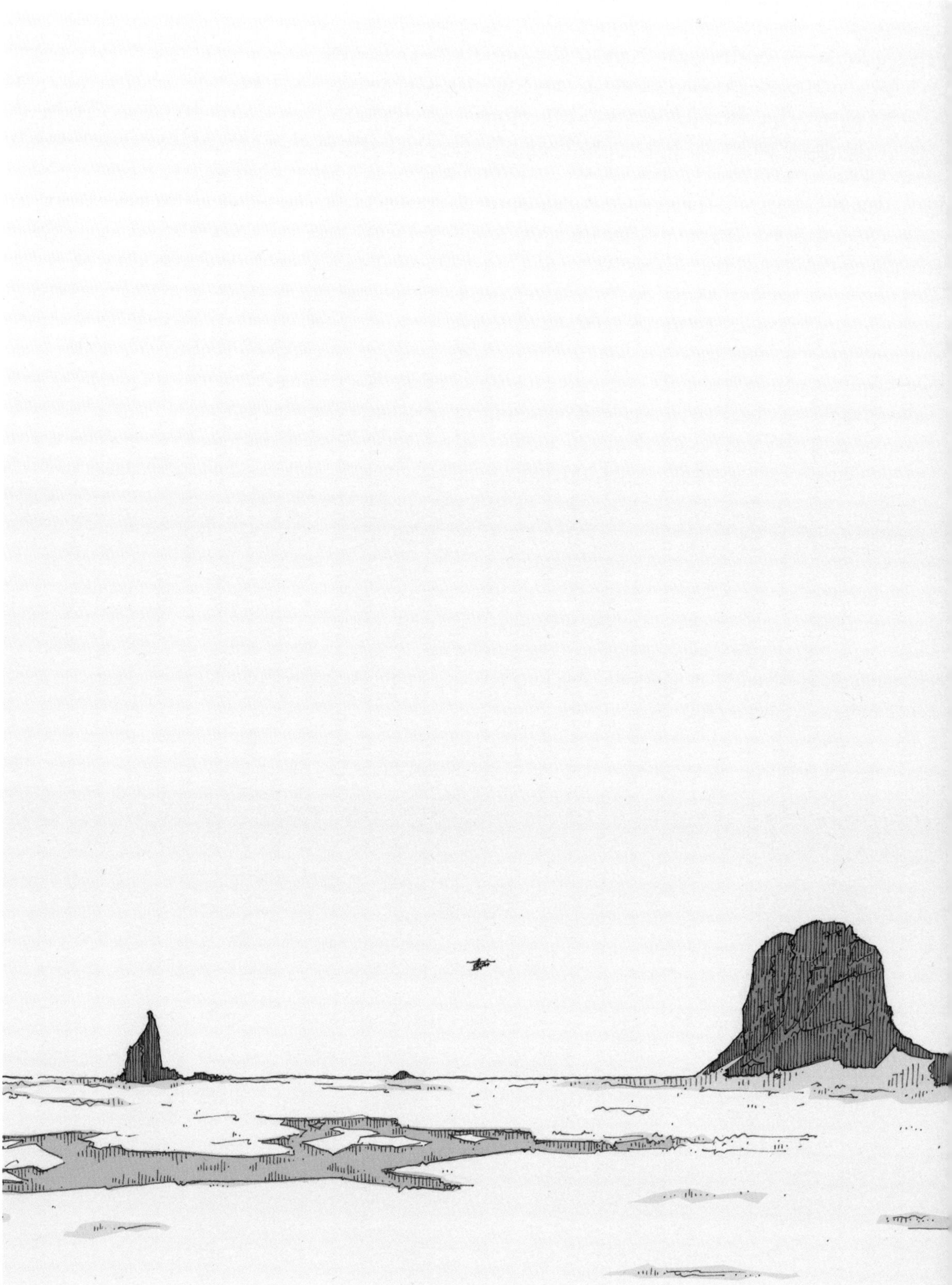

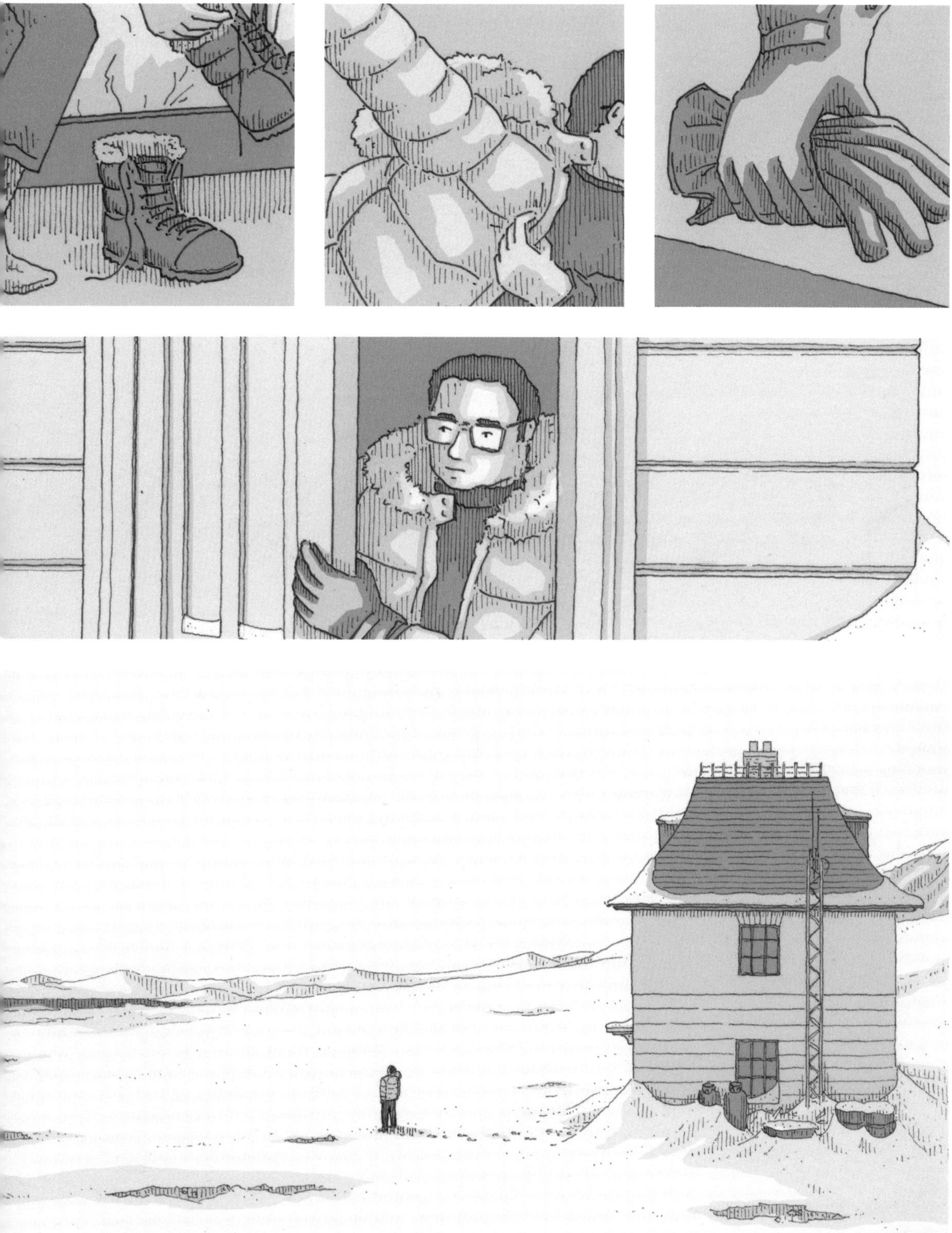

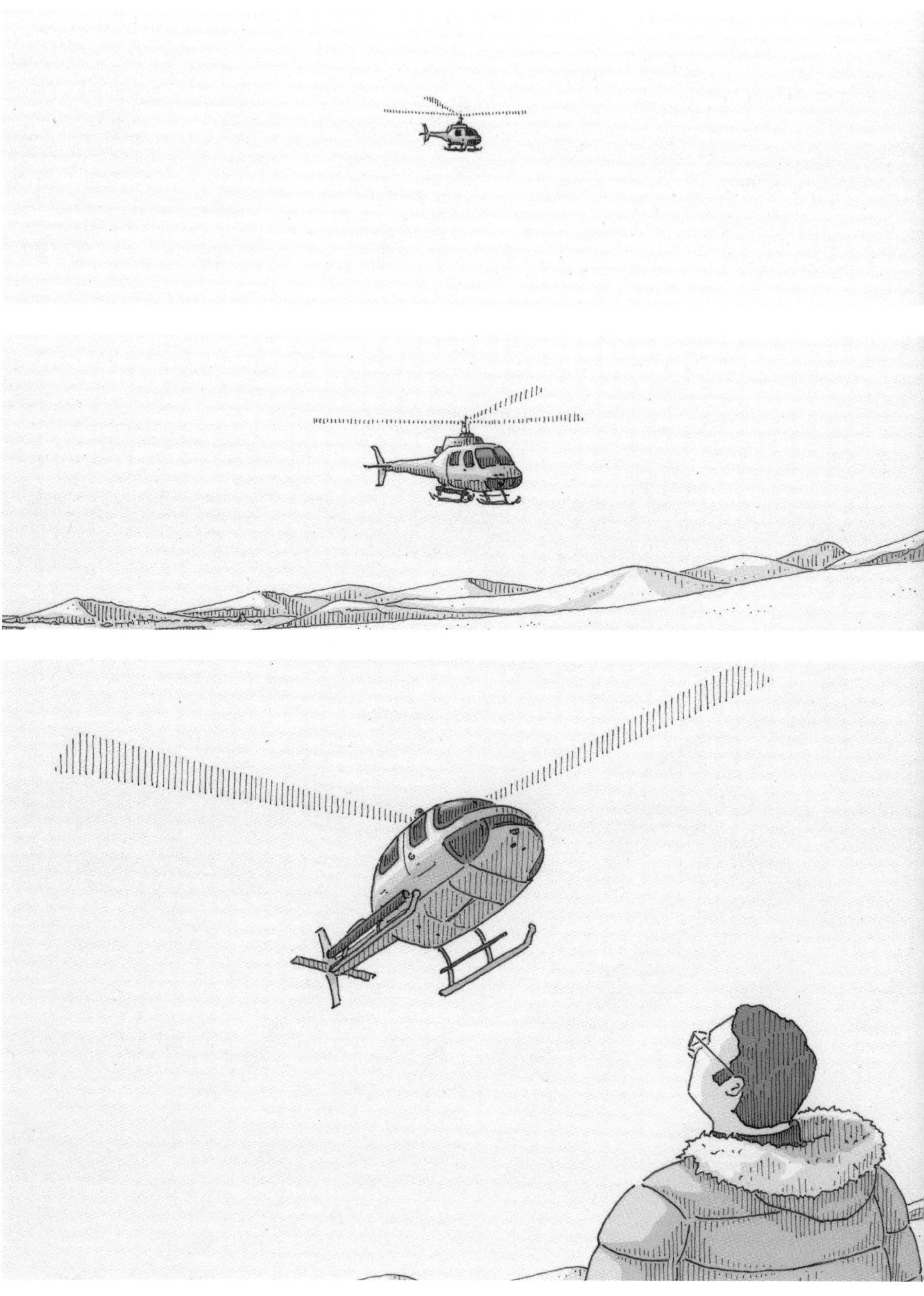

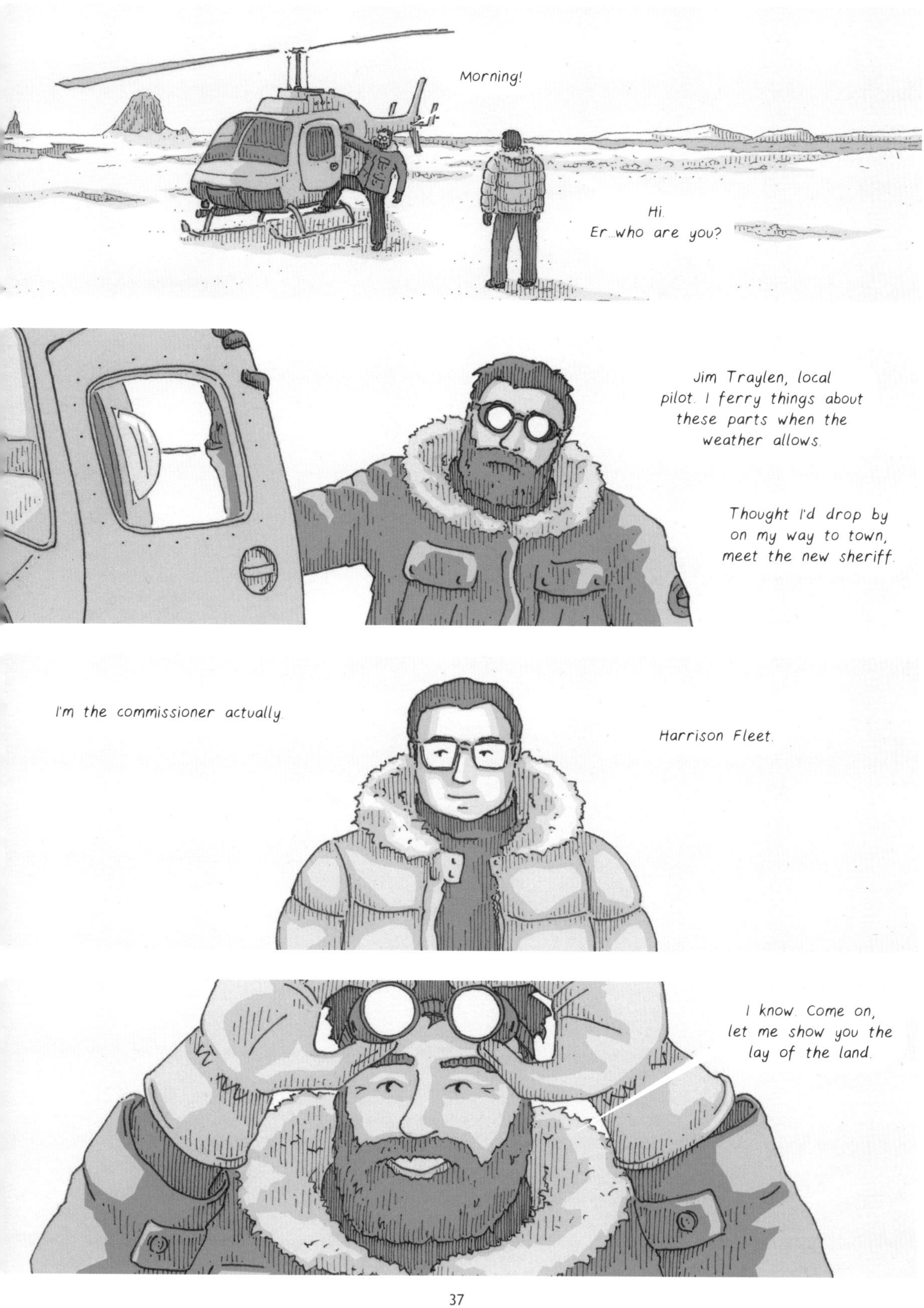

Morning!
Hi.
Er...who are you?
Jim Traylen, local pilot. I ferry things about these parts when the weather allows.
Thought I'd drop by on my way to town, meet the new sheriff.
I'm the commissioner actually.
Harrison Fleet.
I know. Come on, let me show you the lay of the land.

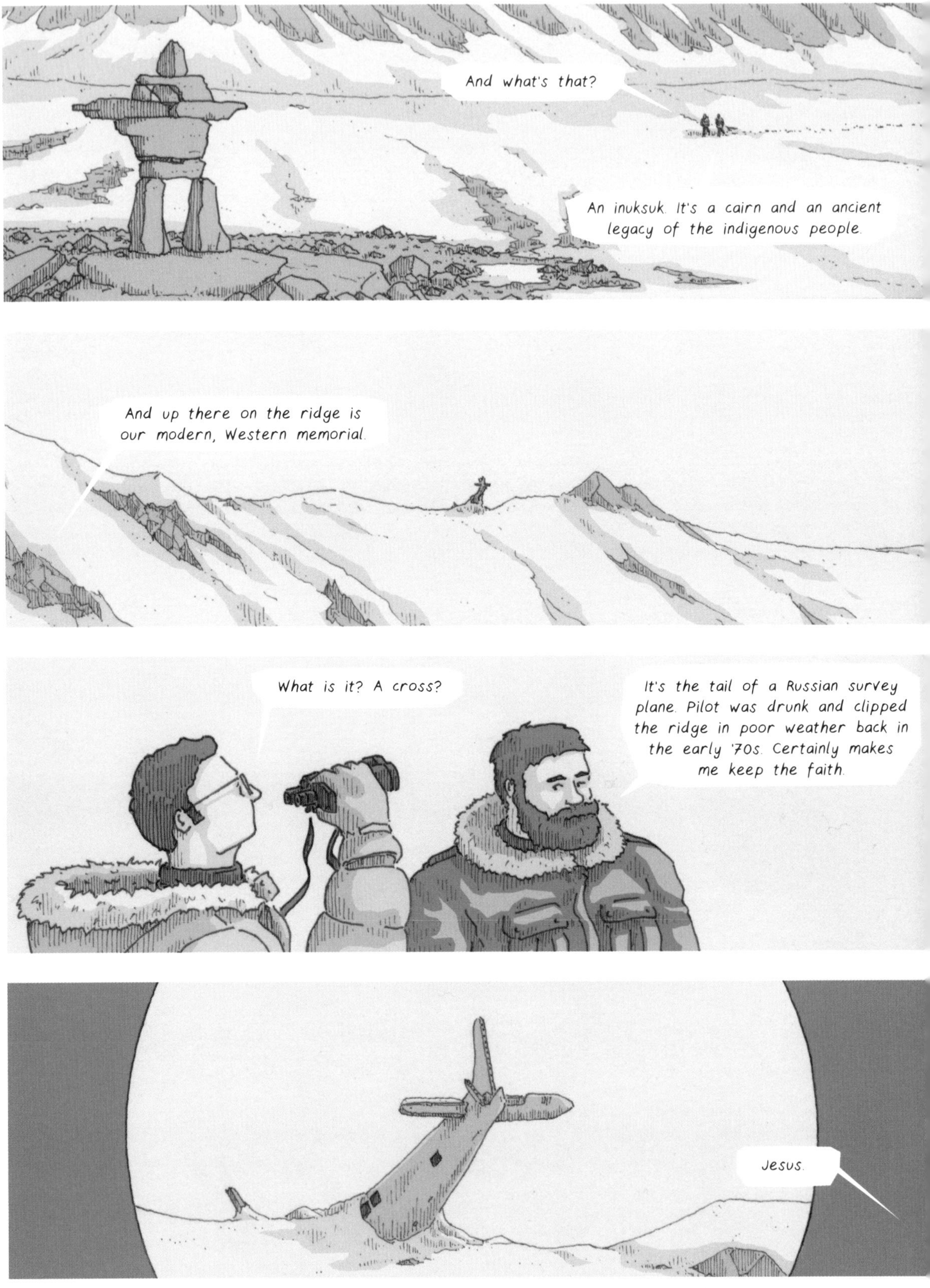
And what's that?
An inuksuk. It's a cairn and an ancient legacy of the indigenous people.
And up there on the ridge is our modern, Western memorial.
What is it? A cross?
It's the tail of a Russian survey plane. Pilot was drunk and clipped the ridge in poor weather back in the early '70s. Certainly makes me keep the faith.
Jesus.

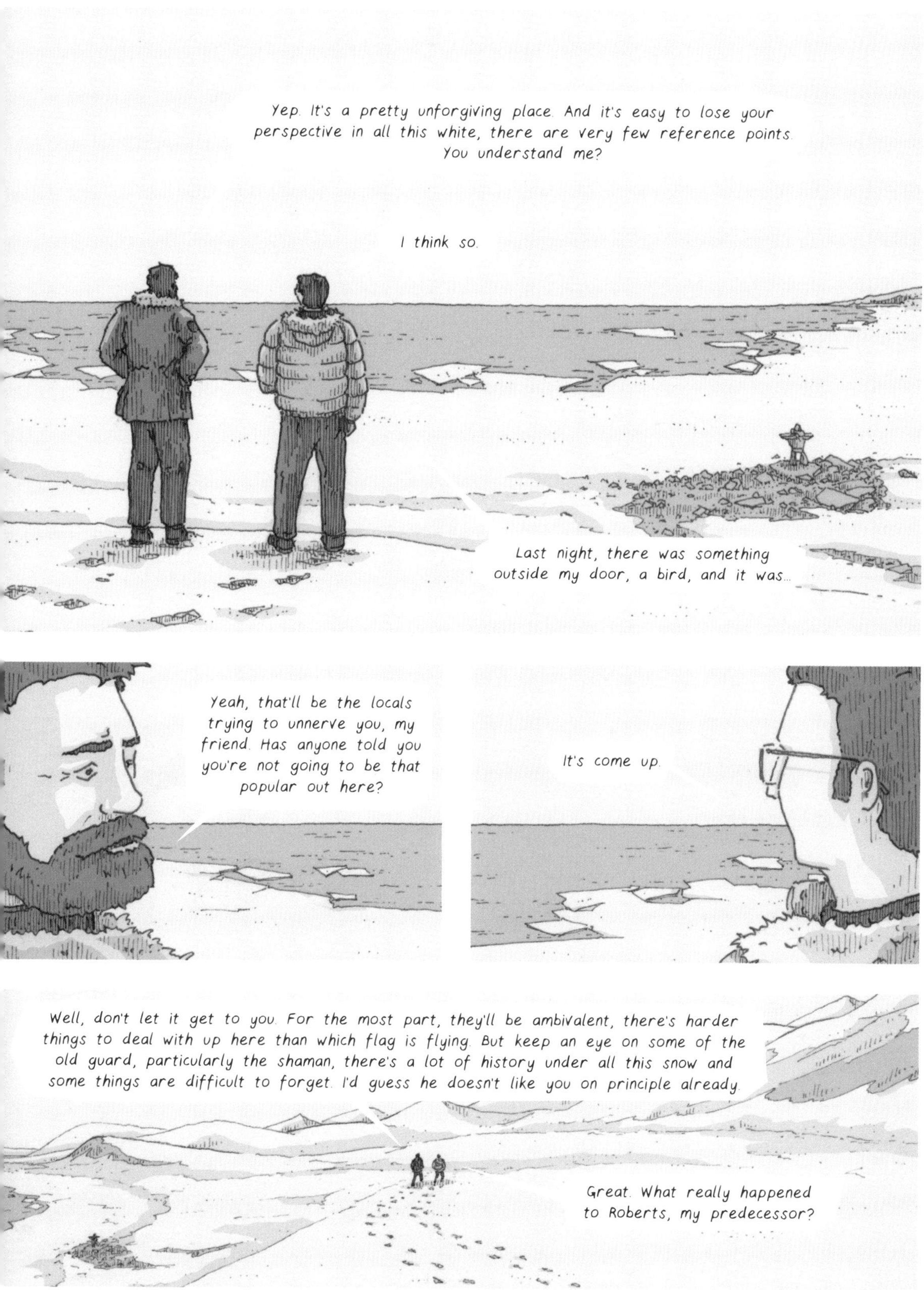
Yep. It's a pretty unforgiving place. And it's easy to lose your perspective in all this white, there are very few reference points. You understand me?
I think so.
Last night, there was something outside my door, a bird, and it was...
Yeah, that'll be the locals trying to unnerve you, my friend. Has anyone told you you're not going to be that popular out here?
It's come up.
Well, don't let it get to you. For the most part, they'll be ambivalent, there's harder things to deal with up here than which flag is flying. But keep an eye on some of the old guard, particularly the shaman, there's a lot of history under all this snow and some things are difficult to forget. I'd guess he doesn't like you on principle already.
Great. What really happened to Roberts, my predecessor?

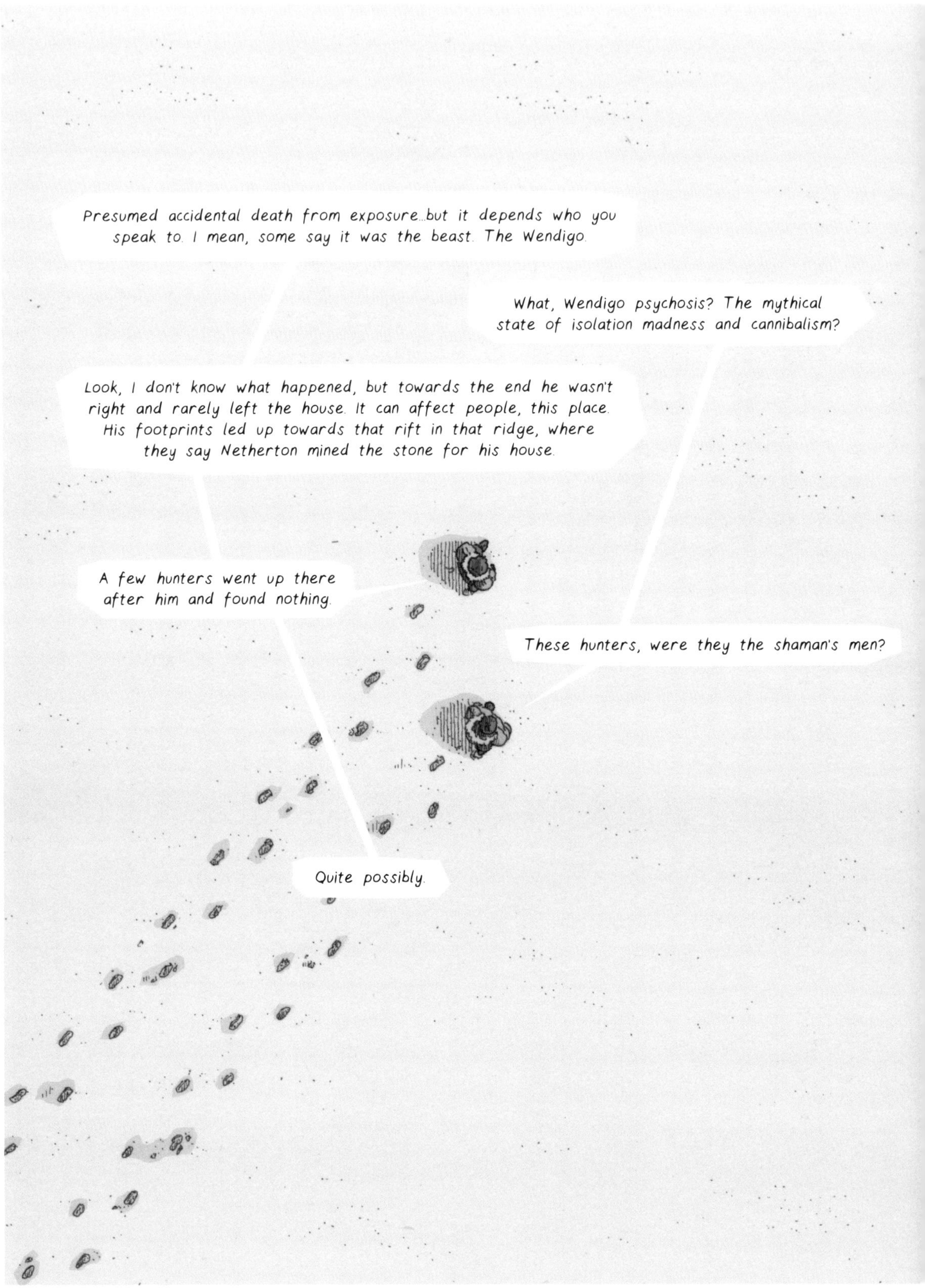
Presumed accidental death from exposure...but it depends who you speak to. I mean, some say it was the beast. The Wendigo.
What, Wendigo psychosis? The mythical state of isolation madness and cannibalism?
Look, I don't know what happened, but towards the end he wasn't right and rarely left the house. It can affect people, this place. His footprints led up towards that rift in that ridge, where they say Netherton mined the stone for his house.
A few hunters went up there after him and found nothing.
These hunters, were they the shaman's men?
Quite possibly.

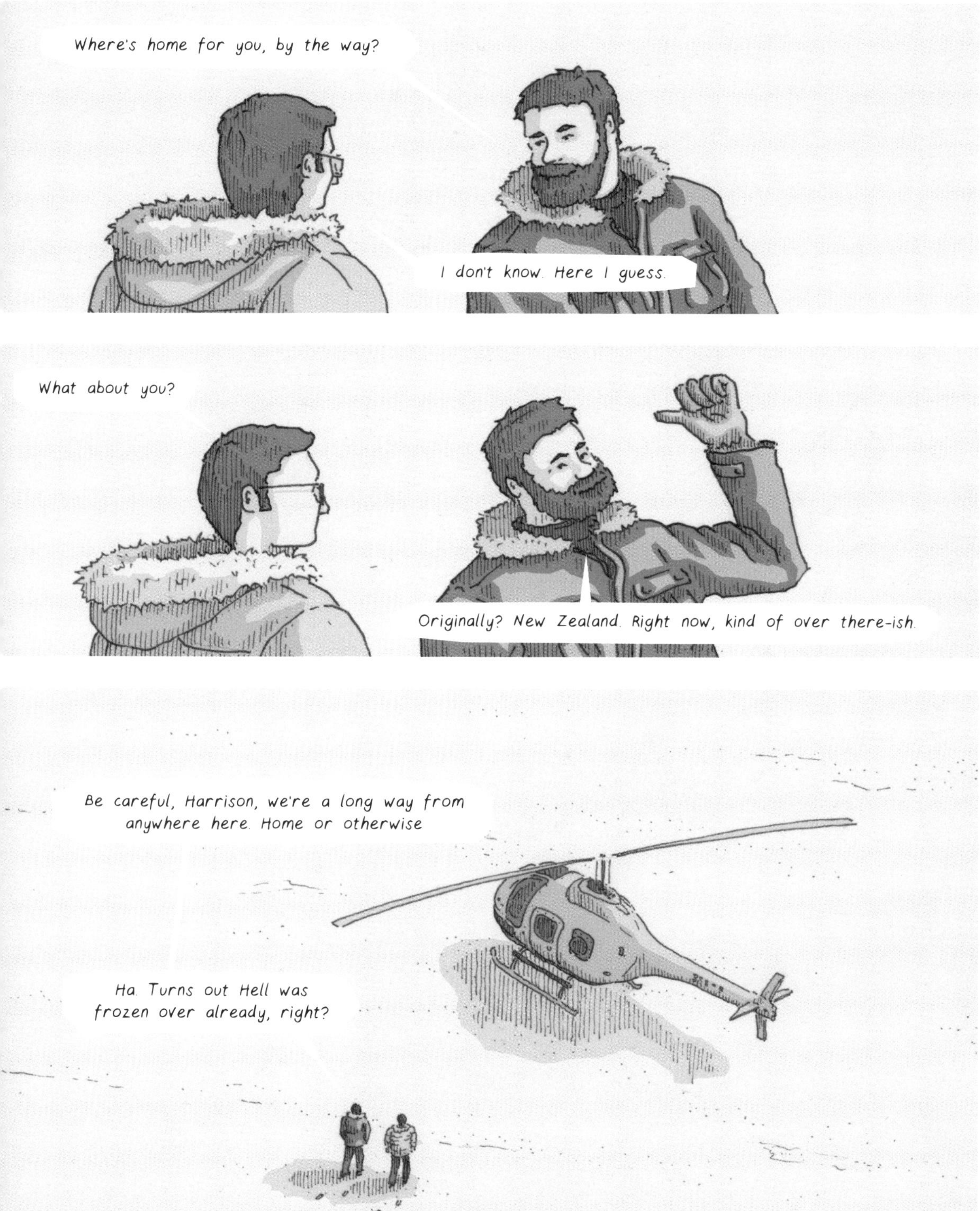
Where's home for you, by the way?
I don't know. Here I guess.
What about you?
Originally? New Zealand. Right now, kind of over there-ish.
Be careful, Harrison, we're a long way from anywhere here. Home or otherwise
Ha. Turns out Hell was frozen over already, right?

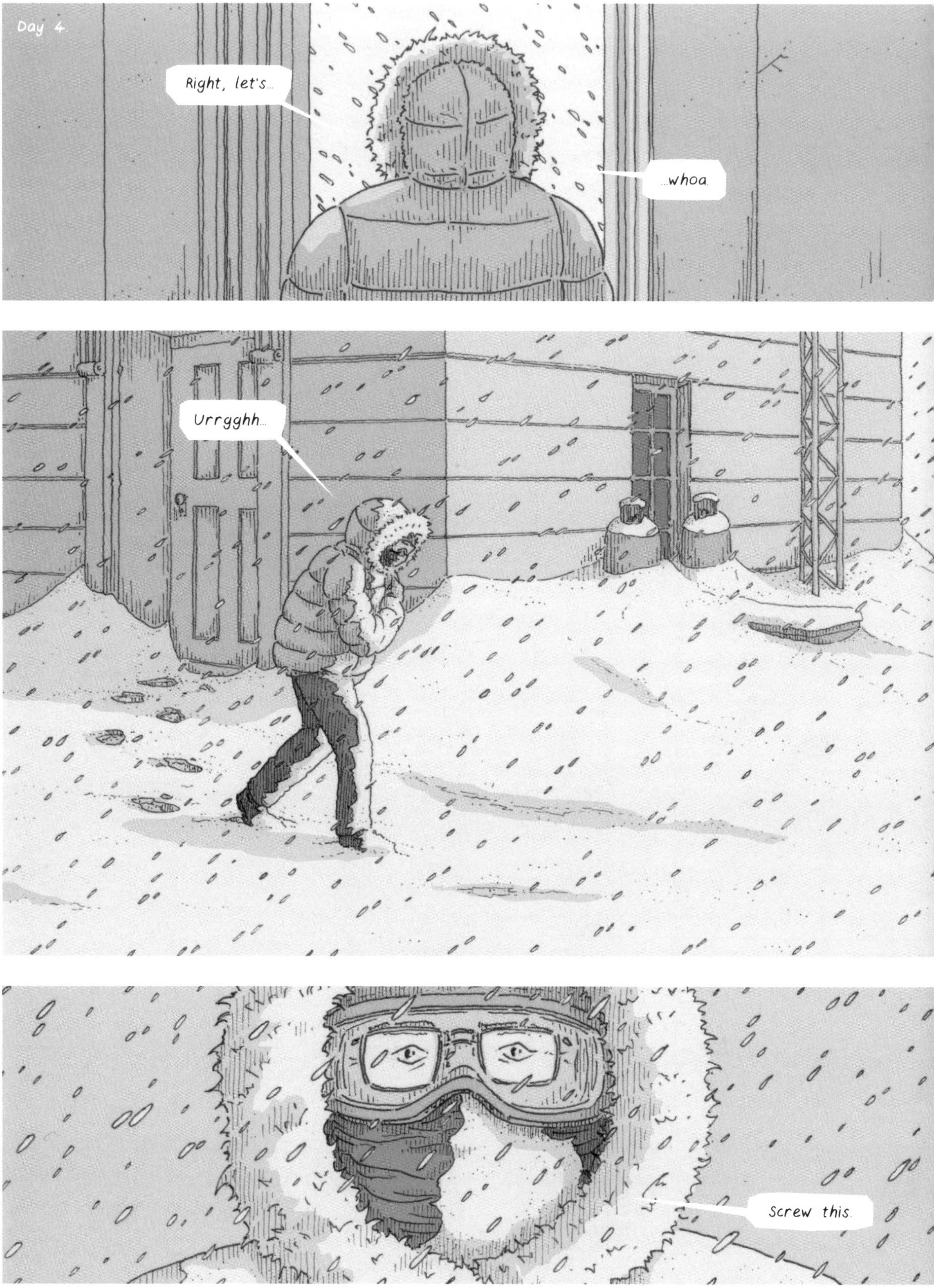
Day 4.
Right, let's...
...whoa.
Urrgghh...
Screw this.

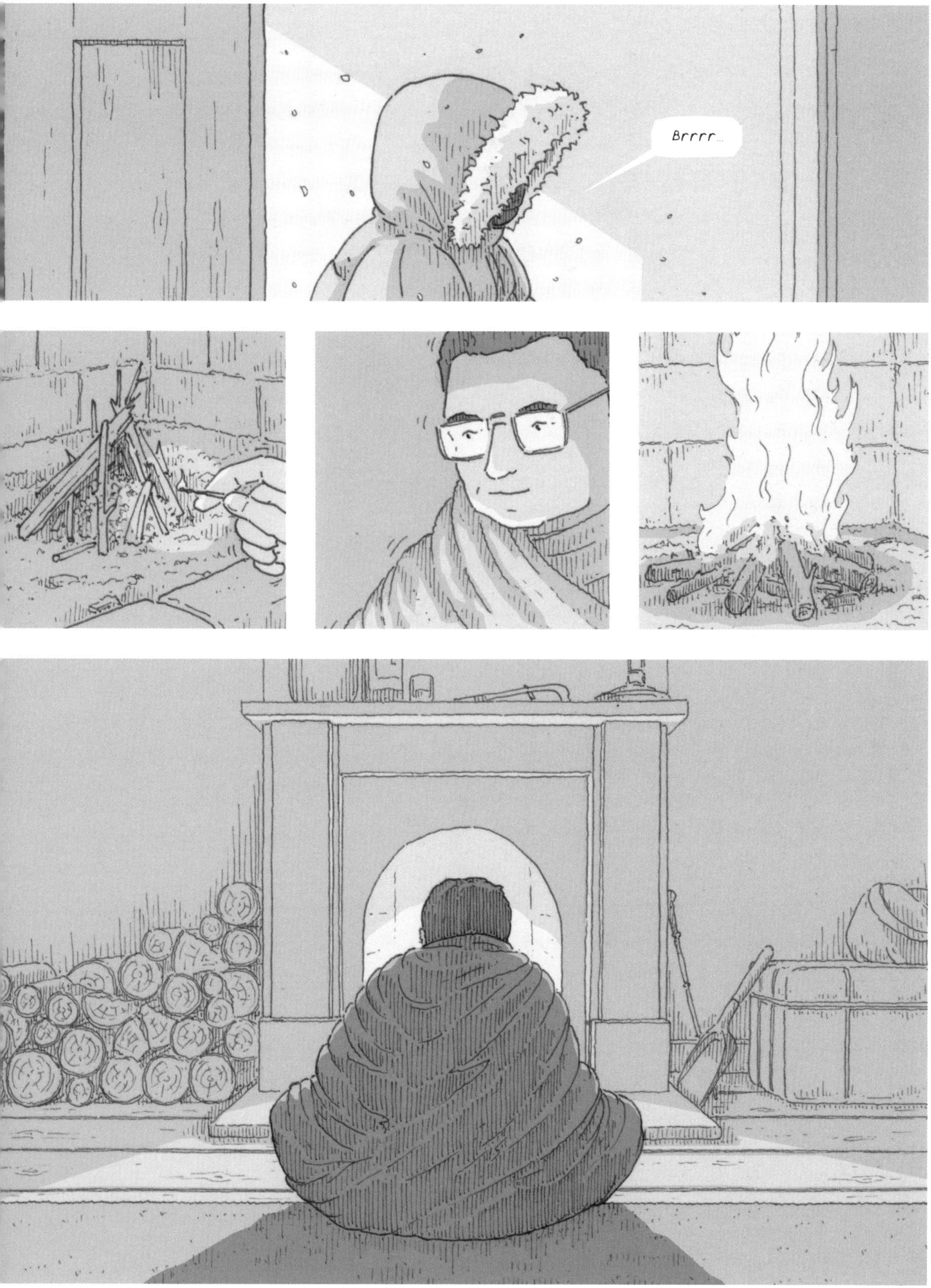
Brrrr...

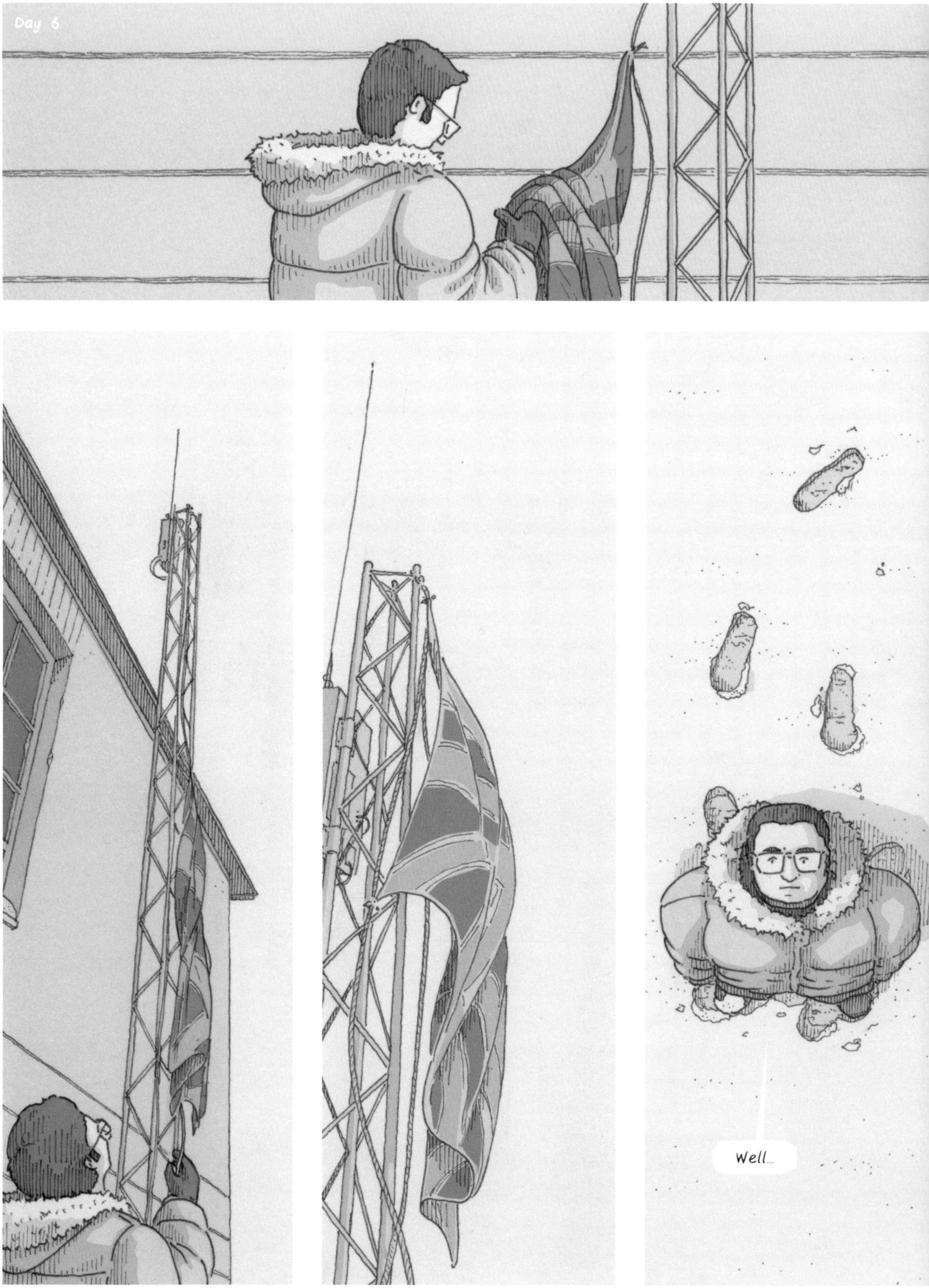
Day 6
Well…

...that's that.

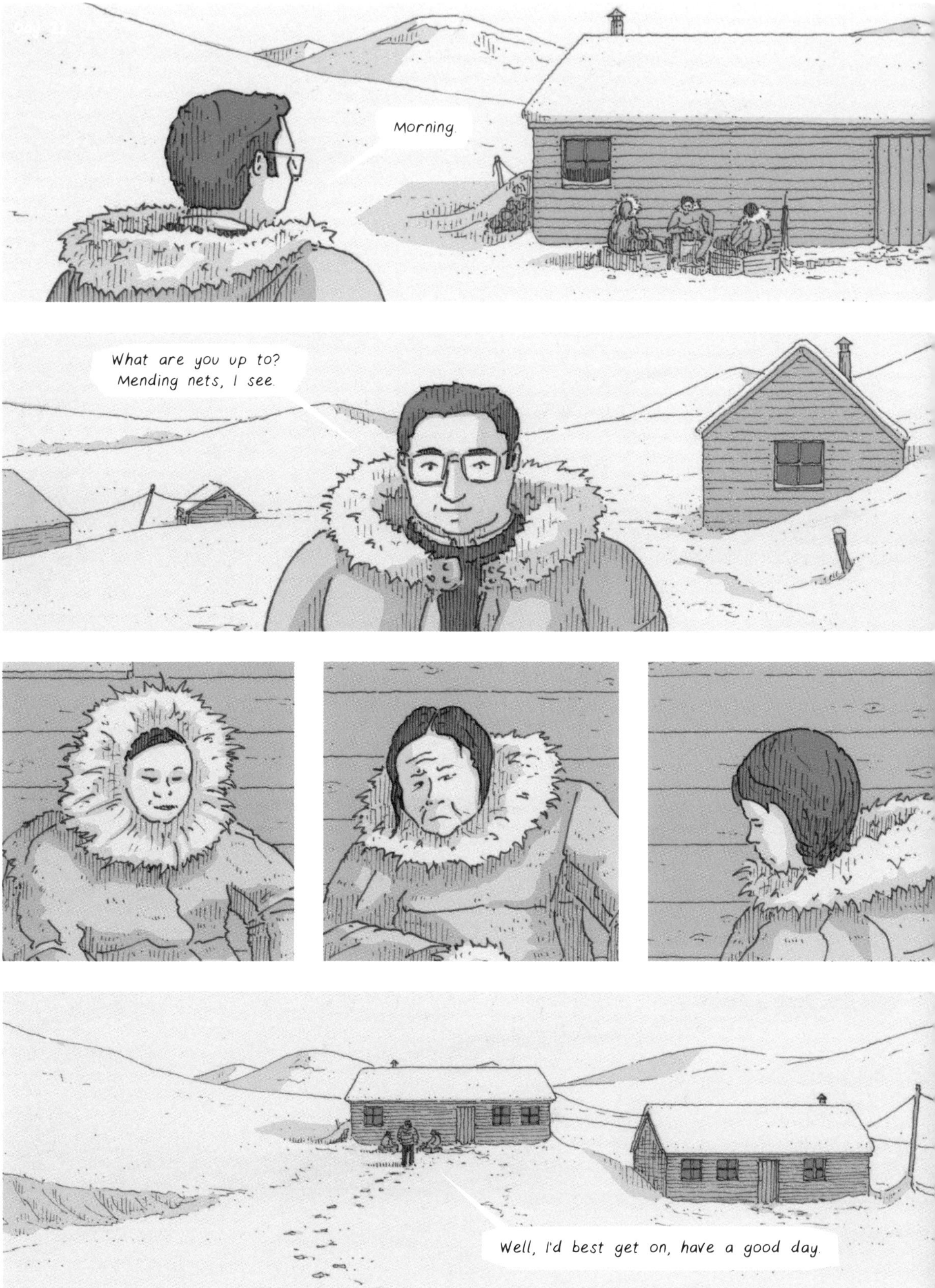
Morning.
What are you up to? Mending nets, I see.
Well, I'd best get on, have a good day.

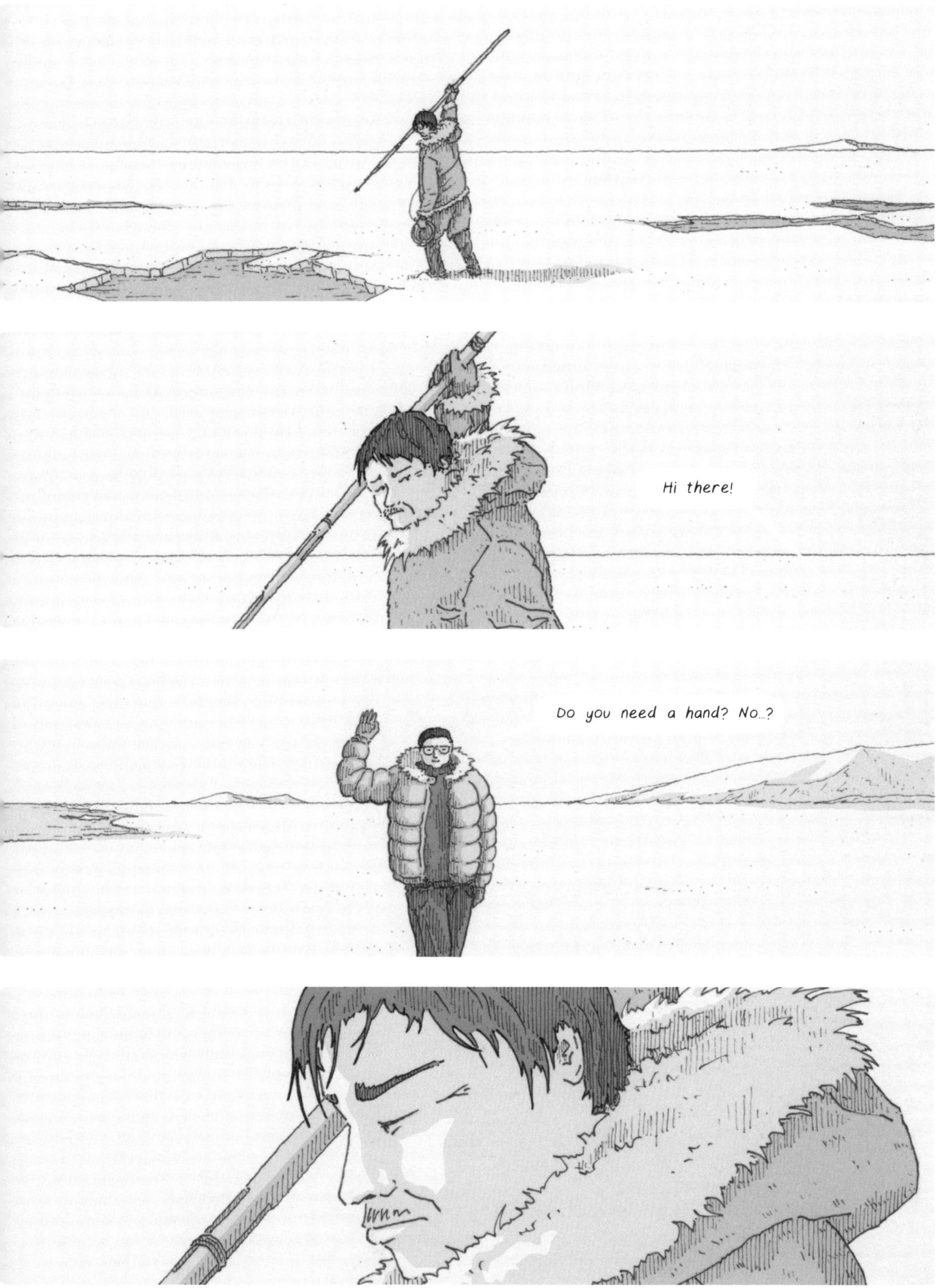
Hi there!
Do you need a hand? No...?

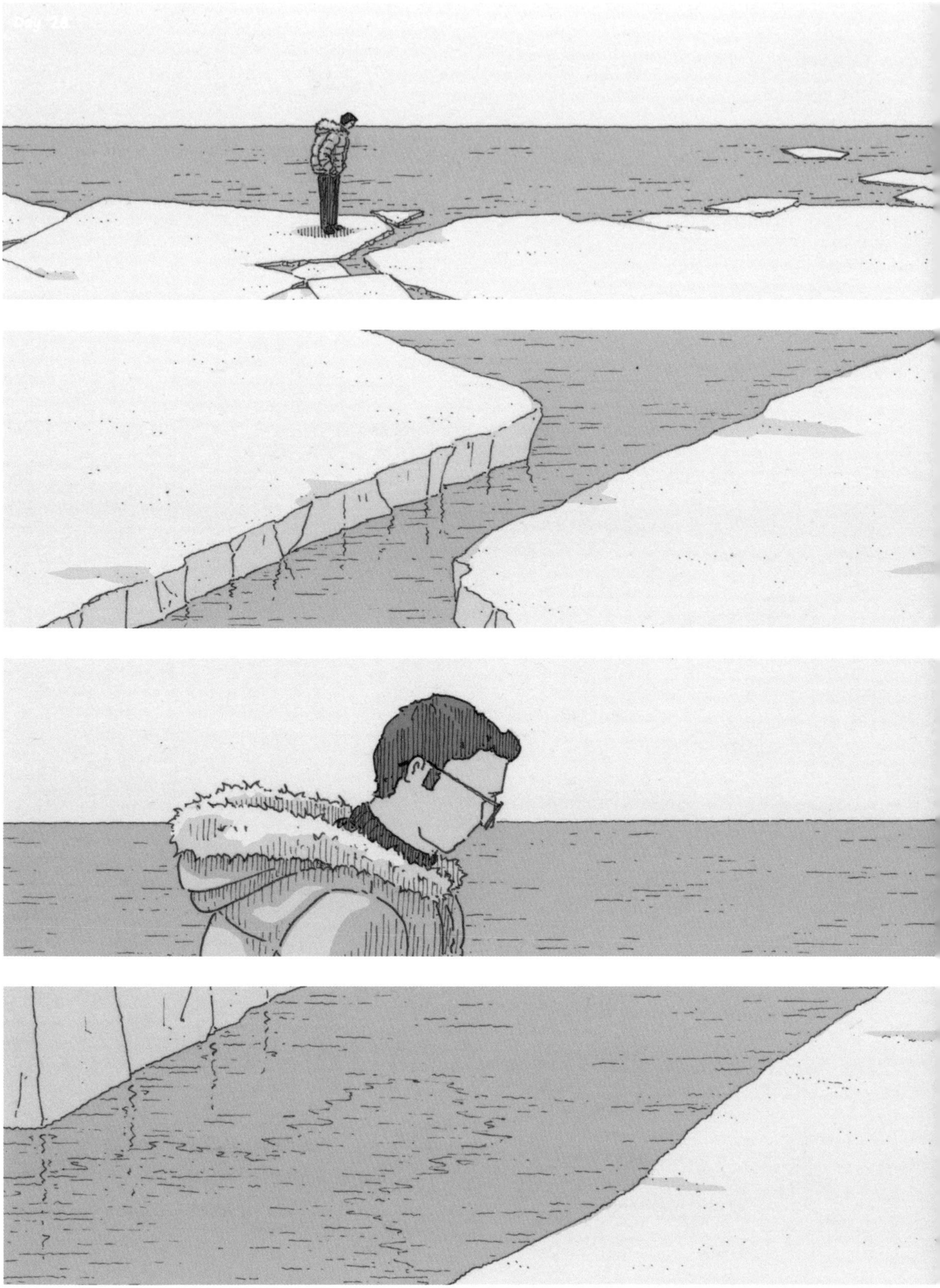

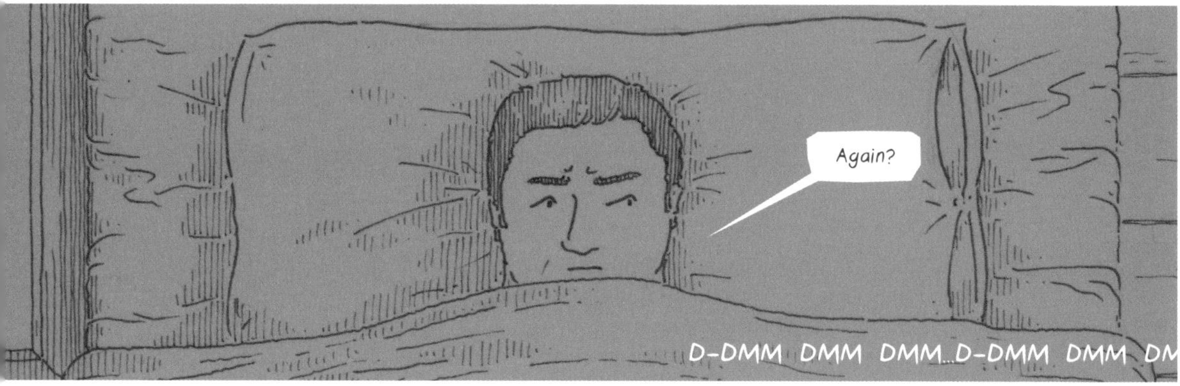
Again?
D-DMM DMM DMM...D-DMM DMM DM

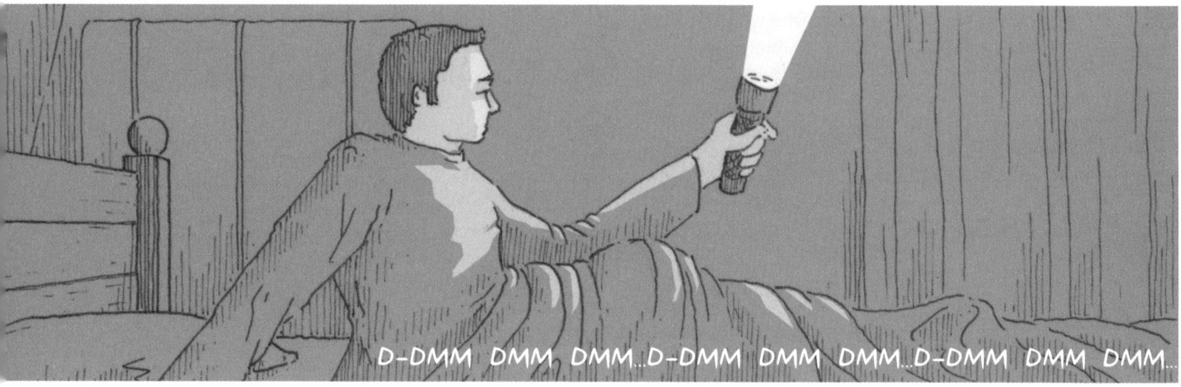
D-DMM DMM DMM...D-DMM DMM DMM...D-DMM DMM DMM...

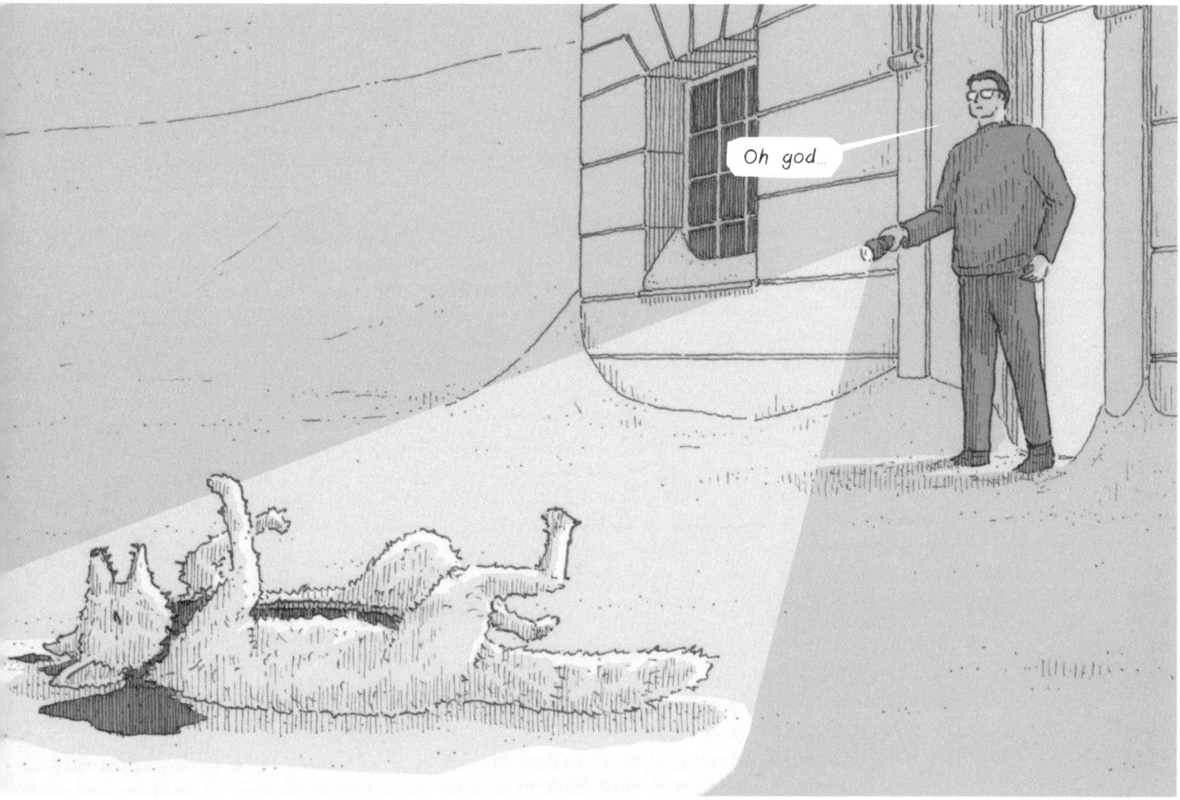
Oh god...

PART II

EXPLORATIONS

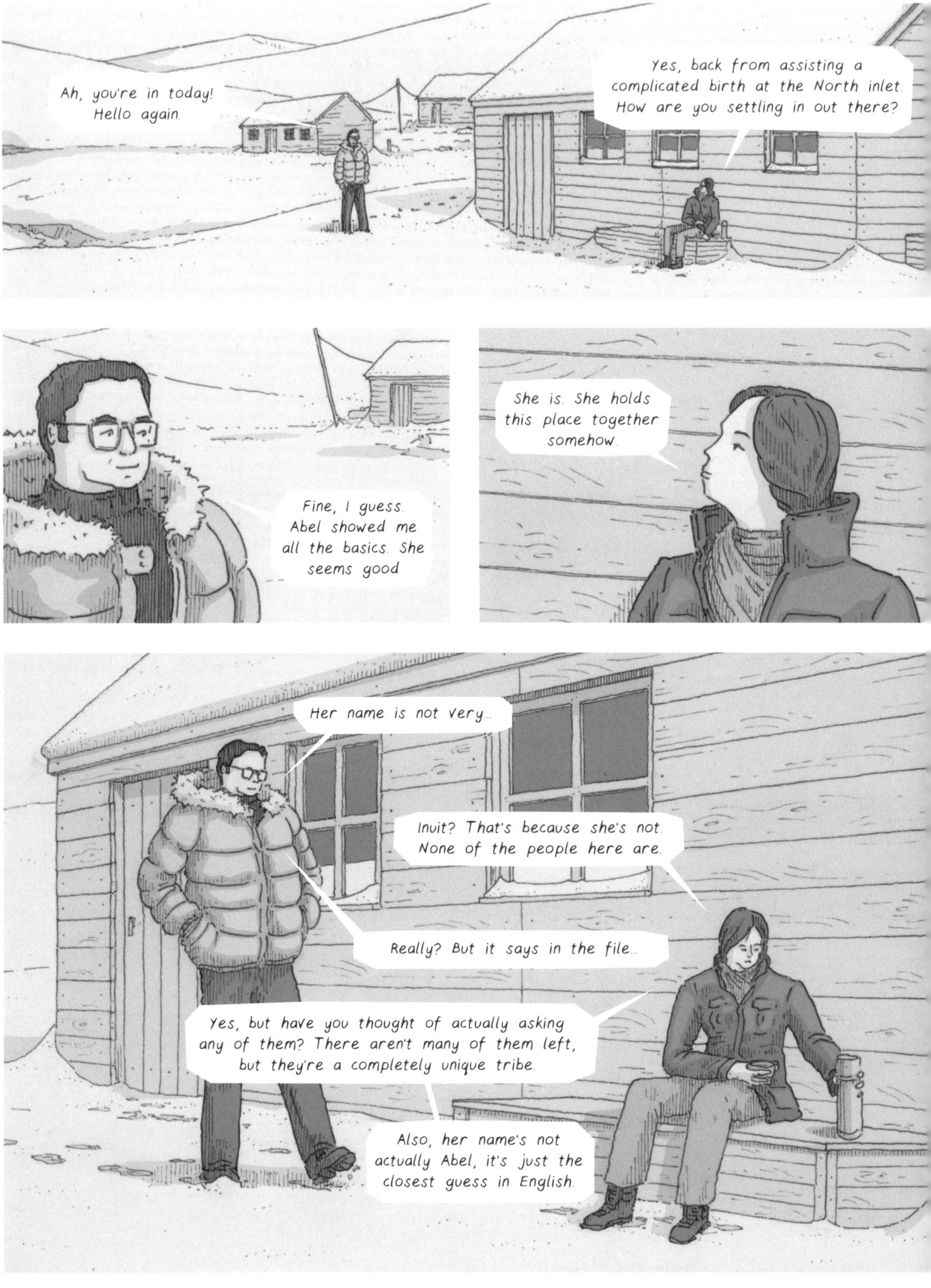
Ah, you're in today! Hello again.
Yes, back from assisting a complicated birth at the North inlet. How are you settling in out there?
Fine, I guess. Abel showed me all the basics. She seems good
She is. She holds this place together somehow.
Her name is not very...
Inuit? That's because she's not. None of the people here are.
Really? But it says in the file...
Yes, but have you thought of actually asking any of them? There aren't many of them left, but they're a completely unique tribe.
Also, her name's not actually Abel, it's just the closest guess in English.

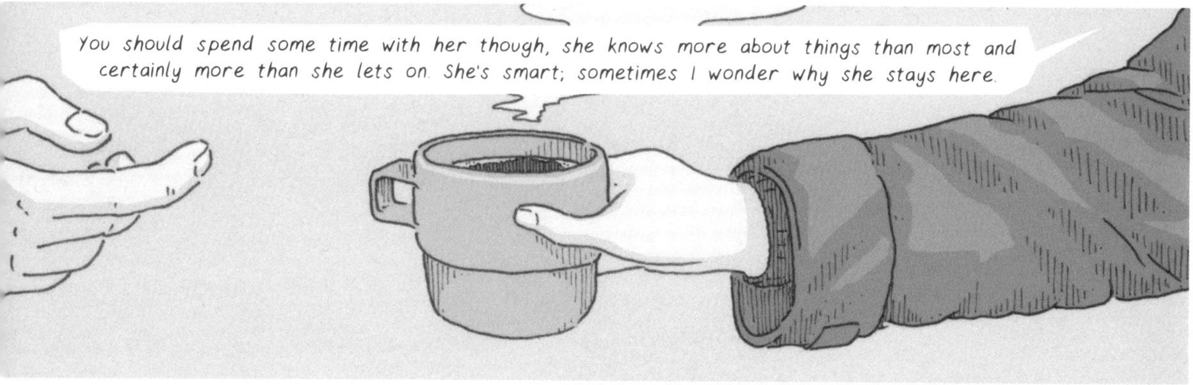
You should spend some time with her though, she knows more about things than most and certainly more than she lets on. She's smart; sometimes I wonder why she stays here.

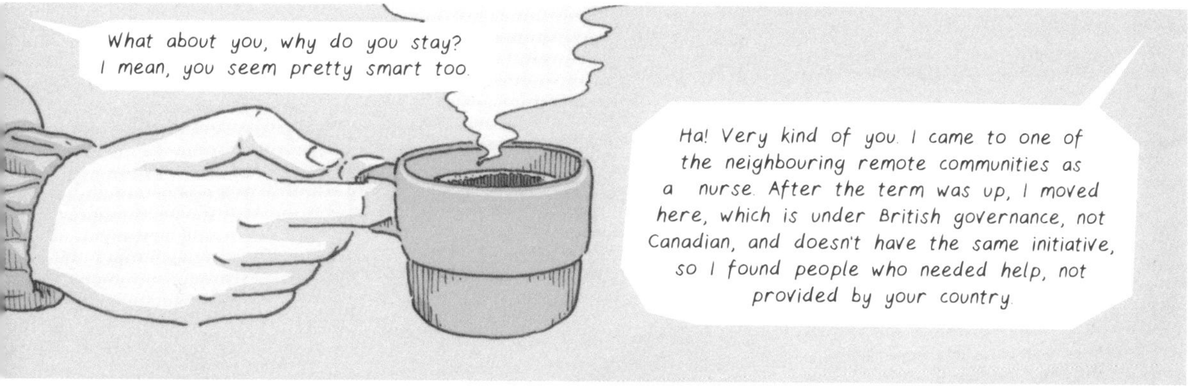
What about you, why do you stay? I mean, you seem pretty smart too.
Ha! Very kind of you. I came to one of the neighbouring remote communities as a nurse. After the term was up, I moved here, which is under British governance, not Canadian, and doesn't have the same initiative, so I found people who needed help, not provided by your country.

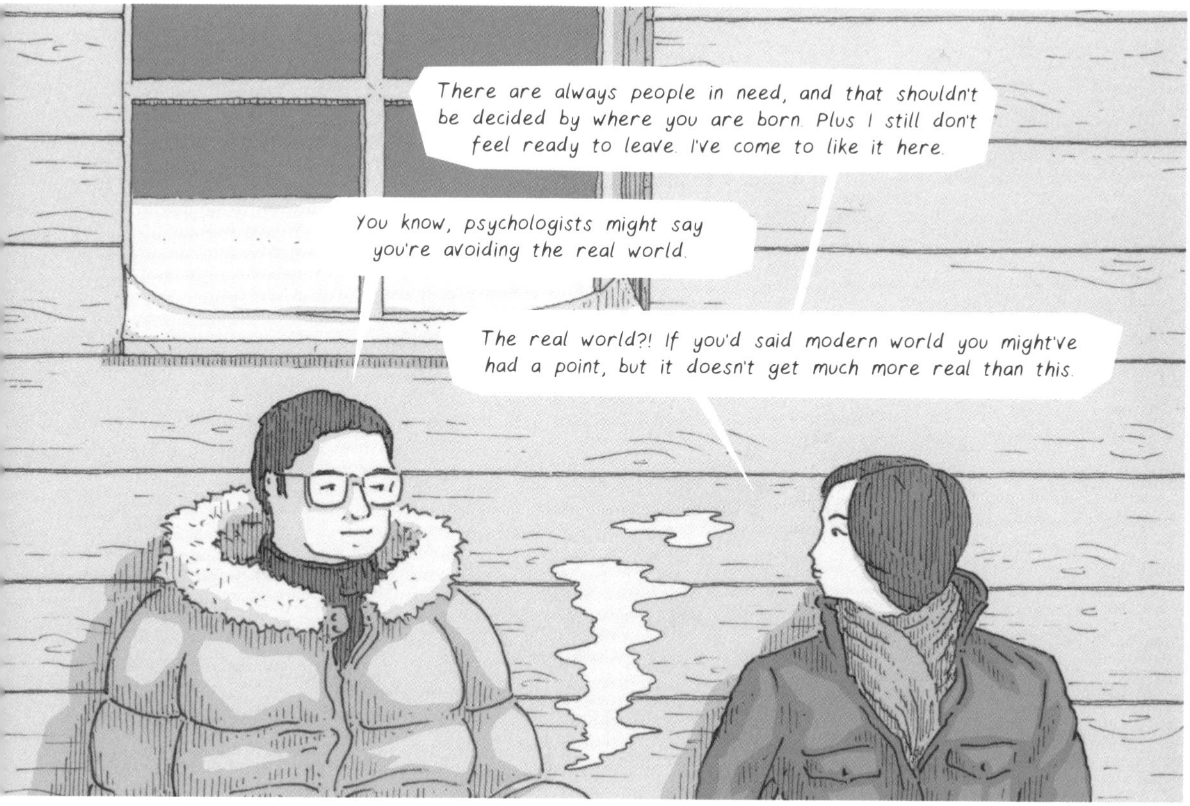
There are always people in need, and that shouldn't be decided by where you are born. Plus I still don't feel ready to leave. I've come to like it here.
You know, psychologists might say you're avoiding the real world.
The real world?! If you'd said modern world you might've had a point, but it doesn't get much more real than this.

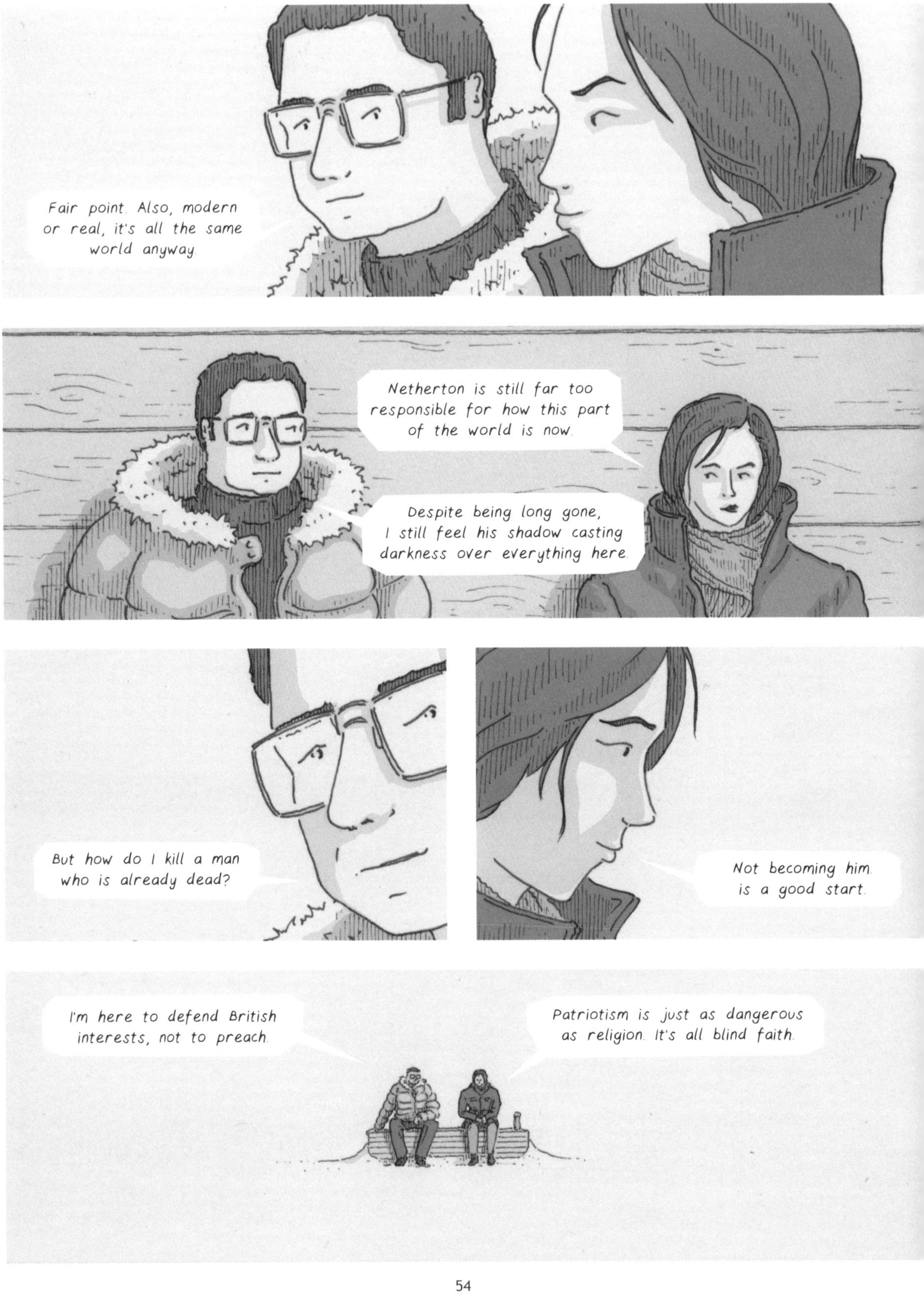
Fair point. Also, modern or real, it's all the same world anyway.
Netherton is still far too responsible for how this part of the world is now.
Despite being long gone, I still feel his shadow casting darkness over everything here.
But how do I kill a man who is already dead?
Not becoming him is a good start.
I'm here to defend British interests, not to preach.
Patriotism is just as dangerous as religion. It's all blind faith.

What really happened?

You should speak to Abel, her great-grandfather was here in Netherton's time.

I will, but it's hard to talk to any of them, they don't really seem to trust me.

Can you blame them?

They have survived by virtue of the fact that they have nothing economic to offer, but it means they are given no help either. They live on a knife's edge. If they are useful, they will be exploited, if they are in the way, they will be disposed of.

I'm only trying to help.

Said like a true missionary.

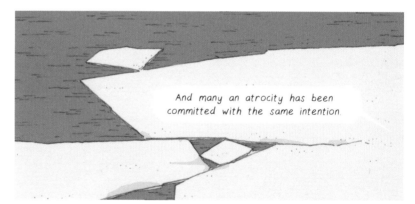

And many an atrocity has been committed with the same intention.

That was good coffee.

It's the only coffee we have.

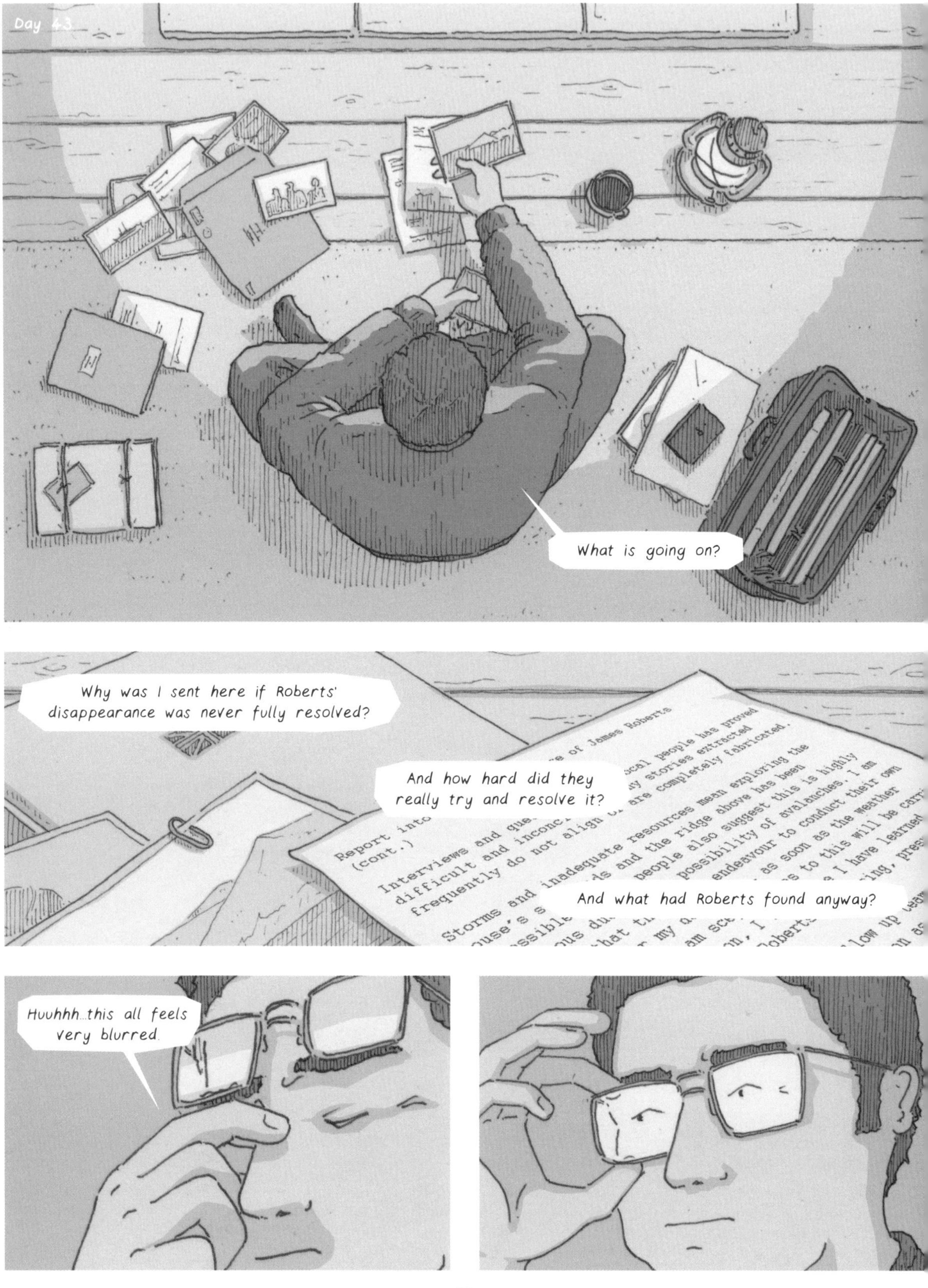
Day 43
What is going on?
Why was I sent here if Roberts' disappearance was never fully resolved?
And how hard did they really try and resolve it?
And what had Roberts found anyway?
Huuhhh...this all feels very blurred.

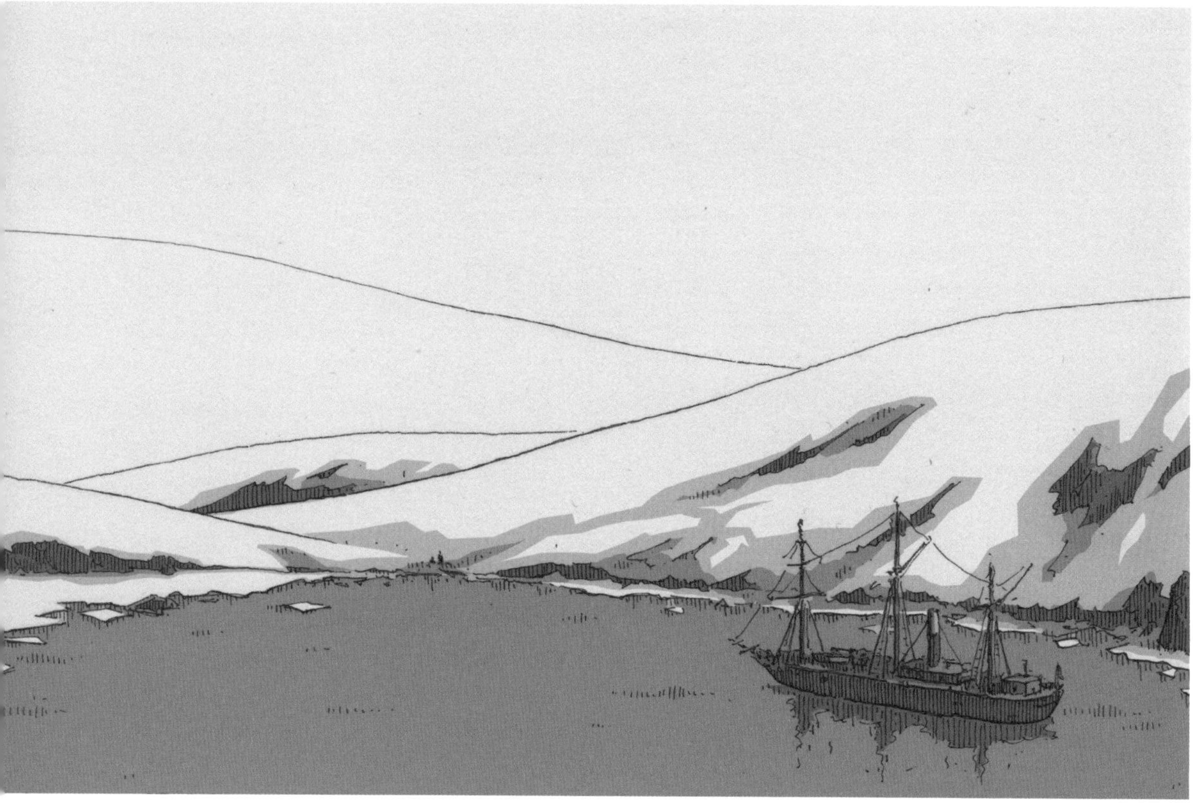

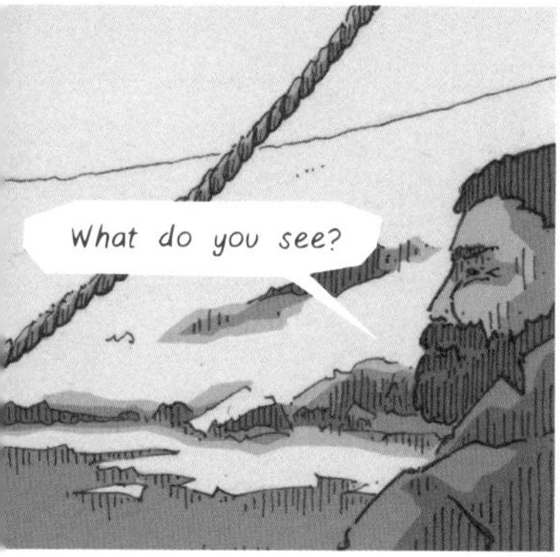
What do you see?

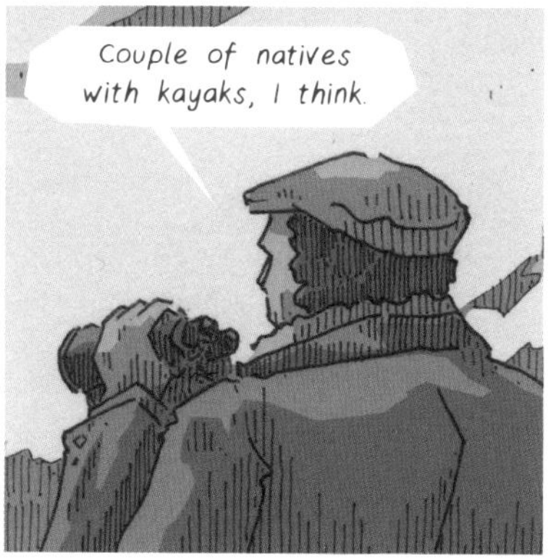
Couple of natives
with kayaks, I think.

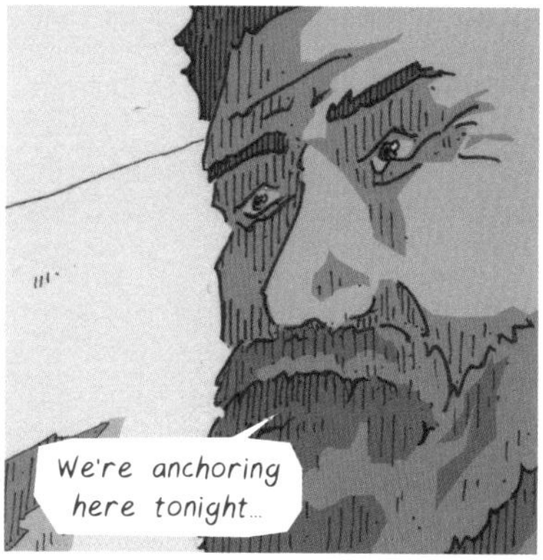
We're anchoring
here tonight...

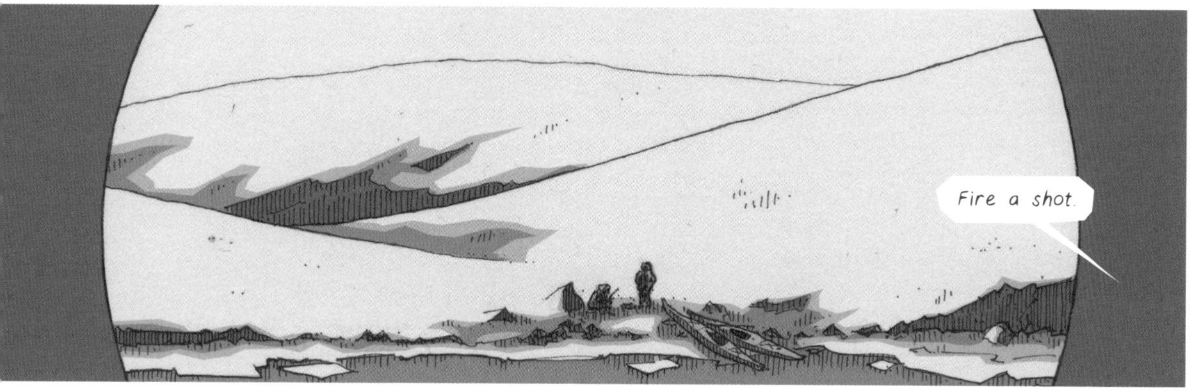
Fire a shot.

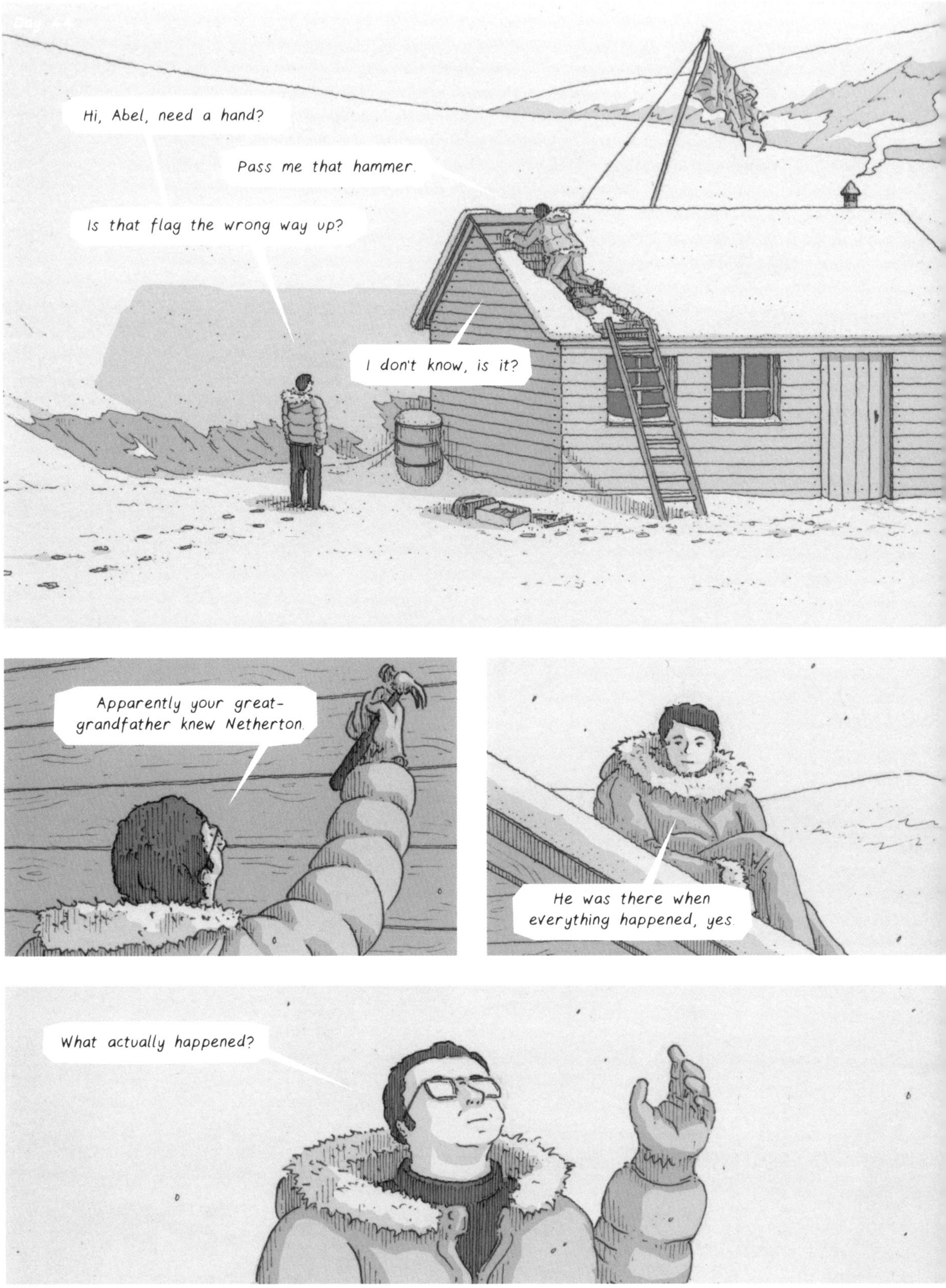
Hi, Abel, need a hand?
Pass me that hammer.
Is that flag the wrong way up?
I don't know, is it?
Apparently your great-grandfather knew Netherton.
He was there when everything happened, yes.
What actually happened?

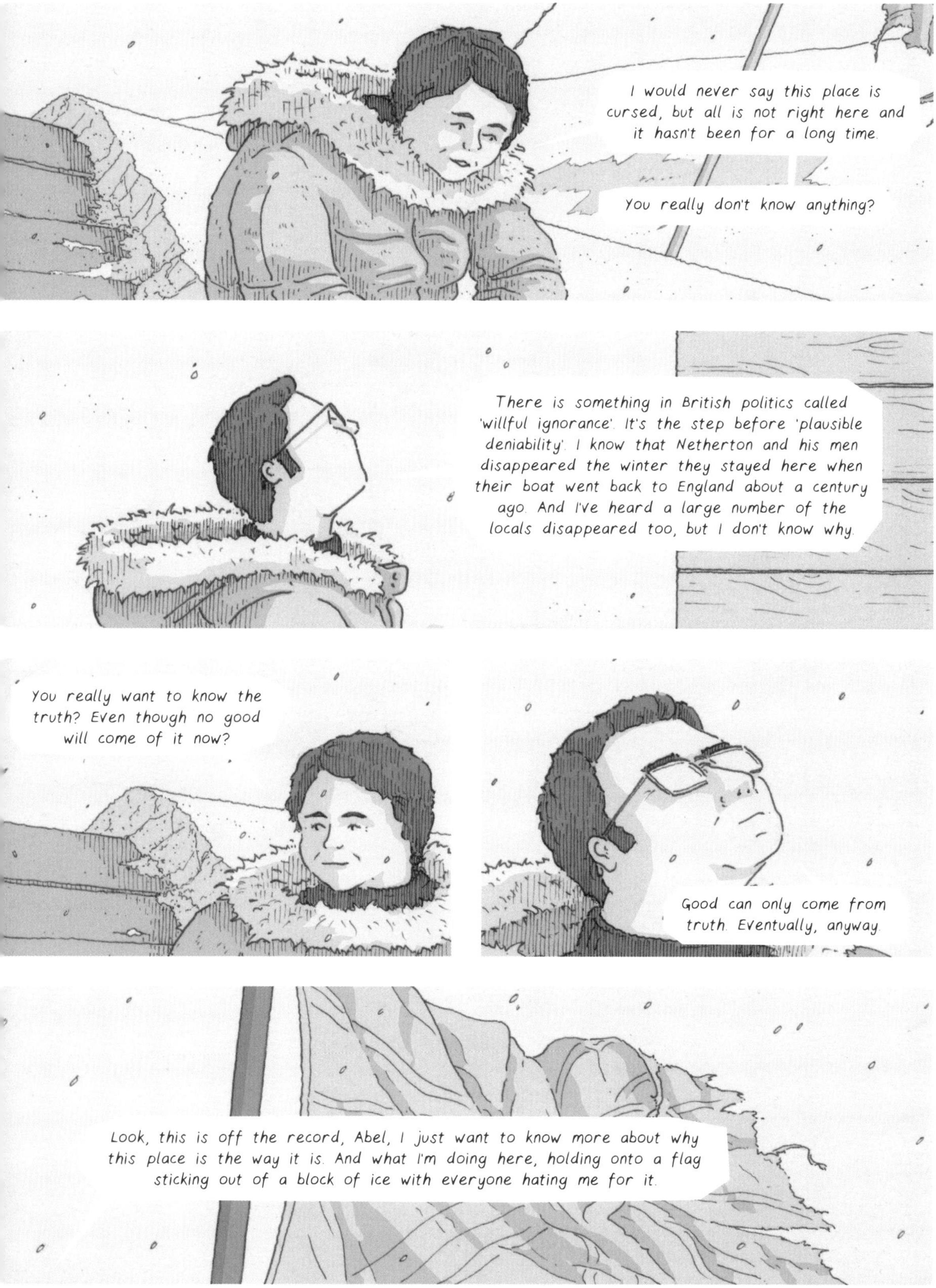
I would never say this place is cursed, but all is not right here and it hasn't been for a long time.
You really don't know anything?
There is something in British politics called 'willful ignorance'. It's the step before 'plausible deniability'. I know that Netherton and his men disappeared the winter they stayed here when their boat went back to England about a century ago. And I've heard a large number of the locals disappeared too, but I don't know why.
You really want to know the truth? Even though no good will come of it now?
Good can only come from truth. Eventually, anyway.
Look, this is off the record, Abel, I just want to know more about why this place is the way it is. And what I'm doing here, holding onto a flag sticking out of a block of ice with everyone hating me for it.

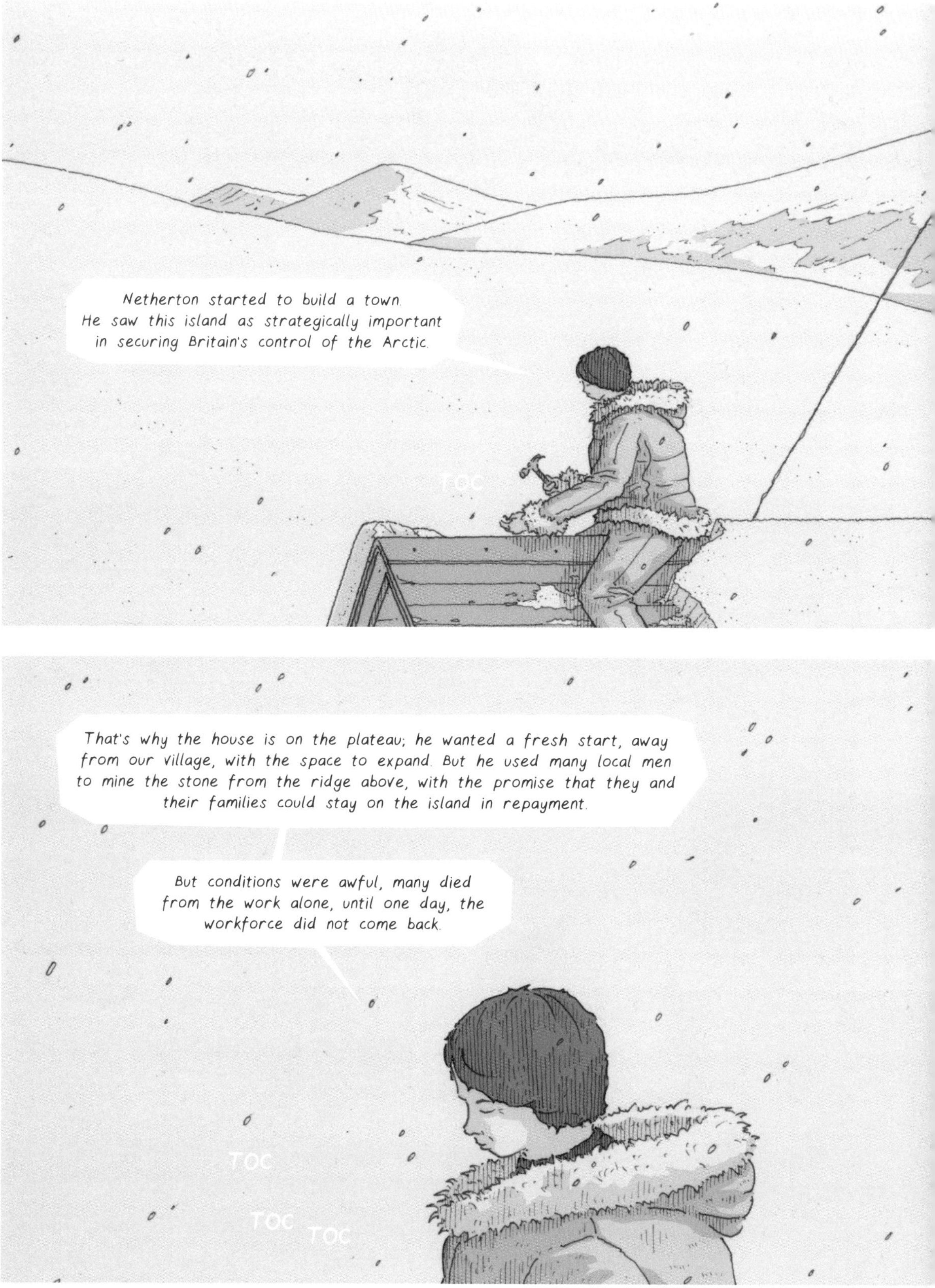
Netherton started to build a town. He saw this island as strategically important in securing Britain's control of the Arctic.
TOC
That's why the house is on the plateau; he wanted a fresh start, away from our village, with the space to expand. But he used many local men to mine the stone from the ridge above, with the promise that they and their families could stay on the island in repayment.
But conditions were awful, many died from the work alone, until one day, the workforce did not come back.
TOC
TOC
TOC

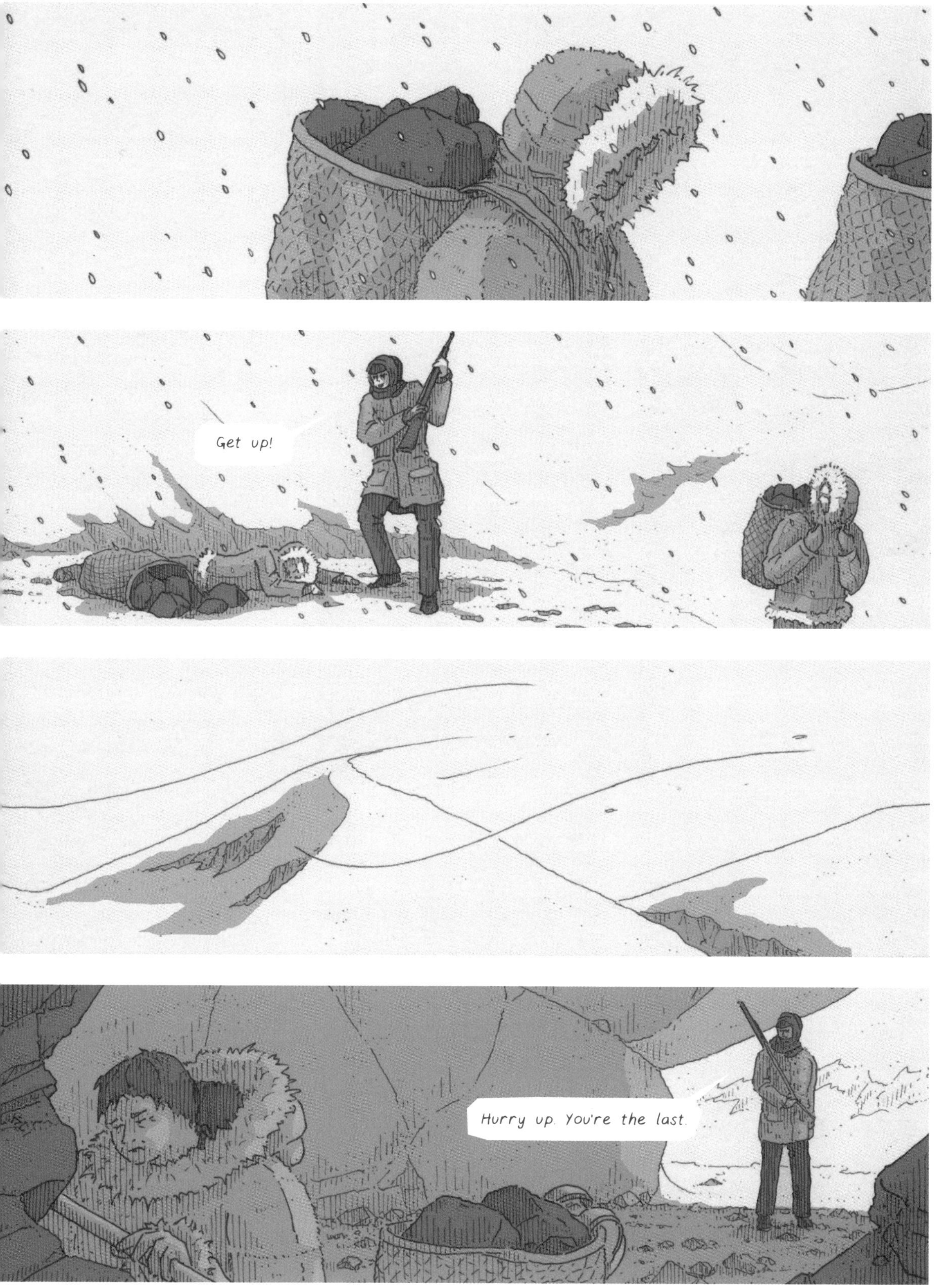
Get up!
Hurry up. You're the last.

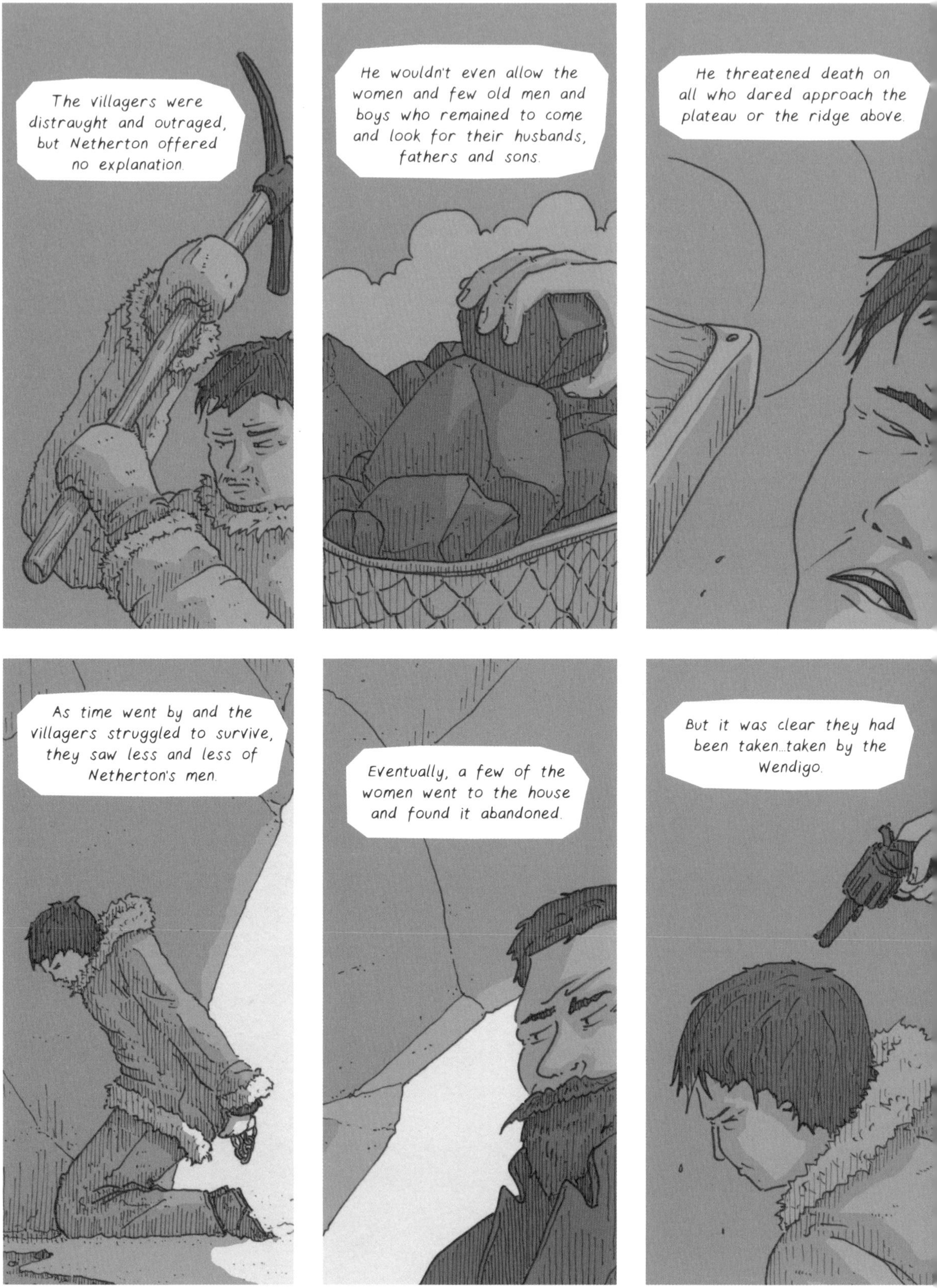
The villagers were distraught and outraged, but Netherton offered no explanation.
He wouldn't even allow the women and few old men and boys who remained to come and look for their husbands, fathers and sons.
He threatened death on all who dared approach the plateau or the ridge above.
As time went by and the villagers struggled to survive, they saw less and less of Netherton's men.
Eventually, a few of the women went to the house and found it abandoned.
But it was clear they had been taken...taken by the Wendigo.

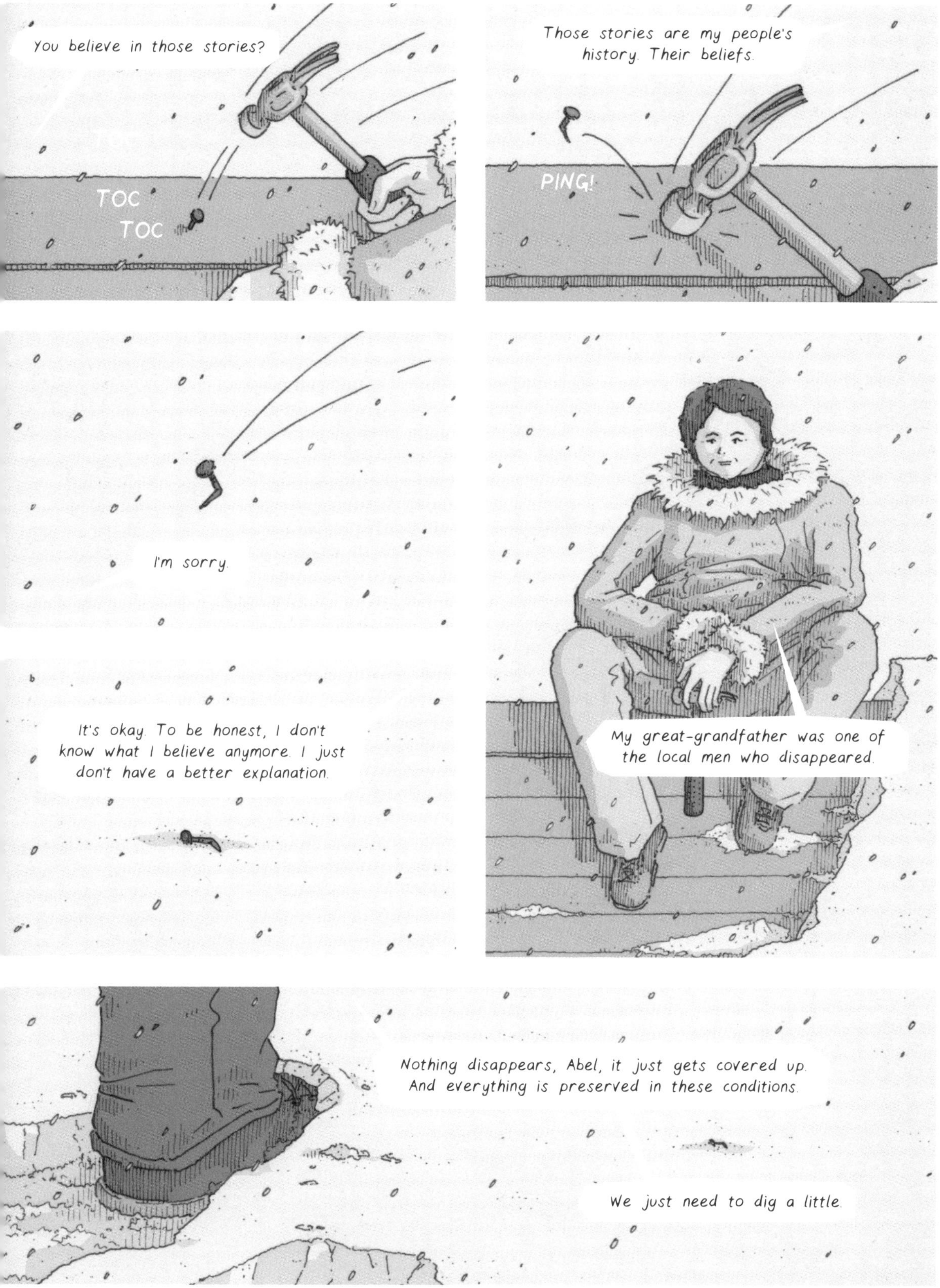
You believe in those stories?
TOC
TOC
Those stories are my people's history. Their beliefs.
PING!
I'm sorry.
It's okay. To be honest, I don't know what I believe anymore. I just don't have a better explanation.
My great-grandfather was one of the local men who disappeared.
Nothing disappears, Abel, it just gets covered up. And everything is preserved in these conditions.
We just need to dig a little.

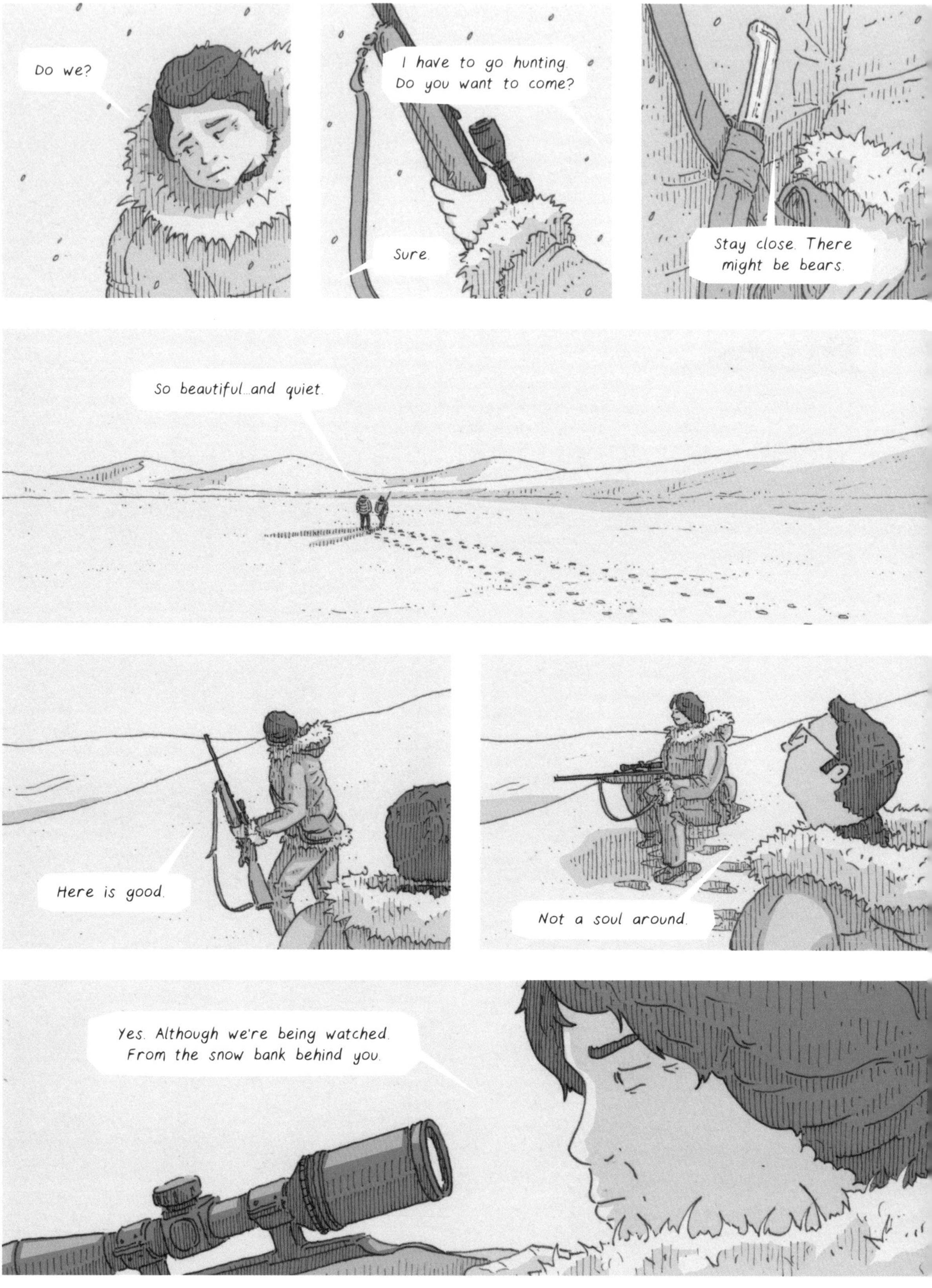
Do we?
I have to go hunting. Do you want to come?
Sure.
Stay close. There might be bears.
So beautiful...and quiet.
Here is good.
Not a soul around.
Yes. Although we're being watched. From the snow bank behind you.

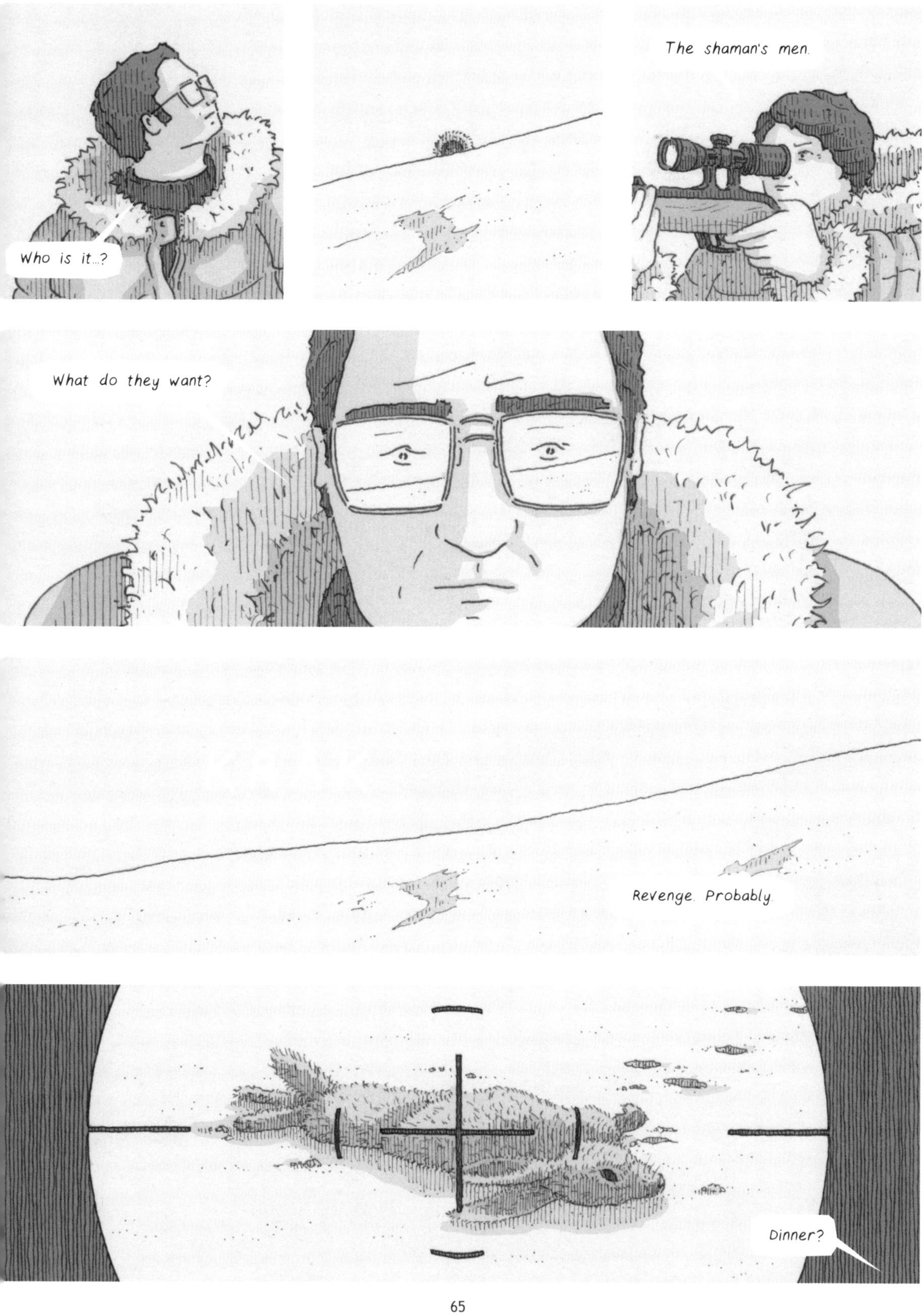
Who is it...?
The shaman's men.
What do they want?
Revenge. Probably.
Dinner?

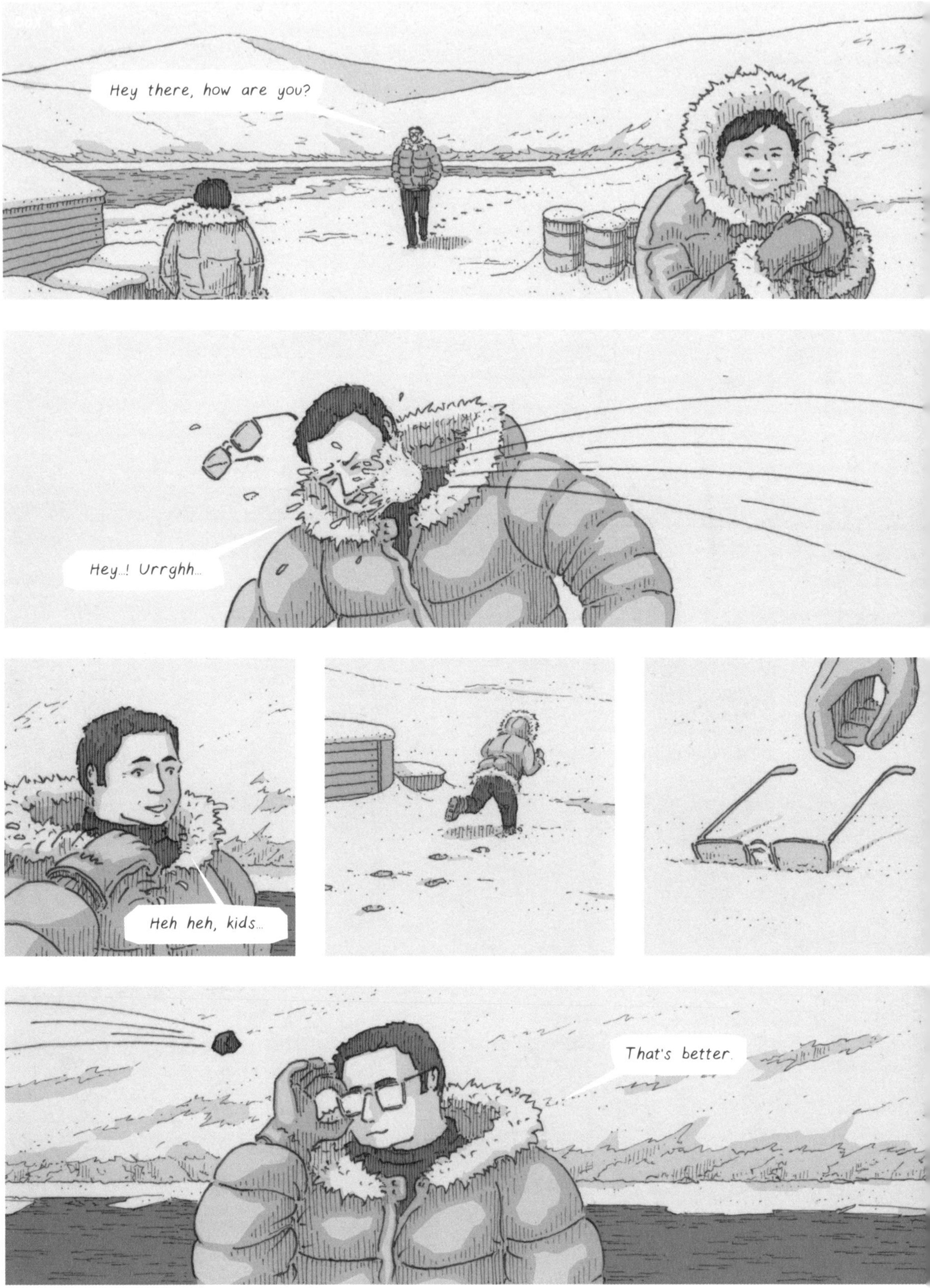
Hey there, how are you?
Hey...! Urrghh...
Heh heh, kids...
That's better.

Christ alive...! What on earth was that?

A rock?!

Who the hell threw it?

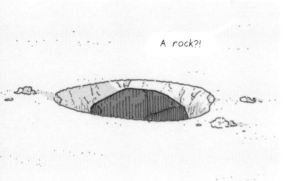

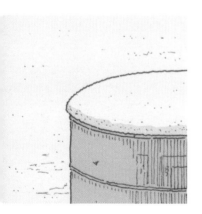

They must be warming to me.

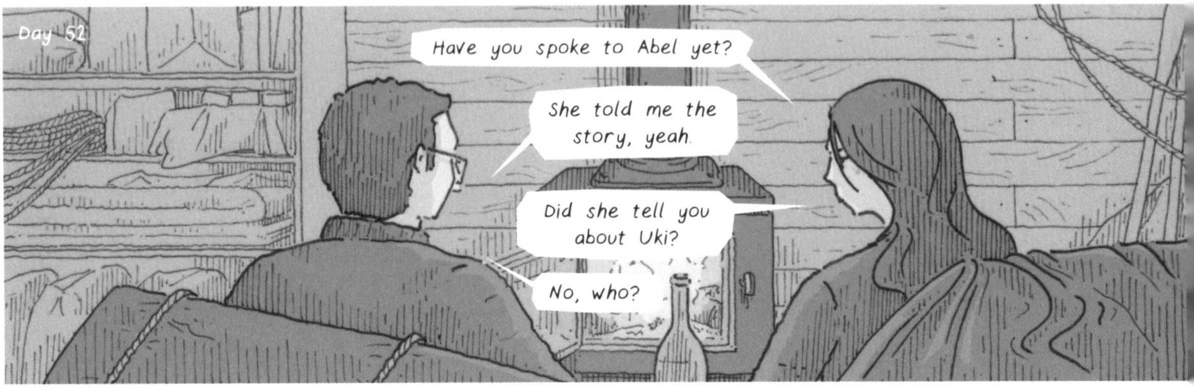
Day 52
Have you spoke to Abel yet?
She told me the story, yeah.
Did she tell you about Uki?
No, who?

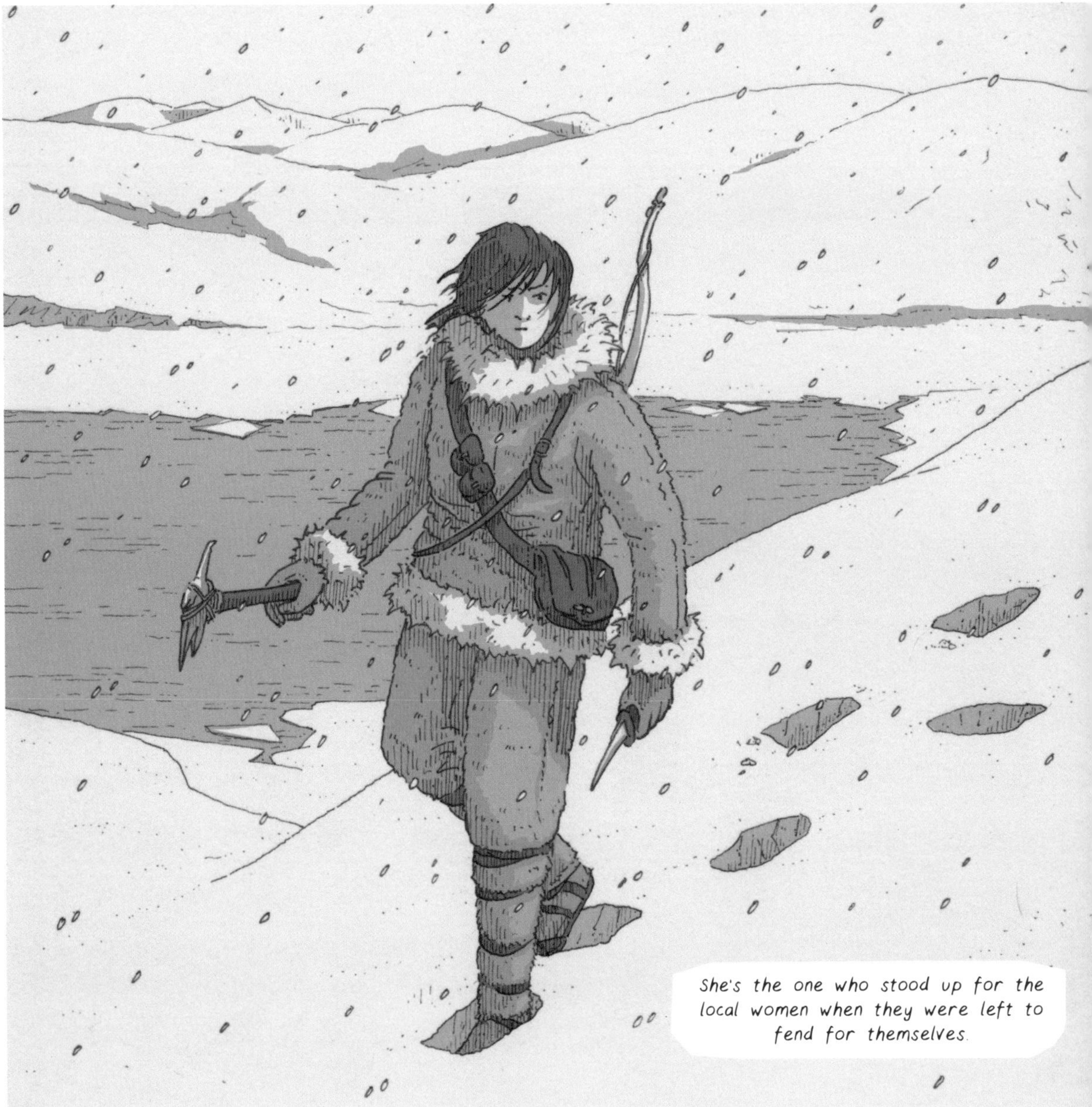
She's the one who stood up for the local women when they were left to fend for themselves.

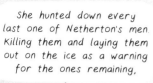

She hunted down every last one of Netherton's men. Killing them and laying them out on the ice as a warning for the ones remaining,

Hrrrrkkk!

until there was only Netherton left, barricaded in the house he'd built. He slowly went insane with fear as she circled her final victim.

They say he took his own life in the end, to spare himself the horror of what Uki had planned.

Bill?!

Jesus, Abel told me it was the 'Wendigo'.

Urrrghh...

She was worse than the Wendigo.

And are you saying a mythical snow beast is more believable than a strong woman?!

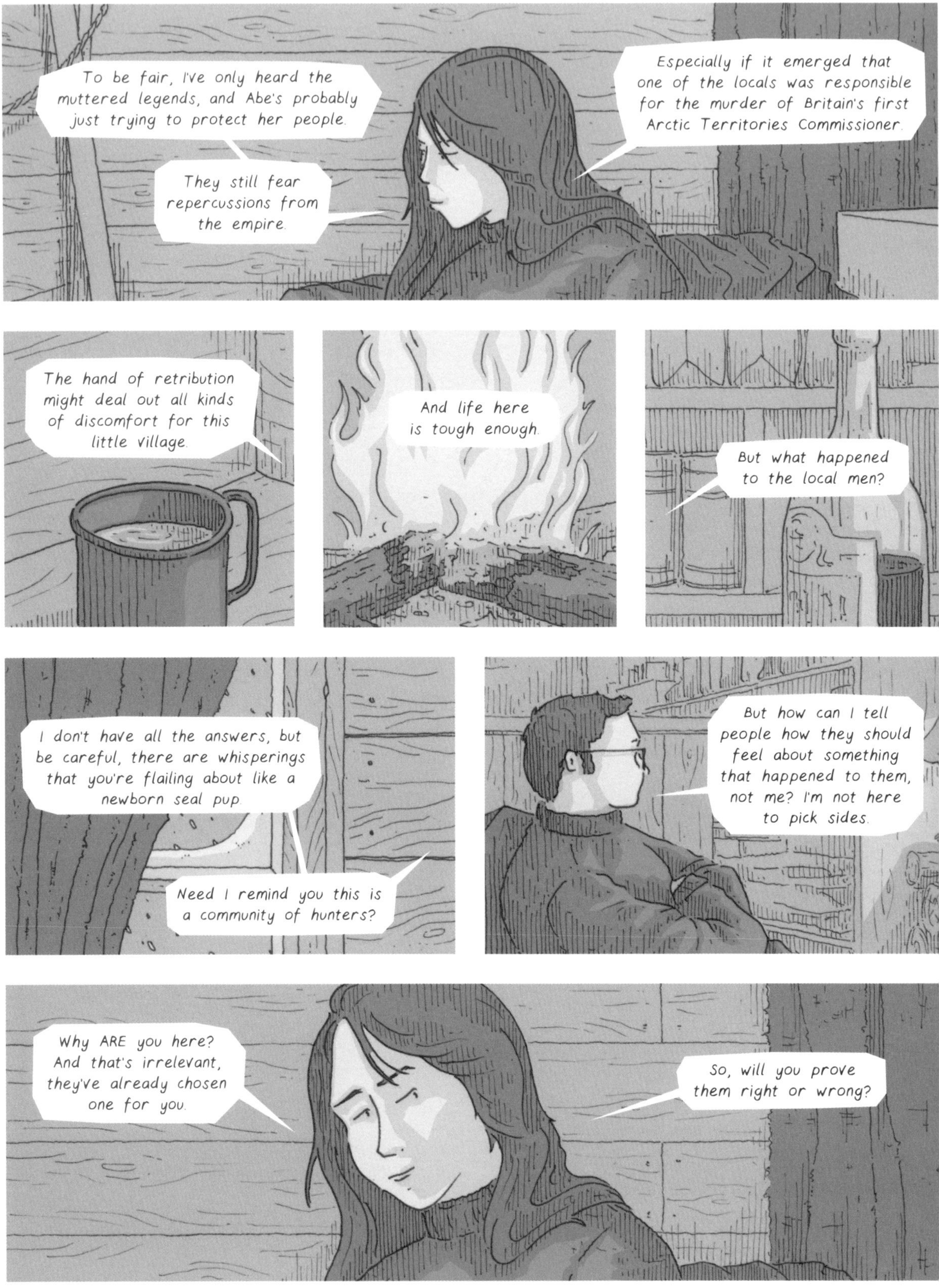
To be fair, I've only heard the muttered legends, and Abe's probably just trying to protect her people.
They still fear repercussions from the empire.
Especially if it emerged that one of the locals was responsible for the murder of Britain's first Arctic Territories Commissioner.
The hand of retribution might deal out all kinds of discomfort for this little village.
And life here is tough enough.
But what happened to the local men?
I don't have all the answers, but be careful, there are whisperings that you're flailing about like a newborn seal pup.
Need I remind you this is a community of hunters?
But how can I tell people how they should feel about something that happened to them, not me? I'm not here to pick sides.
Why ARE you here? And that's irrelevant, they've already chosen one for you.
So, will you prove them right or wrong?

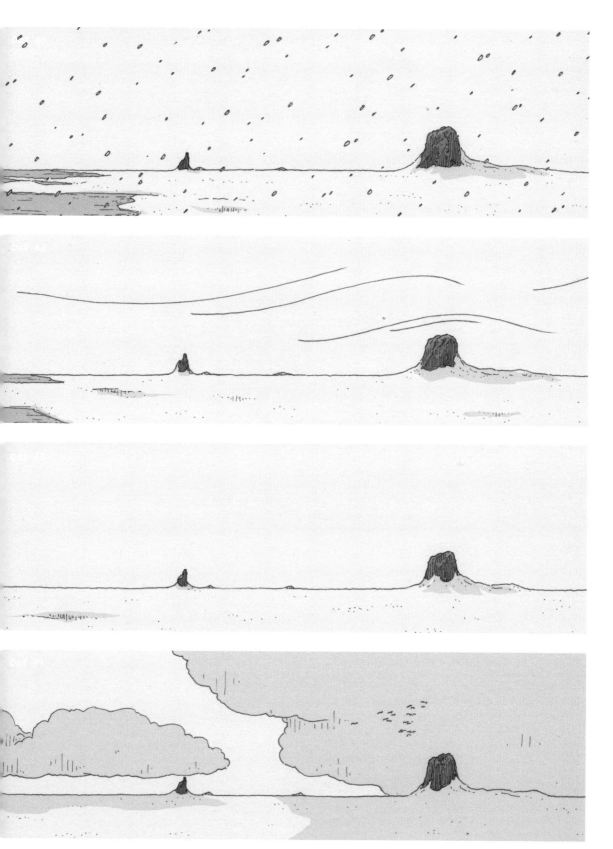

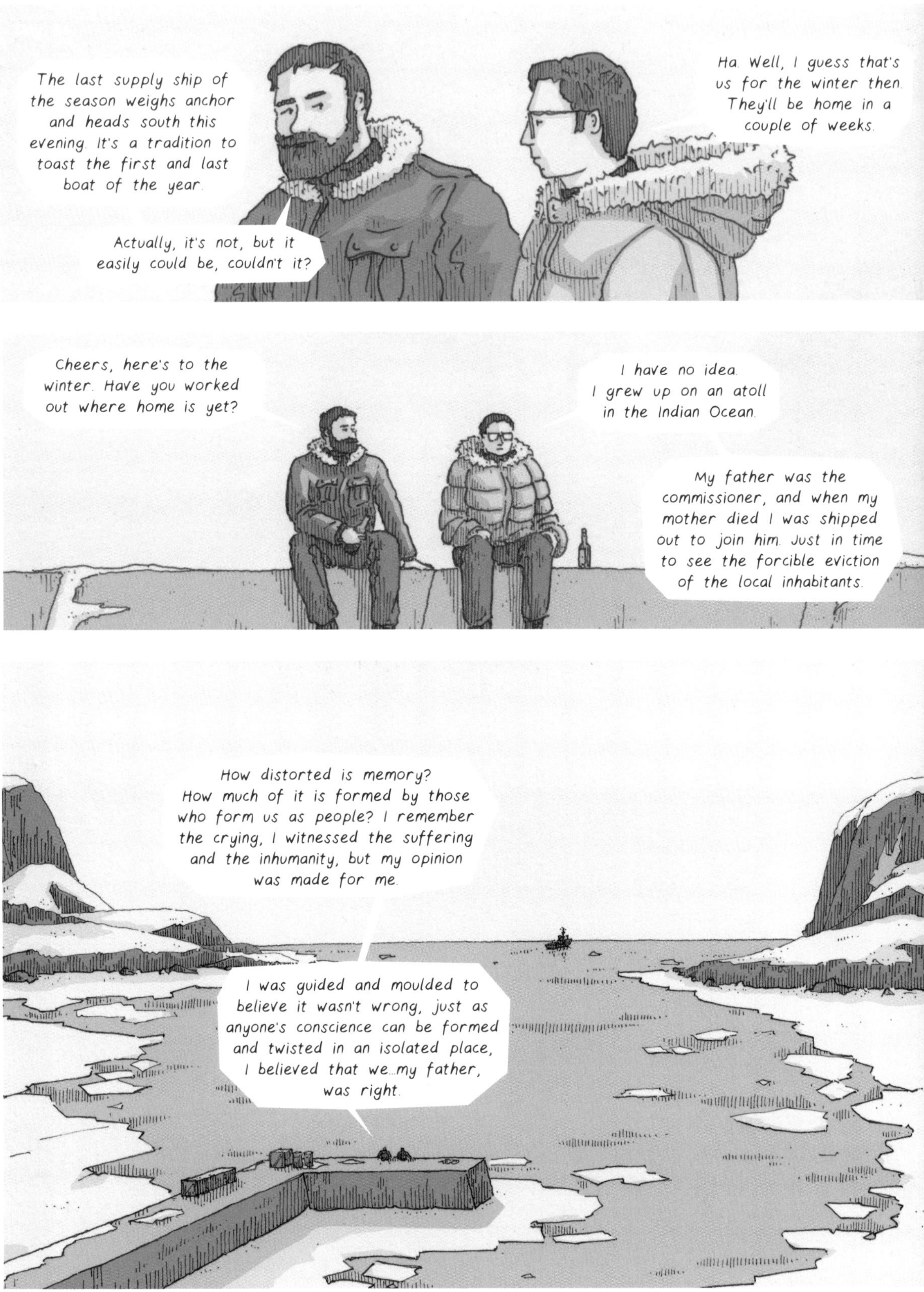

The last supply ship of the season weighs anchor and heads south this evening. It's a tradition to toast the first and last boat of the year.
Ha. Well, I guess that's us for the winter then. They'll be home in a couple of weeks.
Actually, it's not, but it easily could be, couldn't it?
Cheers, here's to the winter. Have you worked out where home is yet?
I have no idea. I grew up on an atoll in the Indian Ocean.
My father was the commissioner, and when my mother died I was shipped out to join him. Just in time to see the forcible eviction of the local inhabitants.
How distorted is memory? How much of it is formed by those who form us as people? I remember the crying, I witnessed the suffering and the inhumanity, but my opinion was made for me.
I was guided and moulded to believe it wasn't wrong, just as anyone's conscience can be formed and twisted in an isolated place, I believed that we...my father, was right.

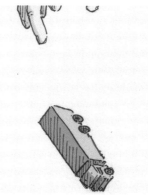

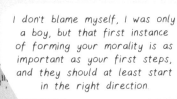

I don't blame myself, I was only a boy, but that first instance of forming your morality is as important as your first steps, and they should at least start in the right direction.

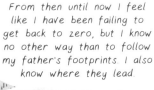

From then until now I feel like I have been failing to get back to zero, but I know no other way than to follow my father's footprints. I also know where they lead.

People's convictions are as unique as snowflakes...

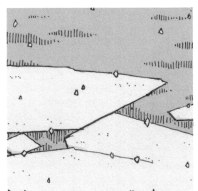

...and equally insignificant when weighed against all the others.

I'm a long way from where I was, but in reality, I'm right back there. Holding a line that this time someone drew in the snow, with tonight's fall it will be covered, and with the morning sun it will melt.

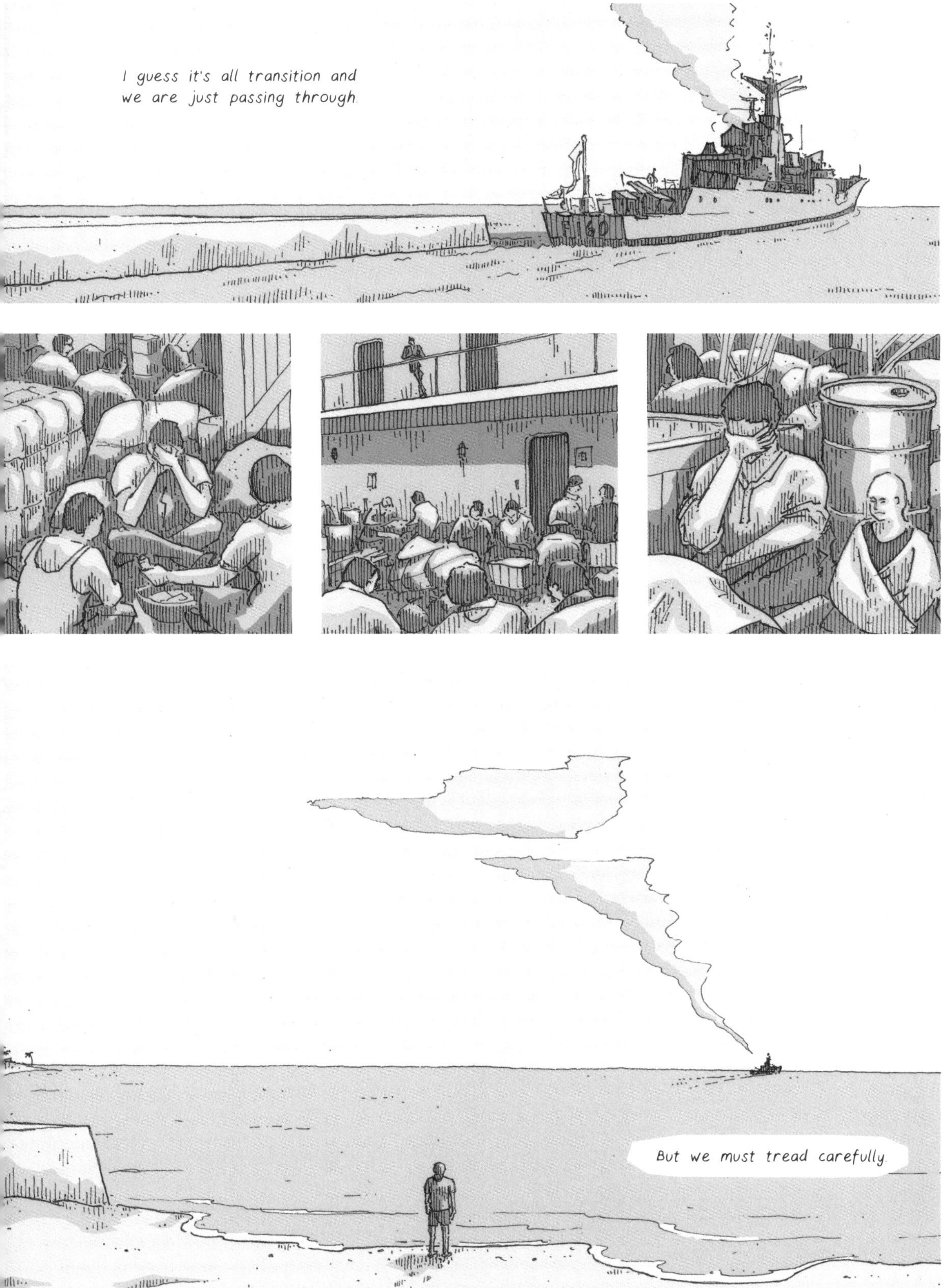
I guess it's all transition and we are just passing through.
F160
But we must tread carefully.

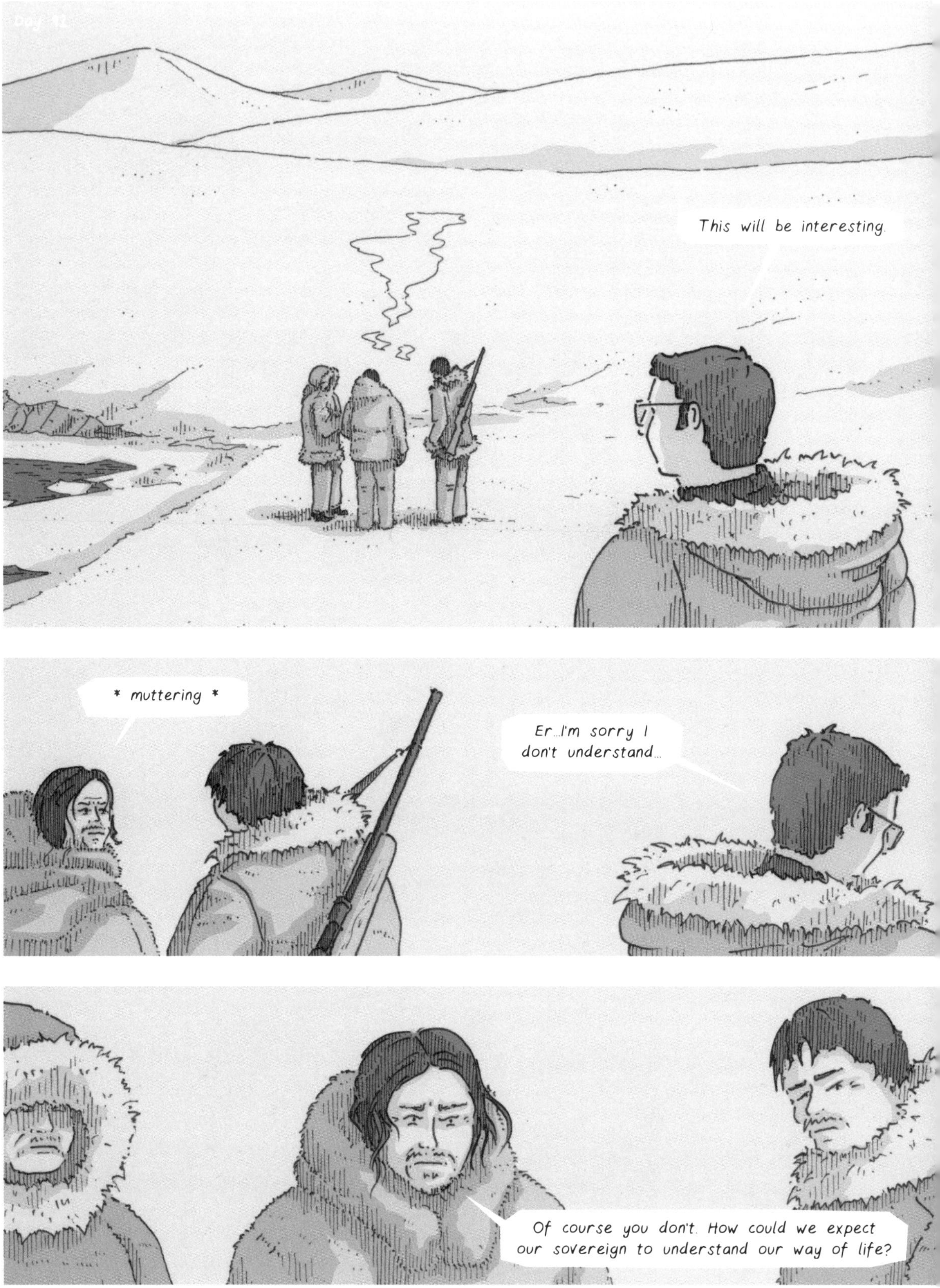
Day 11
This will be interesting.
* muttering *
Er...I'm sorry I don't understand...
Of course you don't. How could we expect our sovereign to understand our way of life?

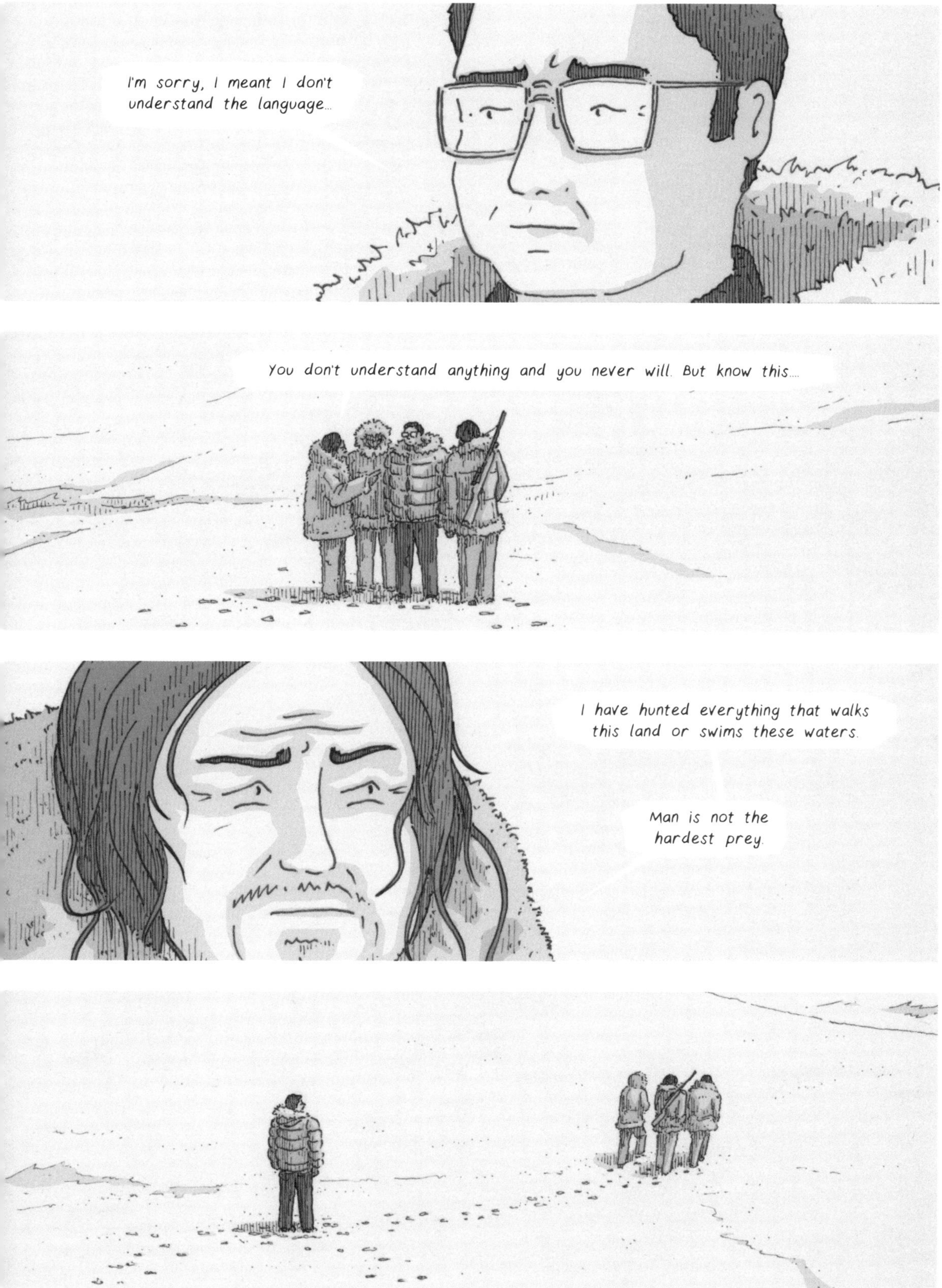
I'm sorry, I meant I don't understand the language...
You don't understand anything and you never will. But know this....
I have hunted everything that walks this land or swims these waters.
Man is not the hardest prey.

Day 93.

Ah!

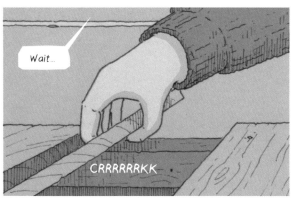

Wait...

CRRRRRKK

'The situation has become desperate.'

'The discovery of the bodies of Williams and Greaves reduces our official numbers to three. Yet, as I write this, Bill Gray and McIroy have failed to return from attempting to get supplies, and I fear the worst.'

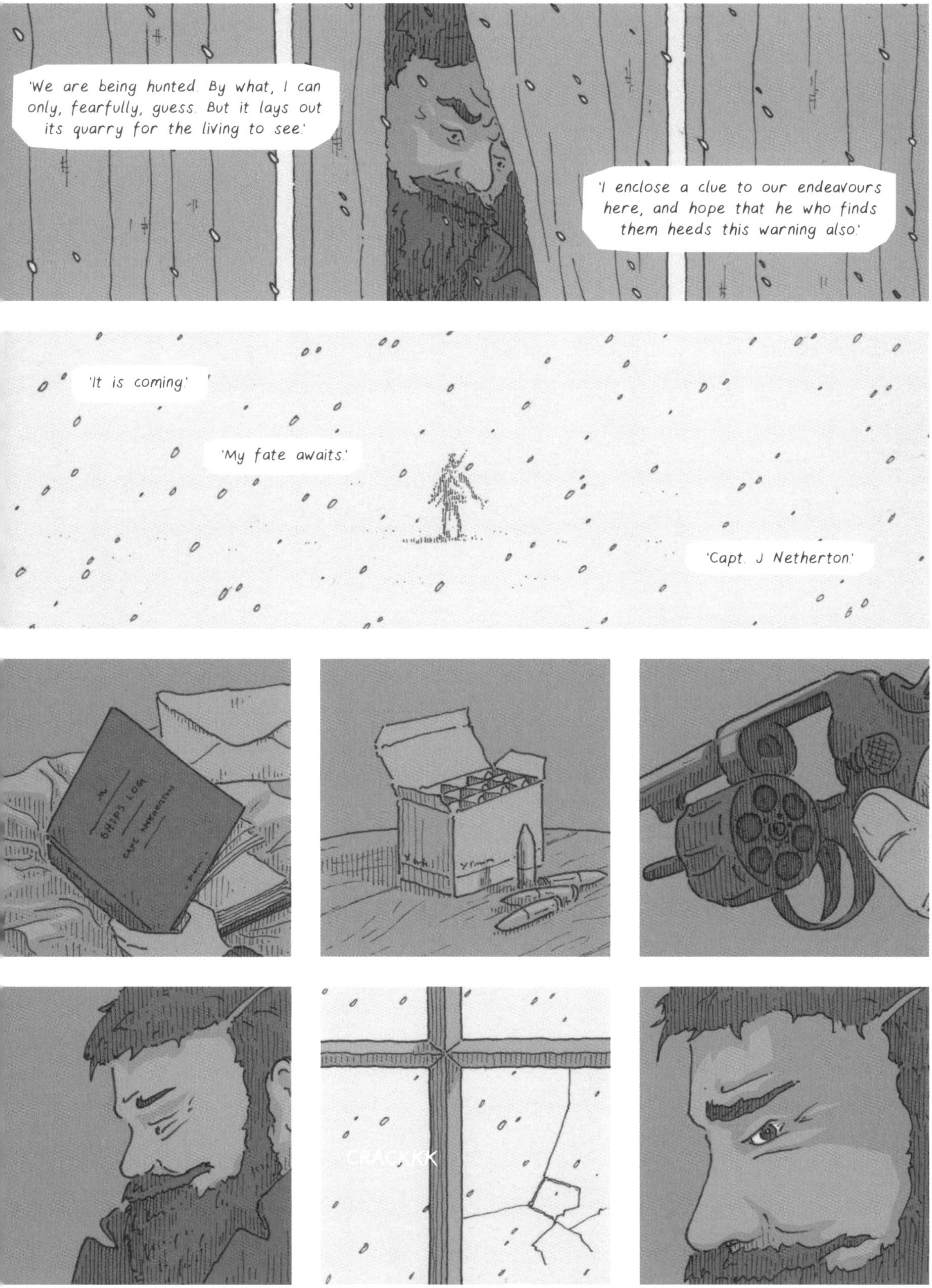
'We are being hunted. By what, I can only, fearfully, guess. But it lays out its quarry for the living to see.'
'I enclose a clue to our endeavours here, and hope that he who finds them heeds this warning also.'
'It is coming.'
'My fate awaits.'
'Capt. J Netherton.'
SHIP'S LOG
CRACKKK

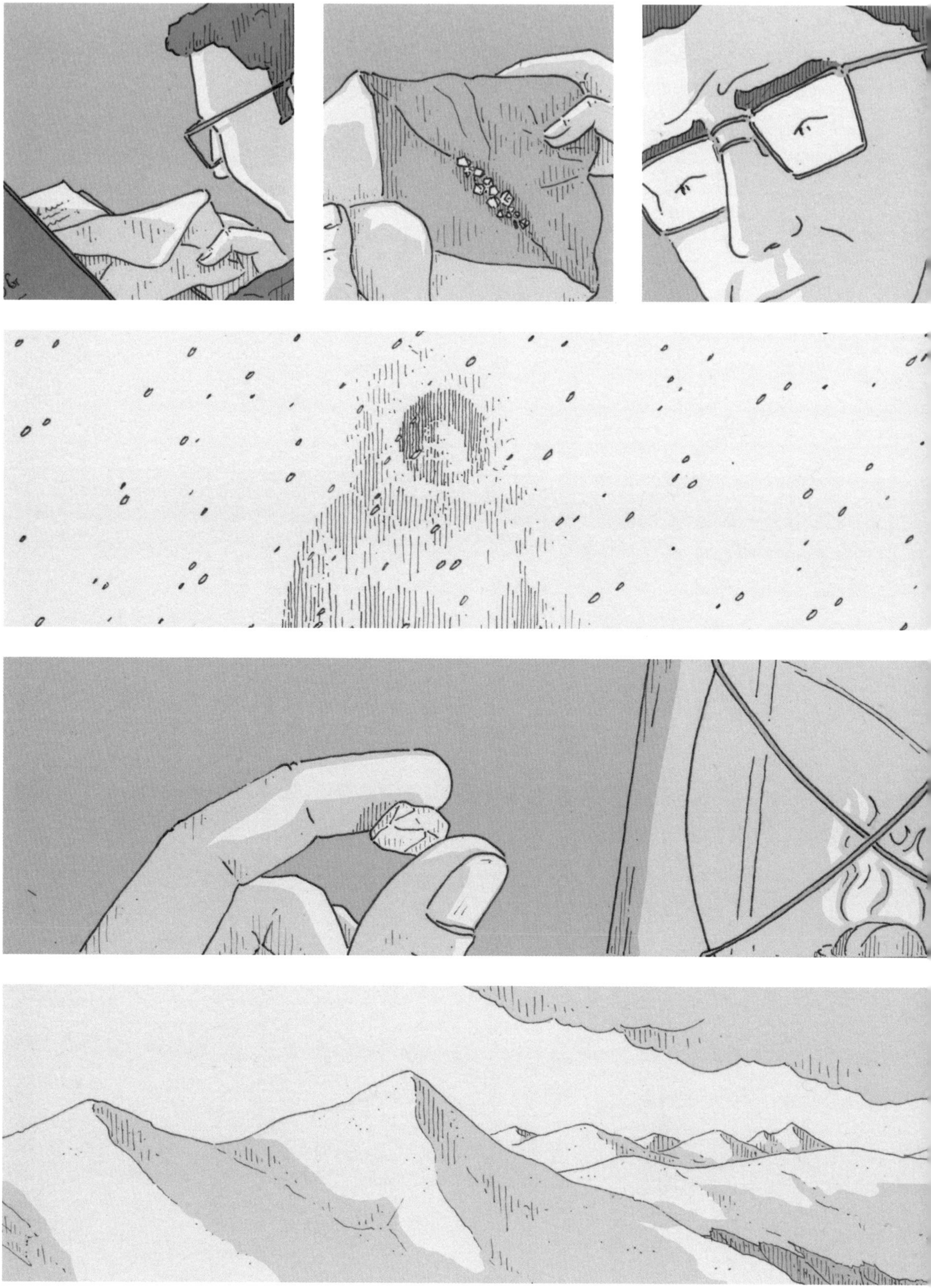

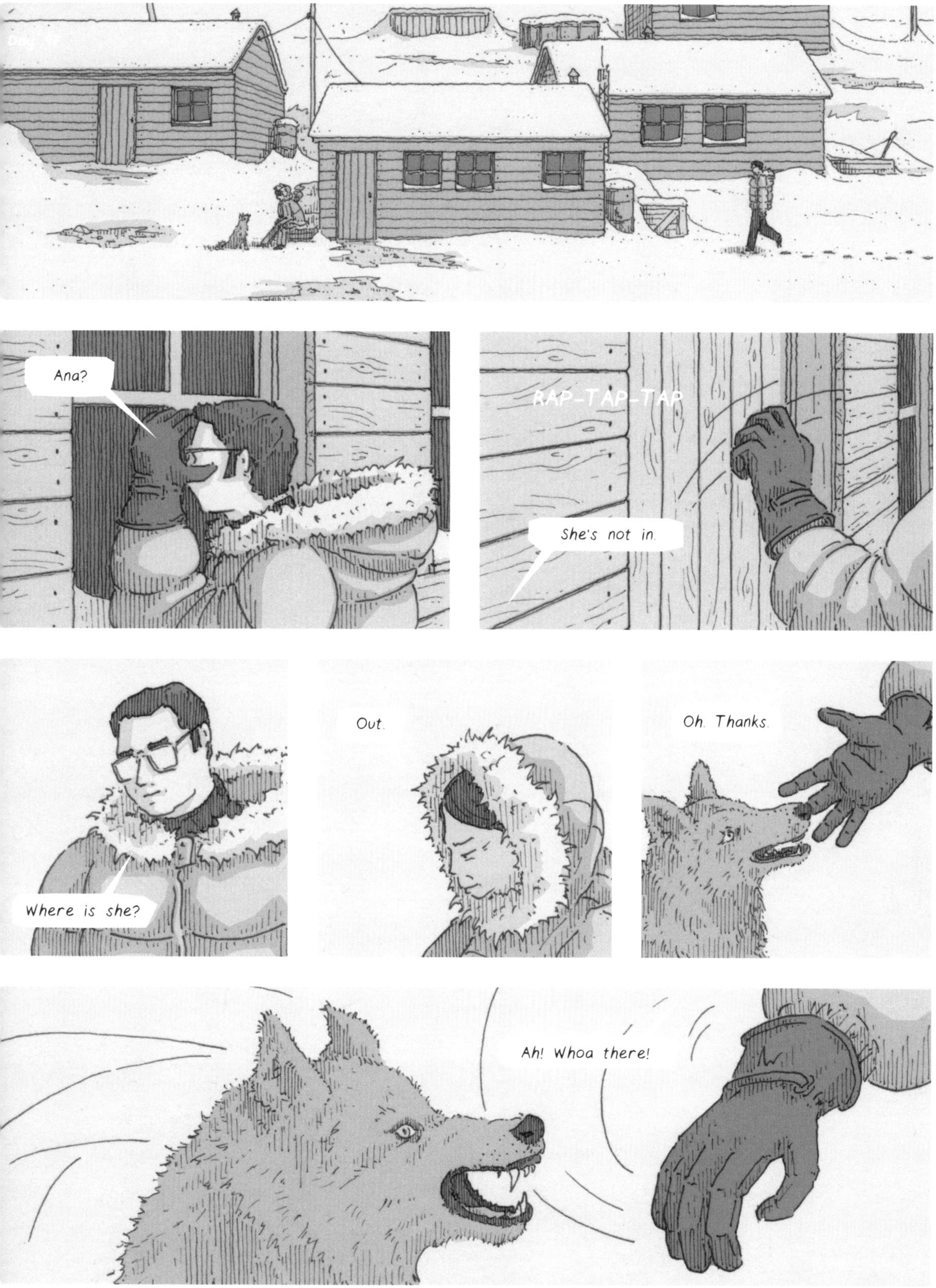
Ana?
RAP-TAP-TAP
She's not in.
Where is she?
Out.
Oh. Thanks.
Ah! Whoa there!

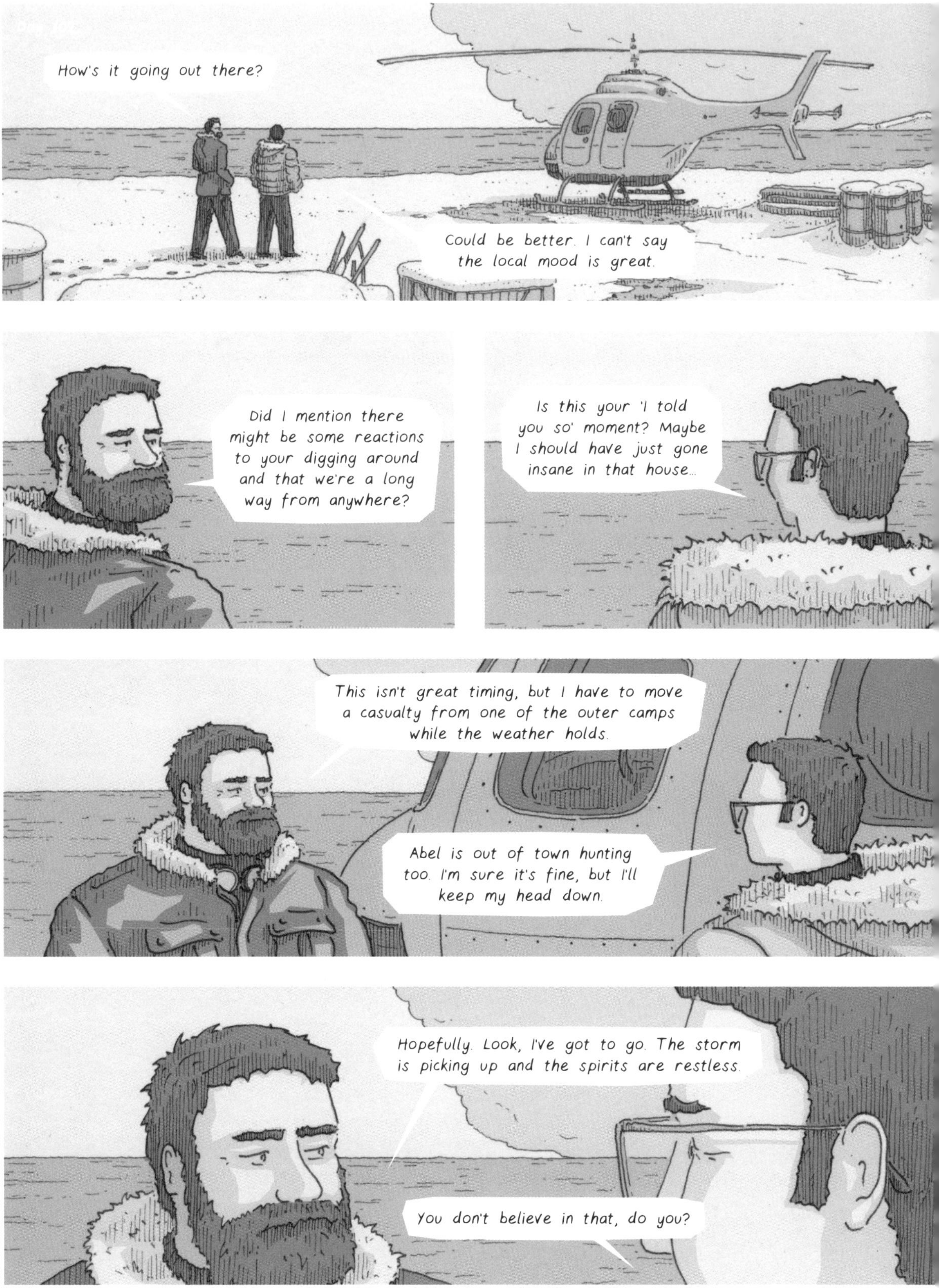
How's it going out there?
Could be better. I can't say the local mood is great.
Did I mention there might be some reactions to your digging around and that we're a long way from anywhere?
Is this your 'I told you so' moment? Maybe I should have just gone insane in that house...
This isn't great timing, but I have to move a casualty from one of the outer camps while the weather holds.
Abel is out of town hunting too. I'm sure it's fine, but I'll keep my head down.
Hopefully. Look, I've got to go. The storm is picking up and the spirits are restless.
You don't believe in that, do you?

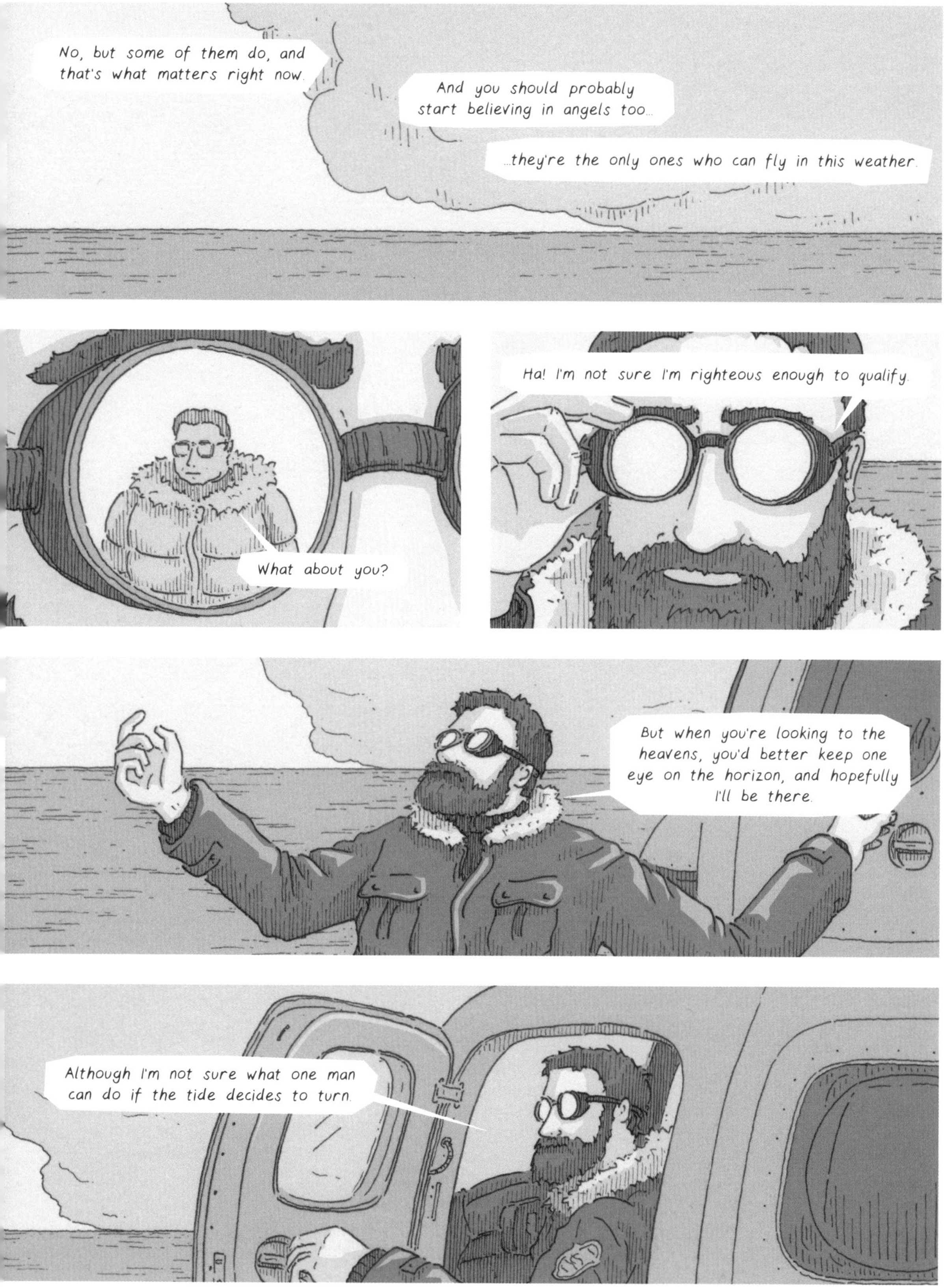
No, but some of them do, and that's what matters right now.
And you should probably start believing in angels too...
...they're the only ones who can fly in this weather.
What about you?
Ha! I'm not sure I'm righteous enough to qualify.
But when you're looking to the heavens, you'd better keep one eye on the horizon, and hopefully I'll be there.
Although I'm not sure what one man can do if the tide decides to turn.

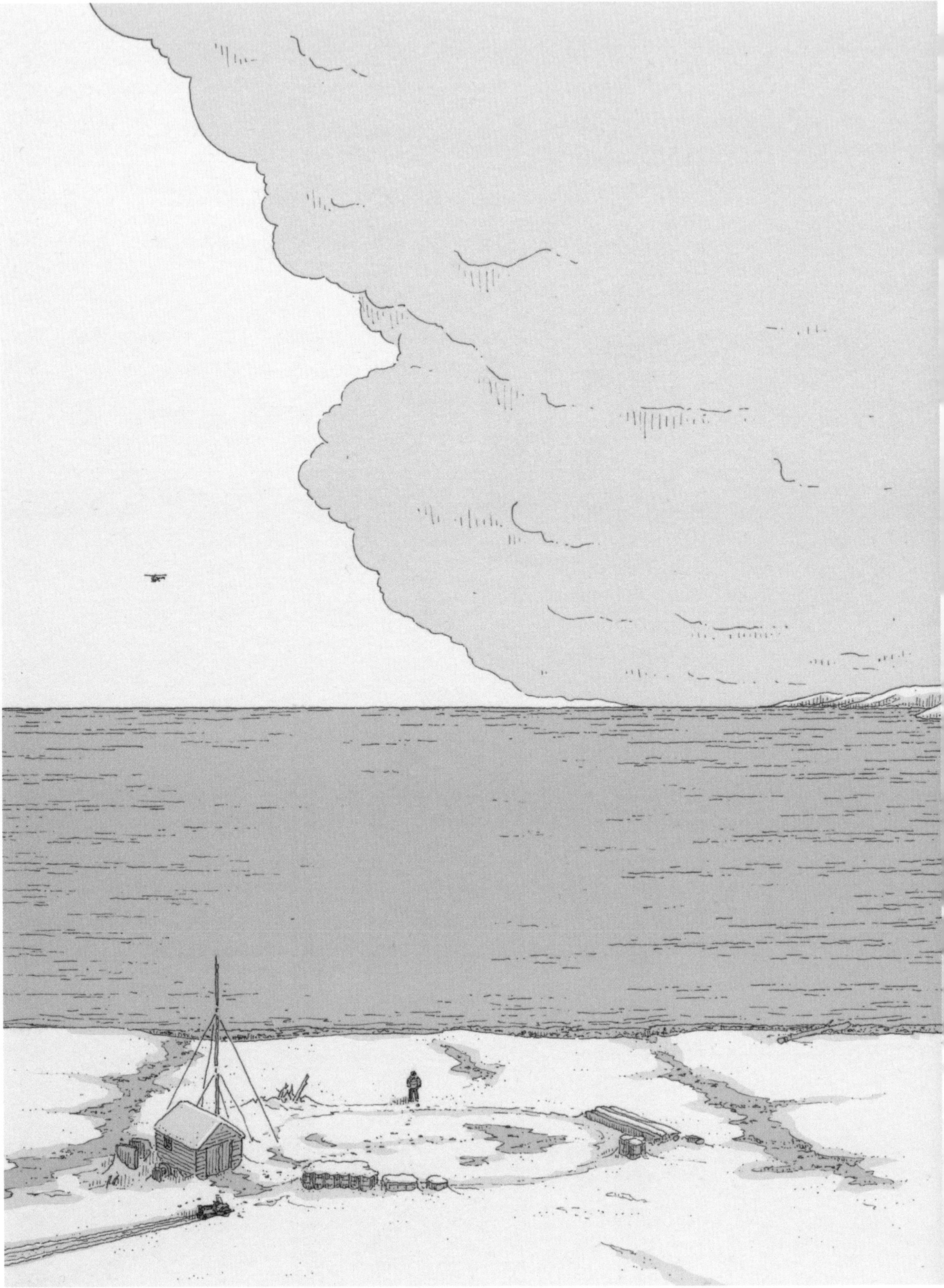

Day 103

D-DMM DMM DMM D-DMM DMM DMM

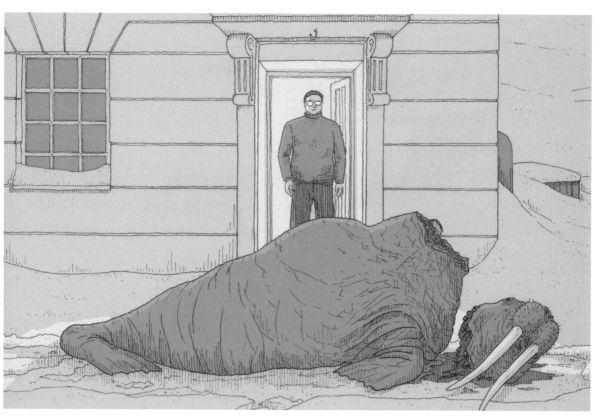

PART III

REVELATIONS

Day 104

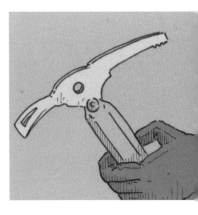

Right. Here goes.

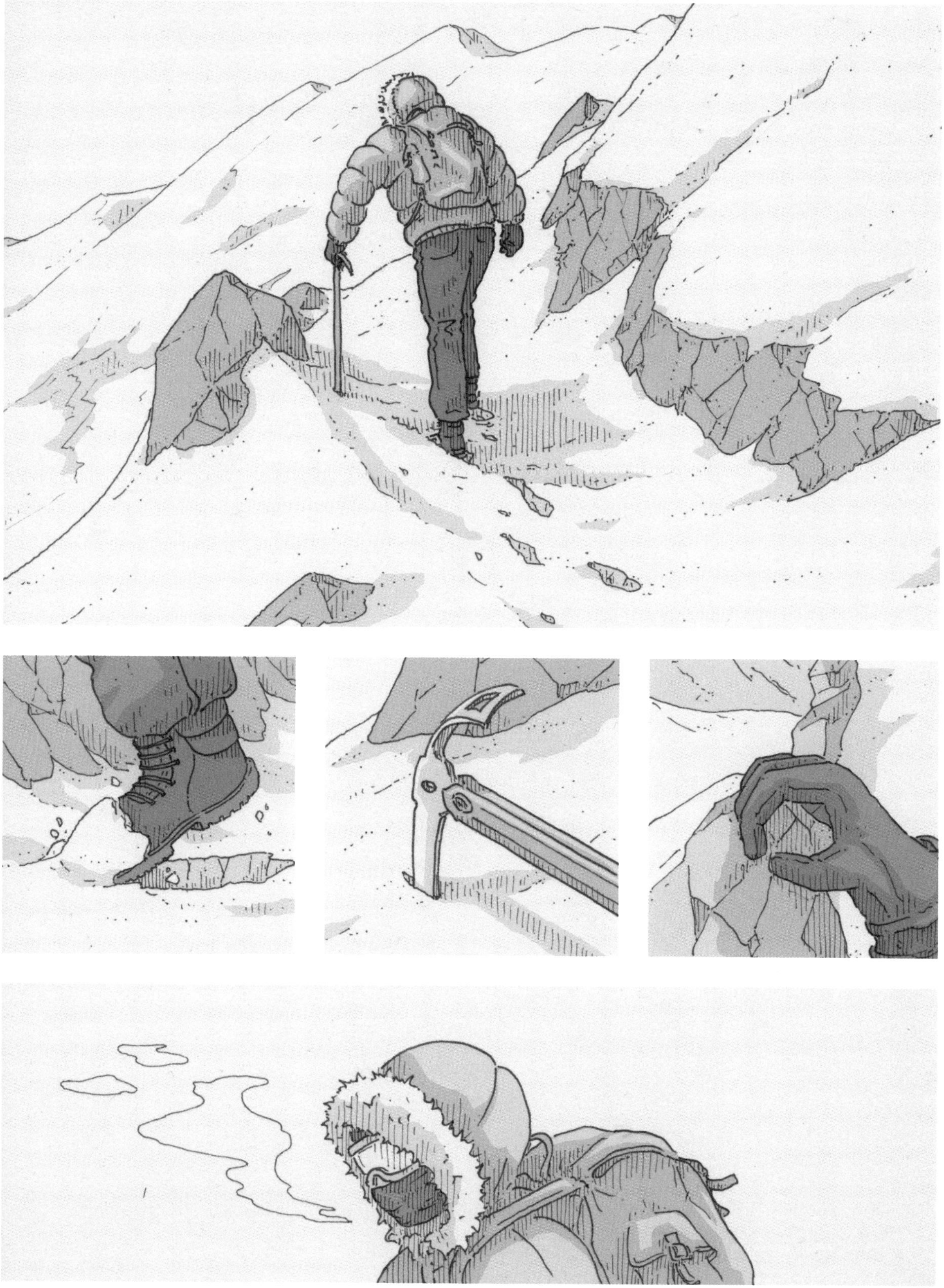

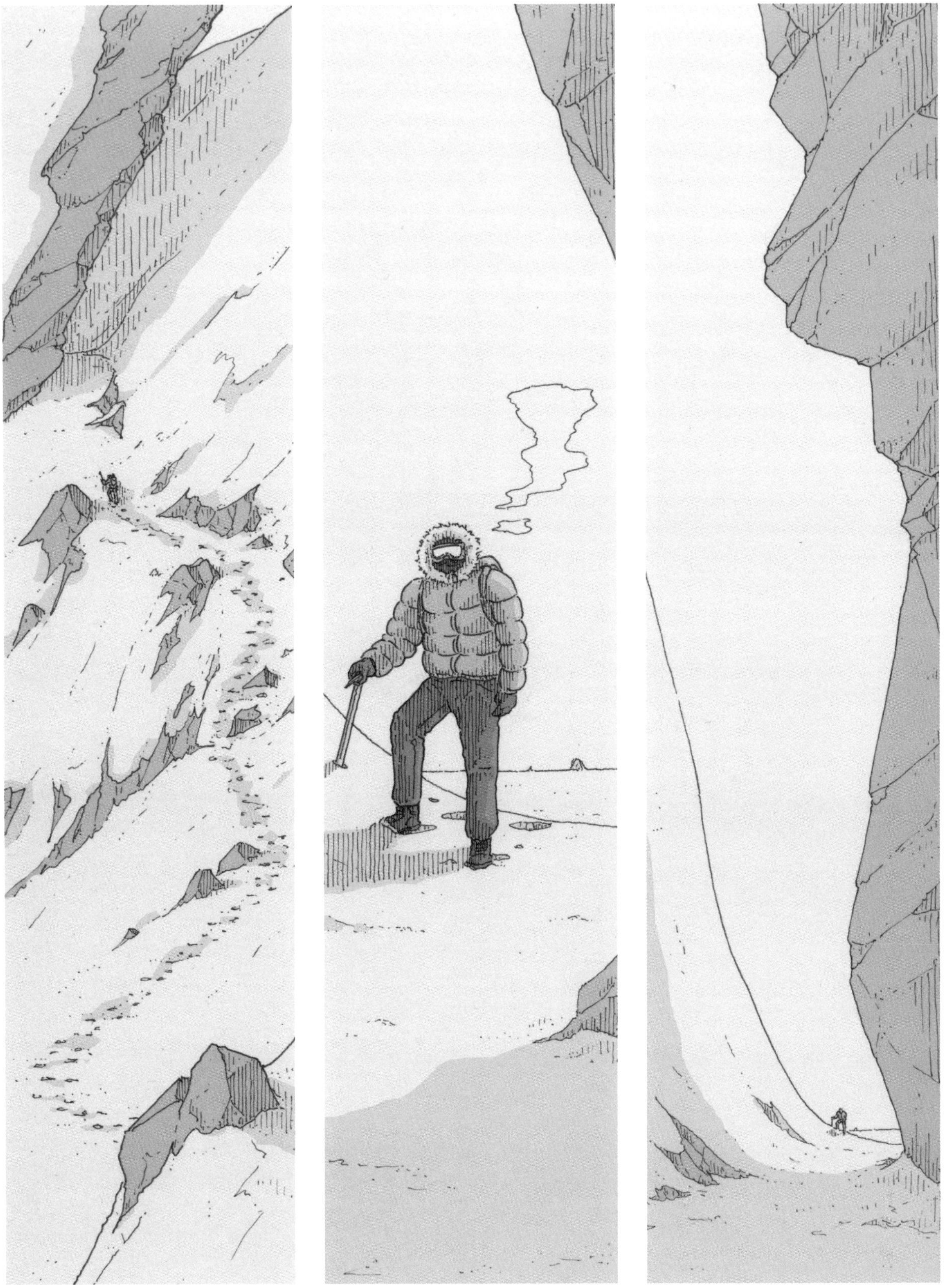

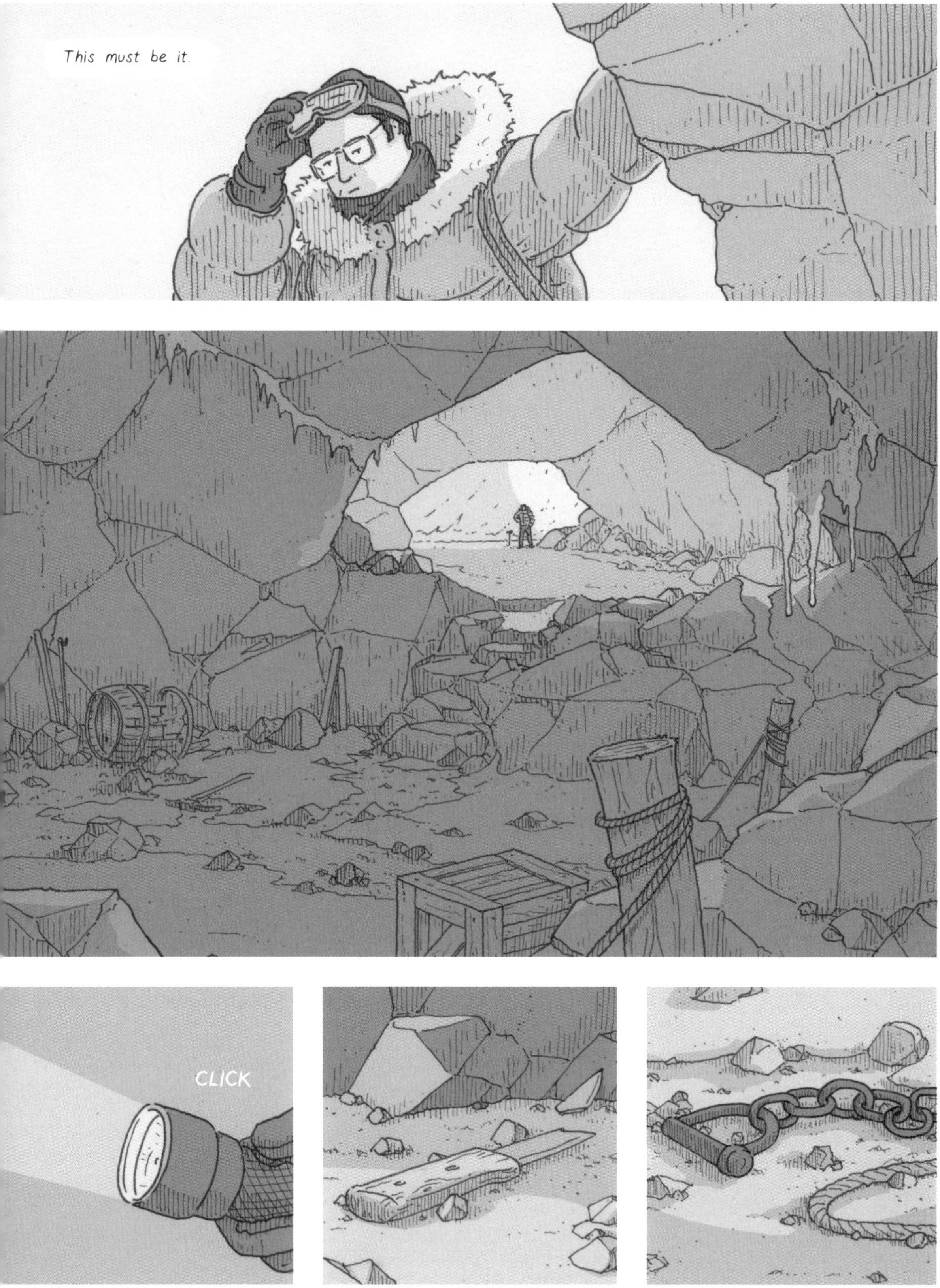
This must be it.
CLICK

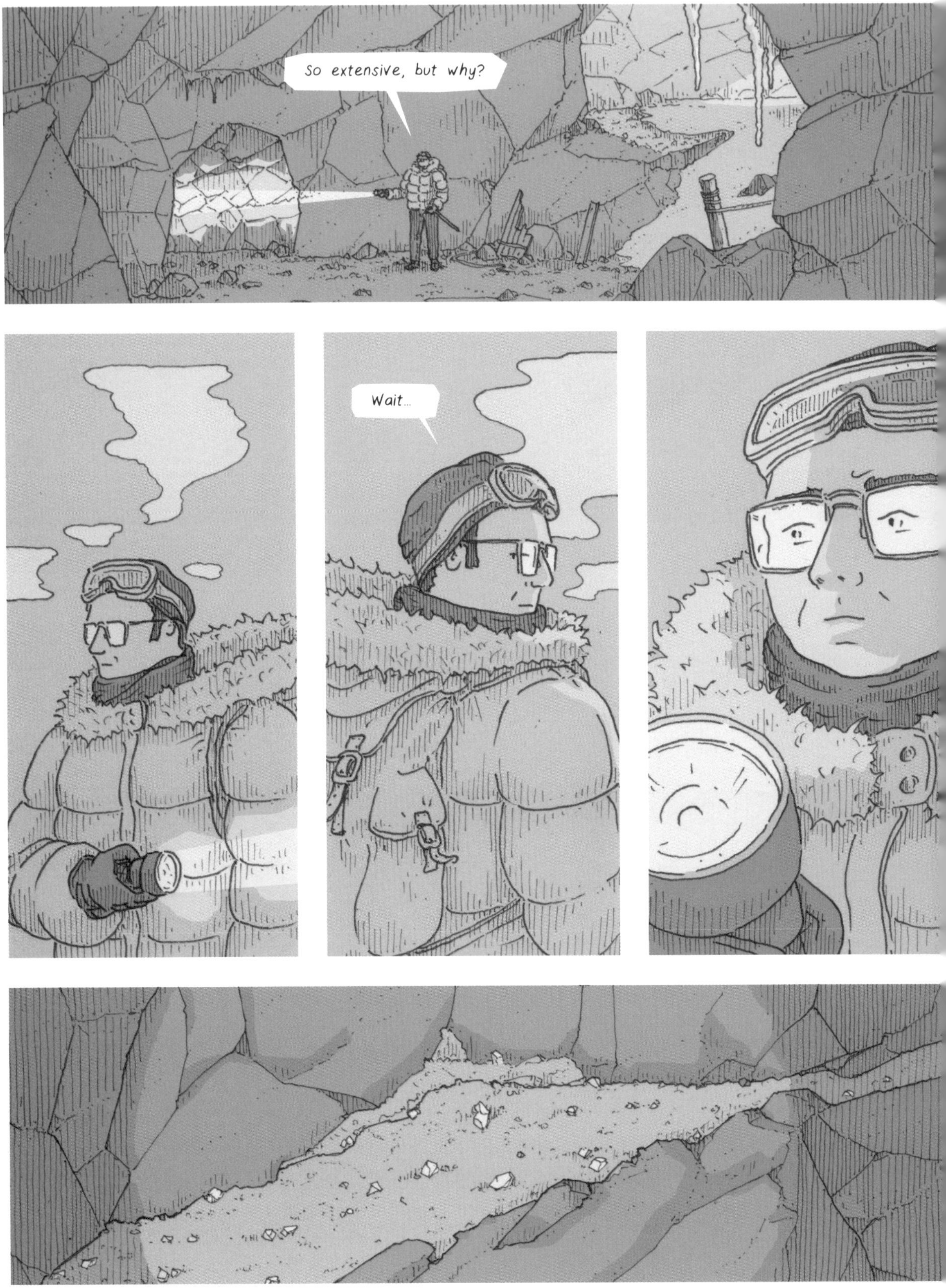

So extensive, but why?
Wait...

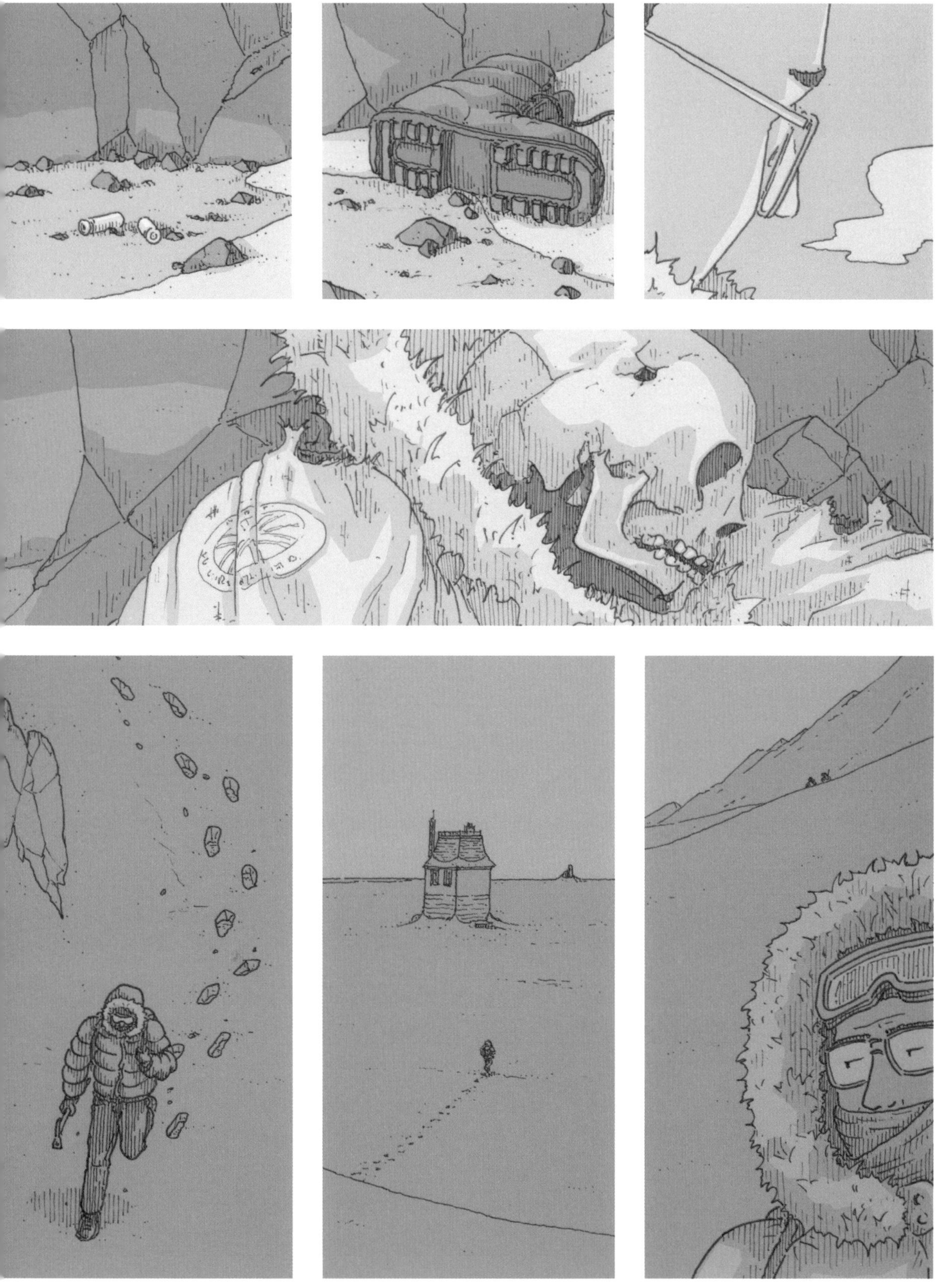

Ana, I'm so glad you're there! I've just got back from the ridge, I've found...hello...hello...?!

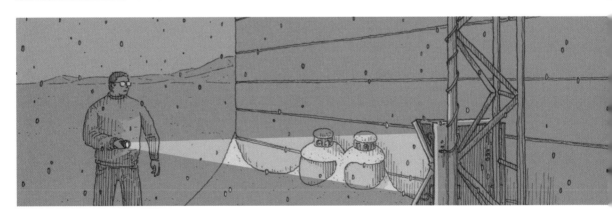

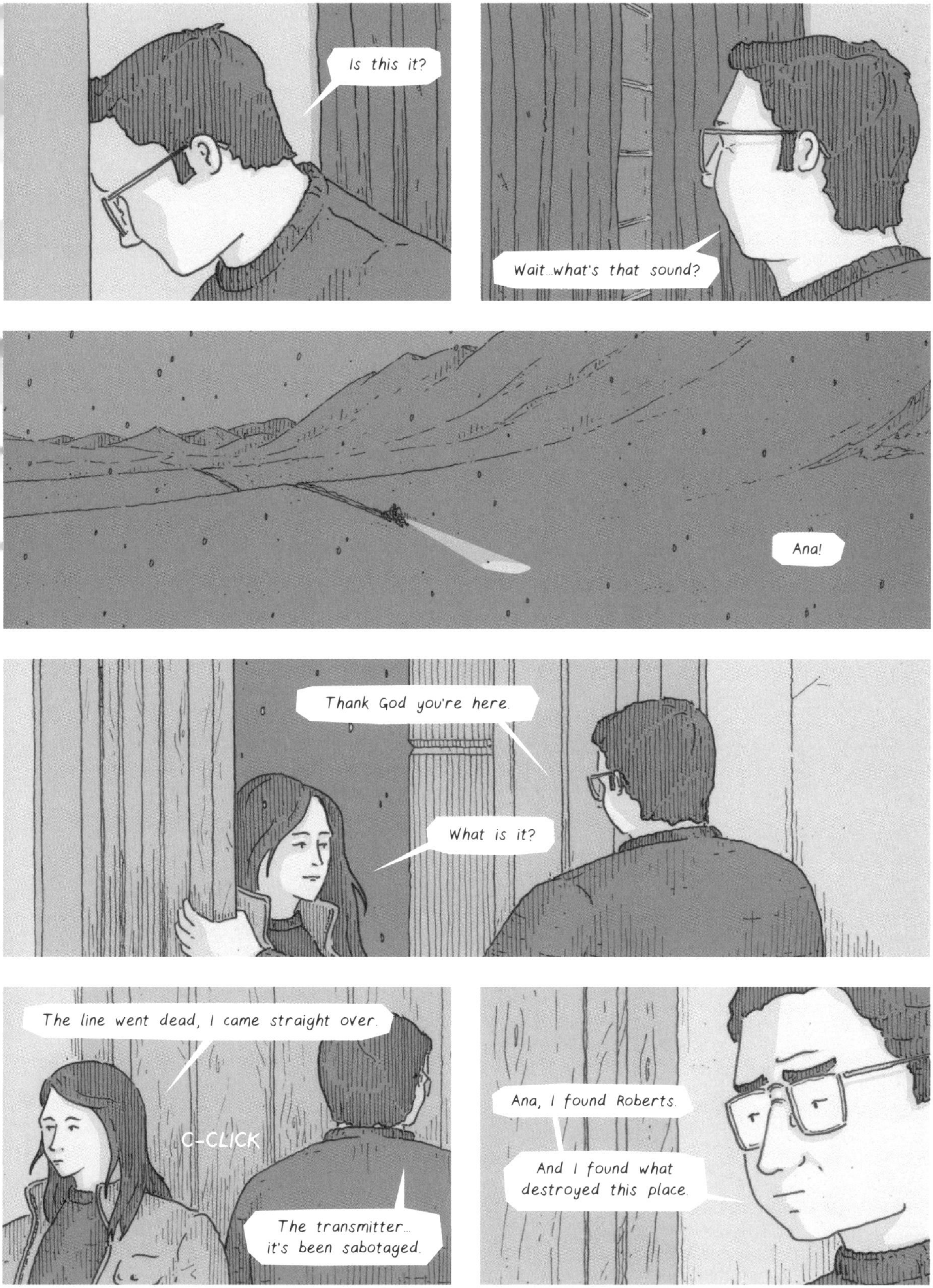

Is this it?
Wait...what's that sound?
Ana!
Thank God you're here.
What is it?
The line went dead, I came straight over.
C-CLICK
The transmitter... it's been sabotaged.
Ana, I found Roberts.
And I found what destroyed this place.

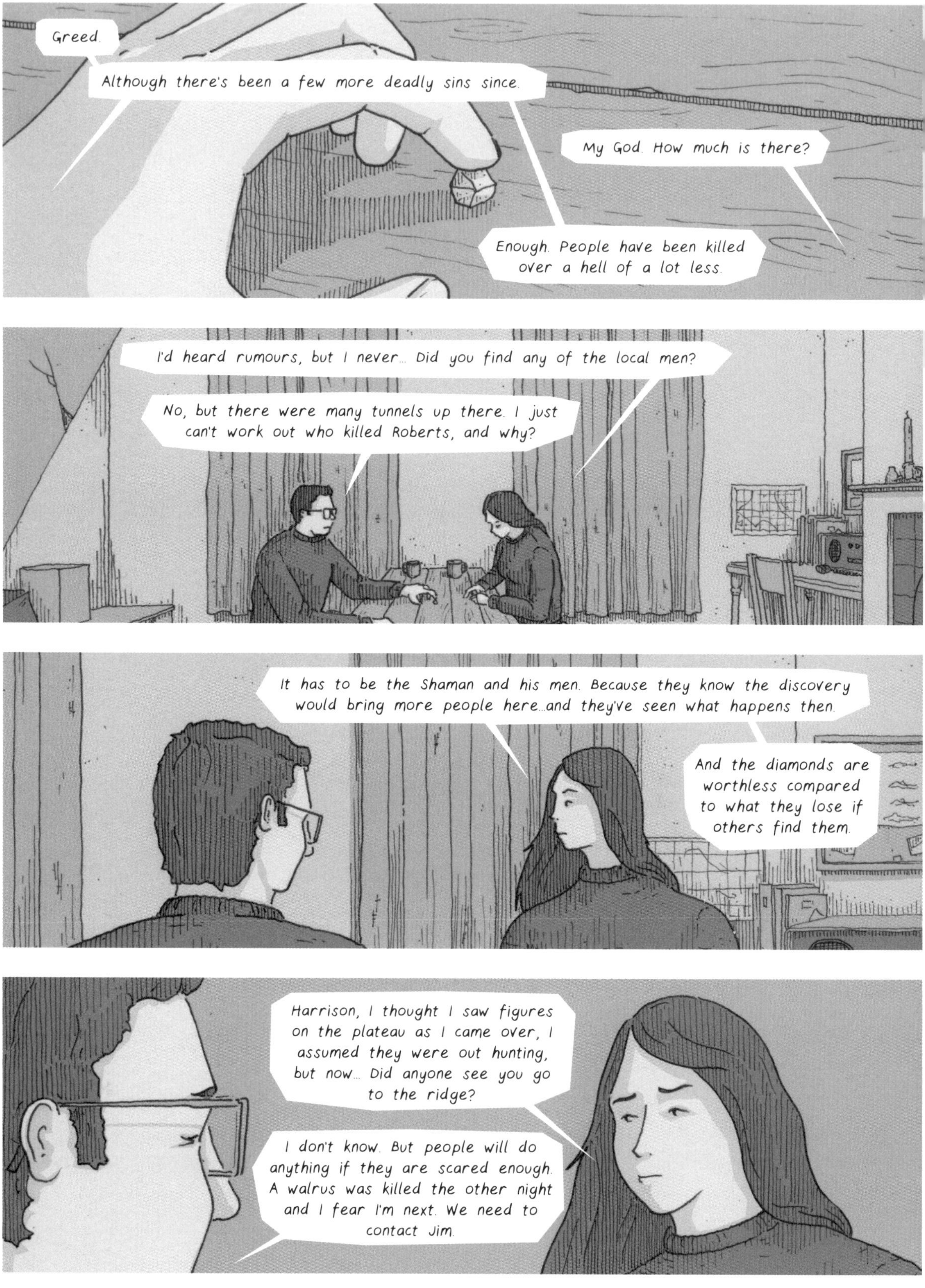
Greed.
Although there's been a few more deadly sins since.
My God. How much is there?
Enough. People have been killed over a hell of a lot less.
I'd heard rumours, but I never... Did you find any of the local men?
No, but there were many tunnels up there. I just can't work out who killed Roberts, and why?
It has to be the Shaman and his men. Because they know the discovery would bring more people here...and they've seen what happens then.
And the diamonds are worthless compared to what they lose if others find them.
Harrison, I thought I saw figures on the plateau as I came over, I assumed they were out hunting, but now... Did anyone see you go to the ridge?
I don't know. But people will do anything if they are scared enough. A walrus was killed the other night and I fear I'm next. We need to contact Jim.

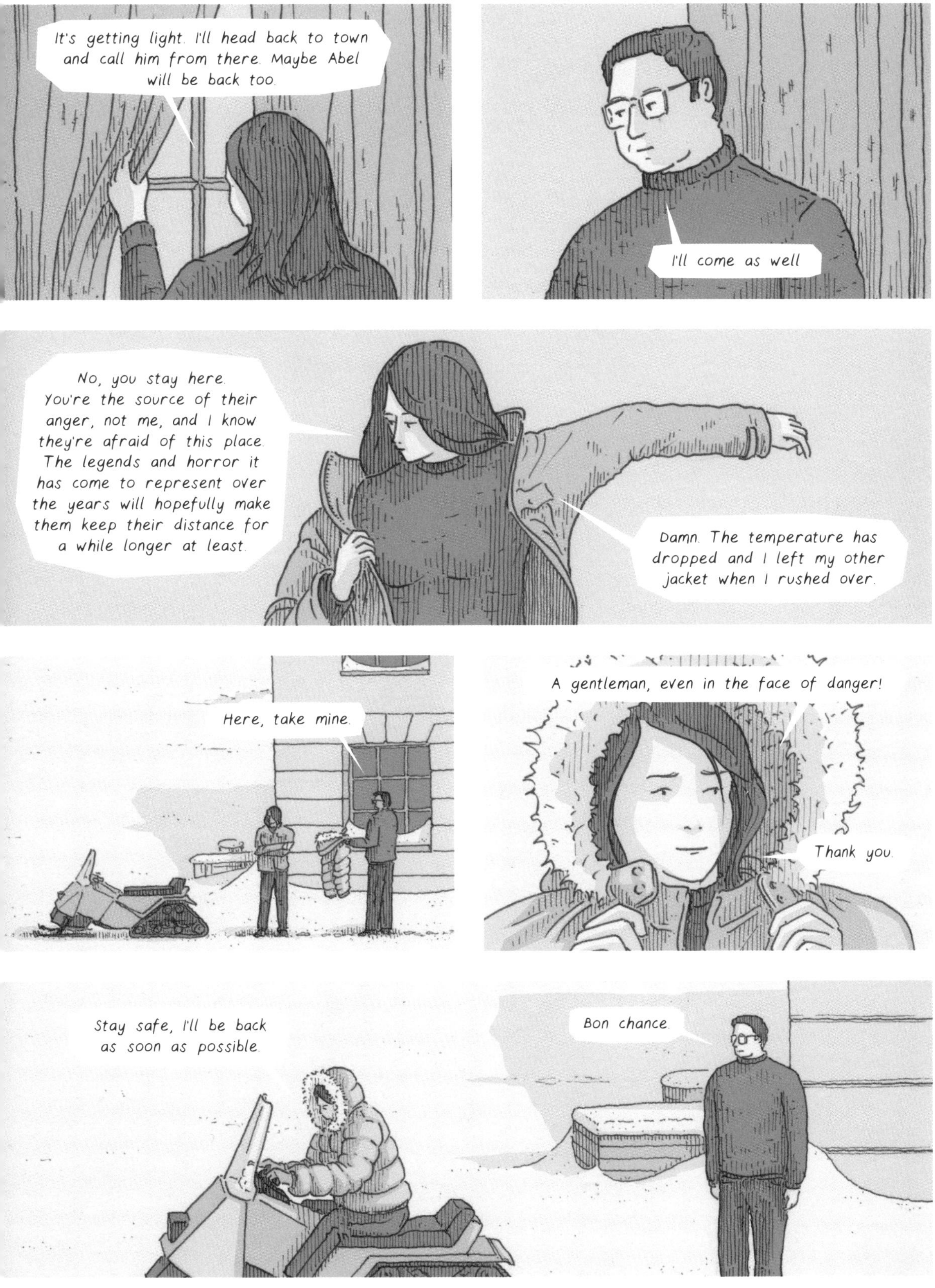
It's getting light. I'll head back to town and call him from there. Maybe Abel will be back too.
I'll come as well
No, you stay here. You're the source of their anger, not me, and I know they're afraid of this place. The legends and horror it has come to represent over the years will hopefully make them keep their distance for a while longer at least.
Damn. The temperature has dropped and I left my other jacket when I rushed over.
Here, take mine.
A gentleman, even in the face of danger!
Thank you.
Stay safe, I'll be back as soon as possible.
Bon chance.

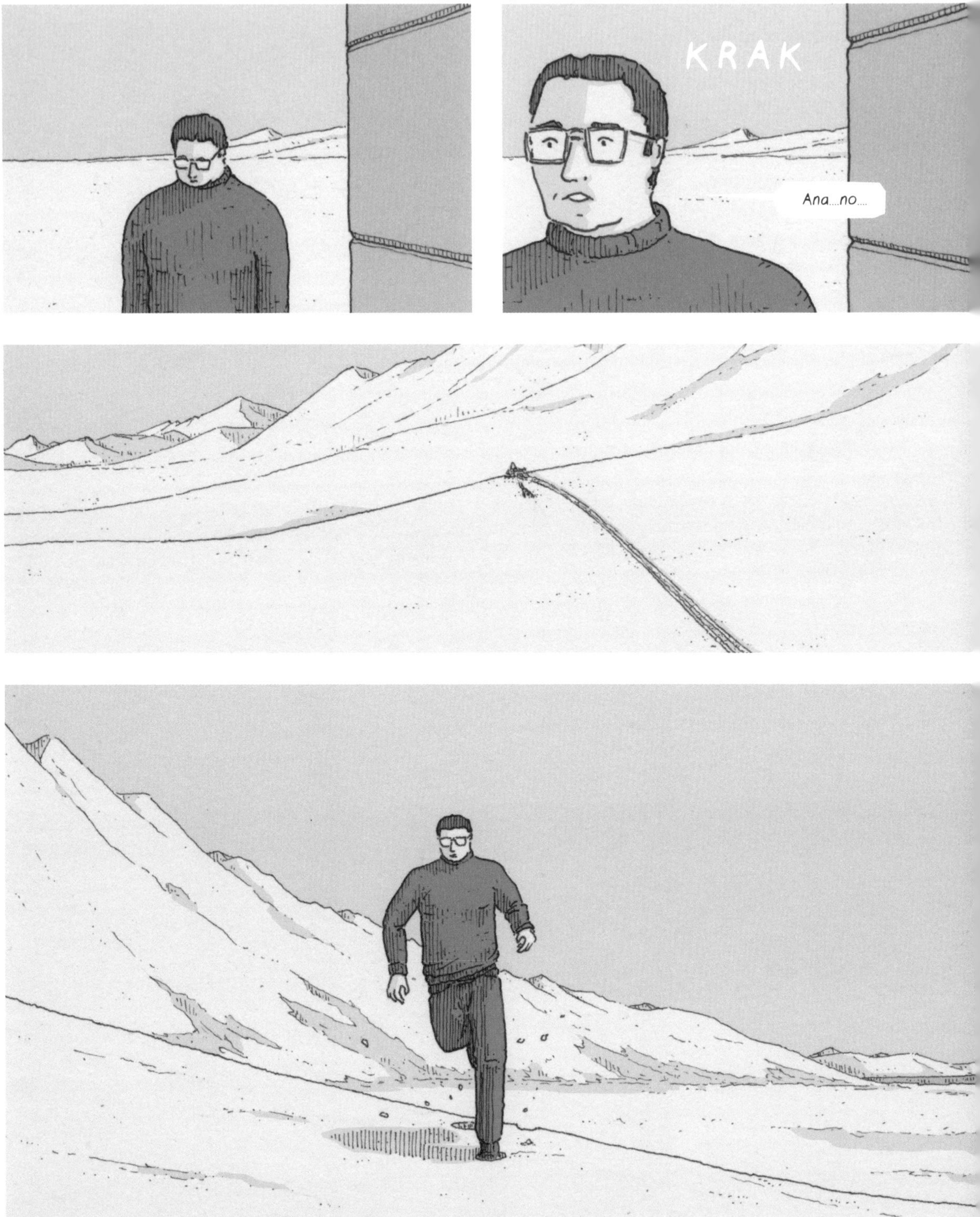
KRAK
Ana....no....

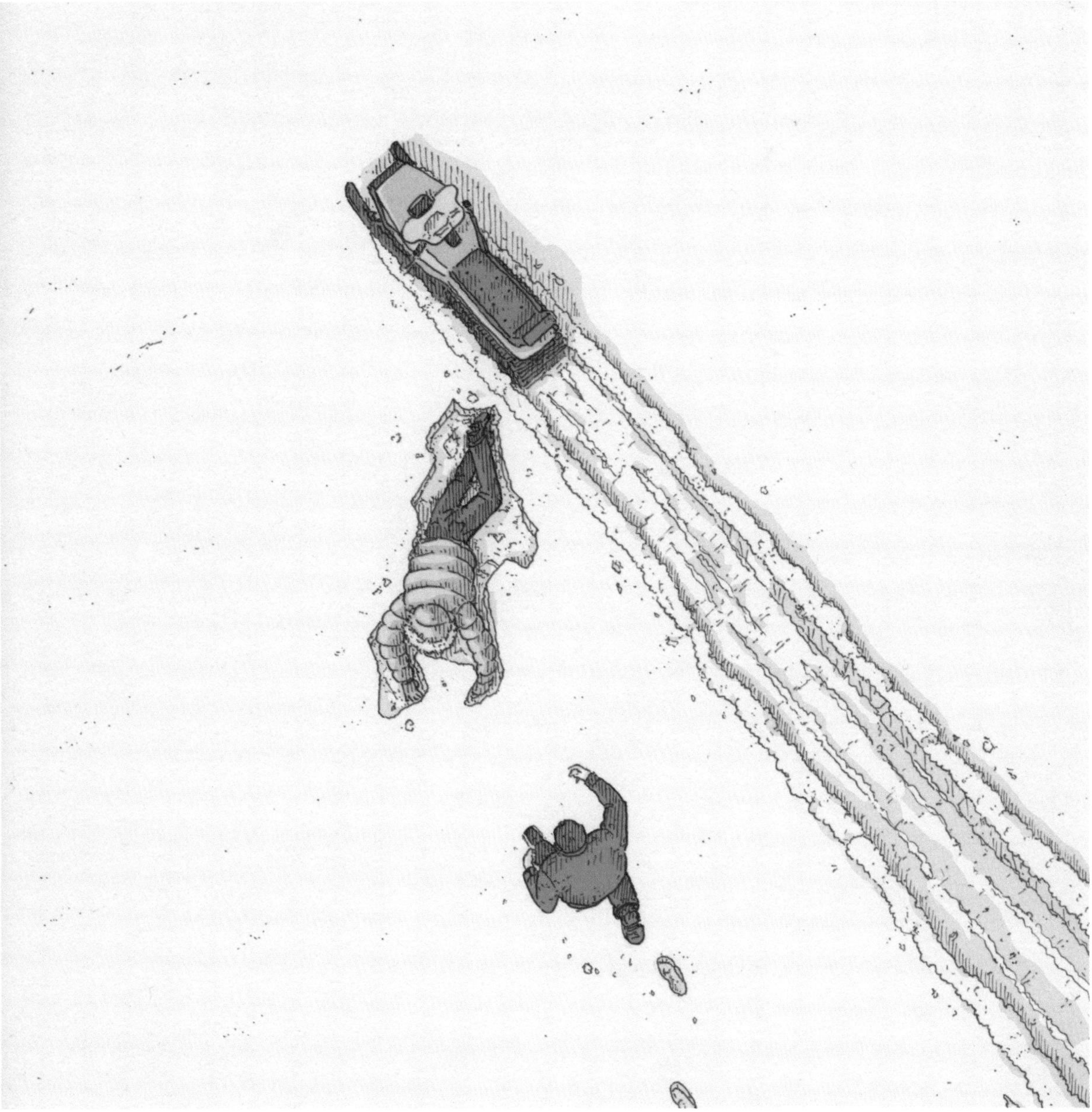

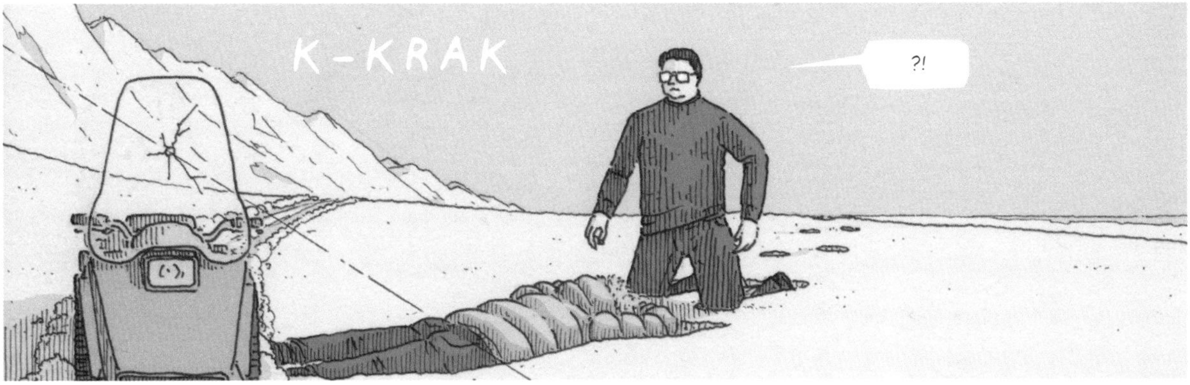
K-KRAK
?!

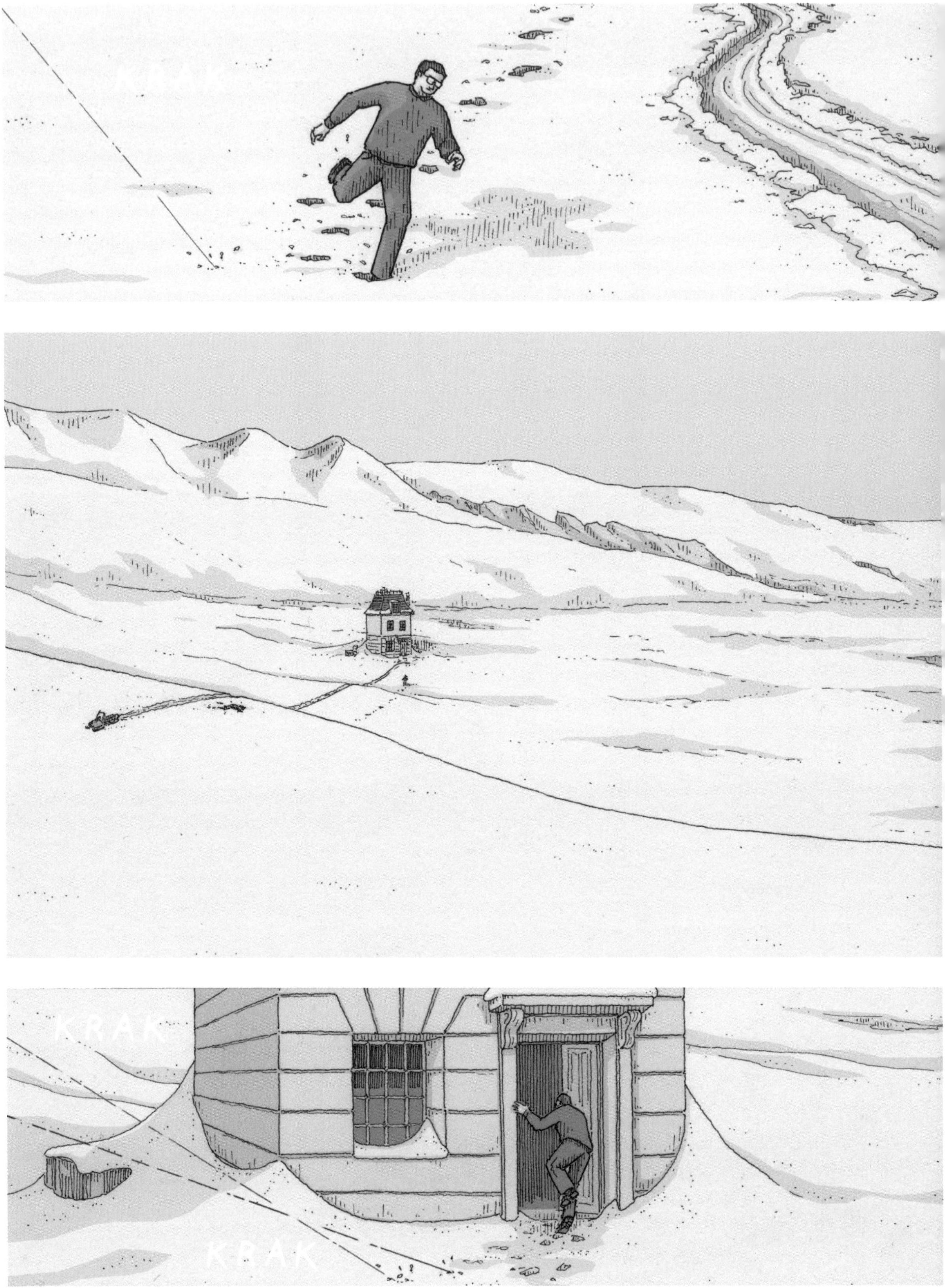
KRAK
KRAK
KRAK

SHHHCK

I'm going to need
more than faith now....

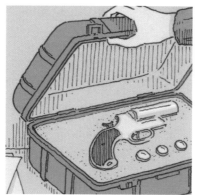

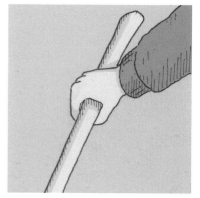

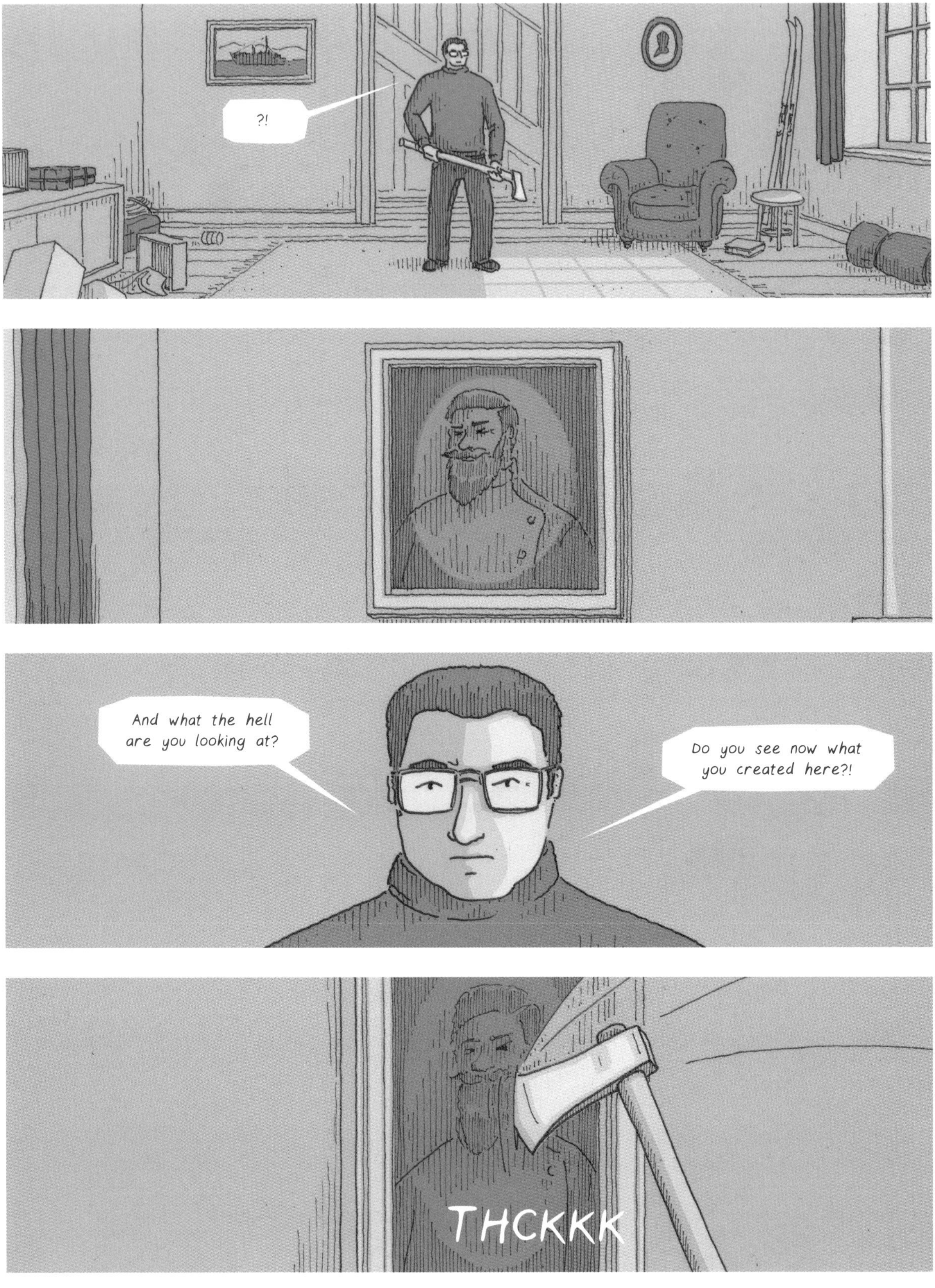
?!
And what the hell are you looking at?
Do you see now what you created here?!
THCKKK

THCK-CHINK
Wait...
Dear God, no...

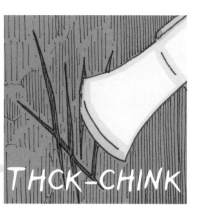

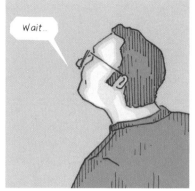

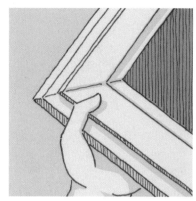

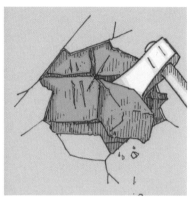

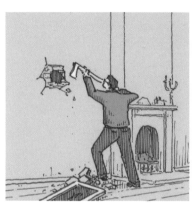

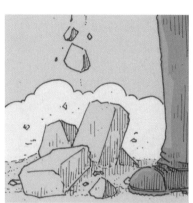

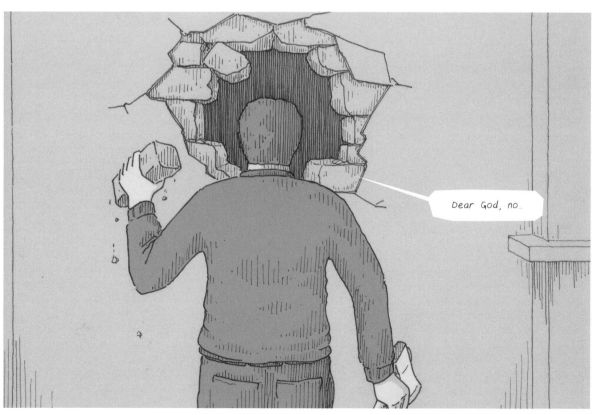

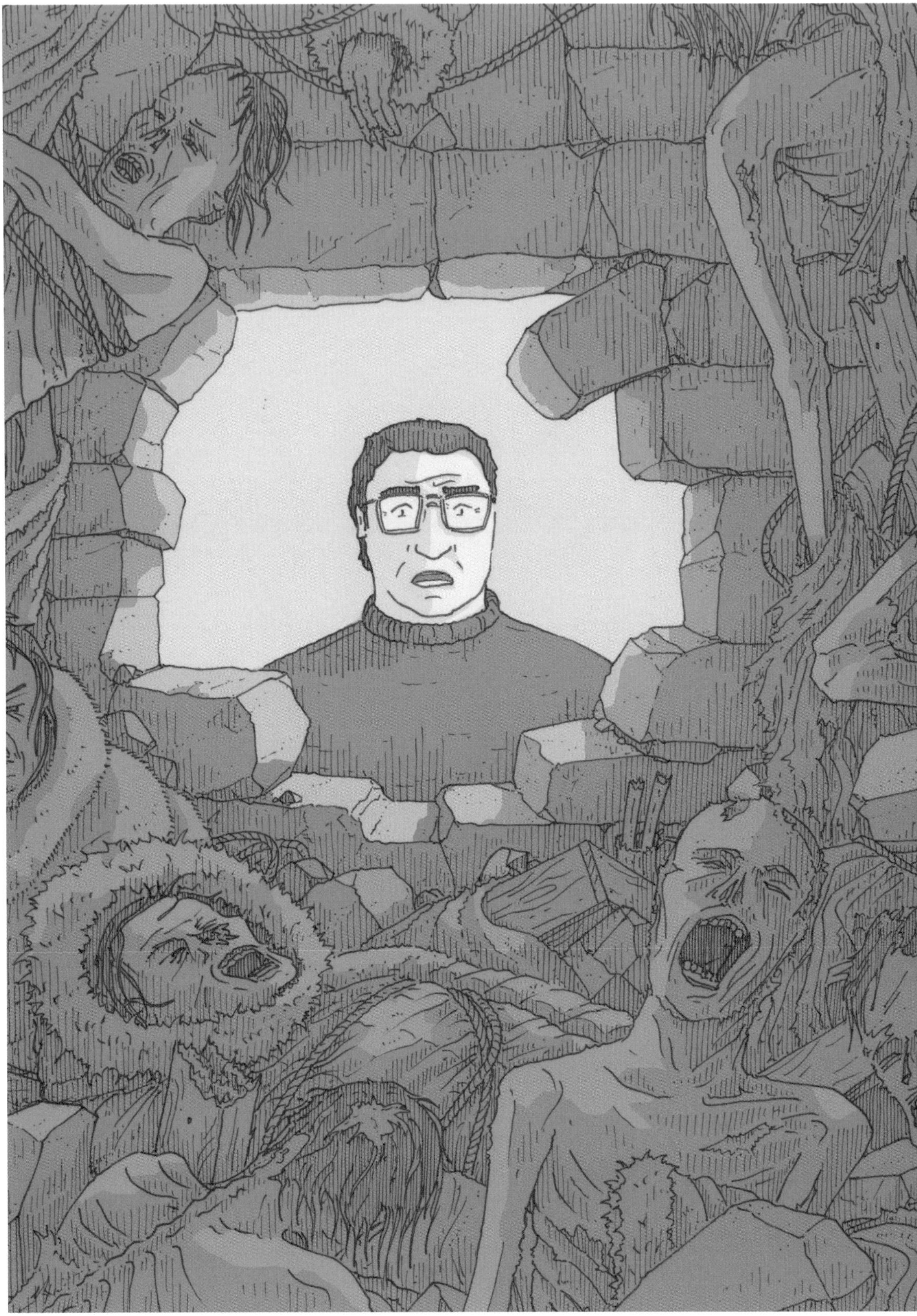

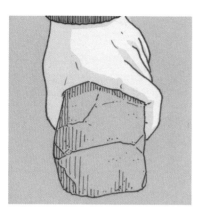 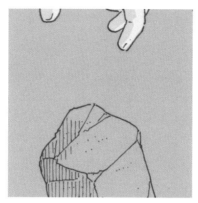 

CLNNK

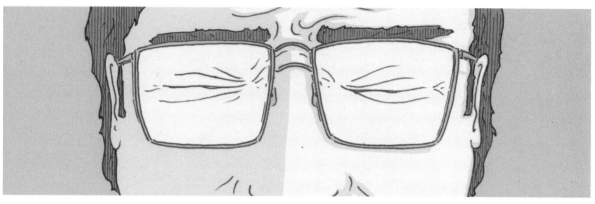

They must be..EVERYWHERE.
What have we done
to this place?

This needs to end now.

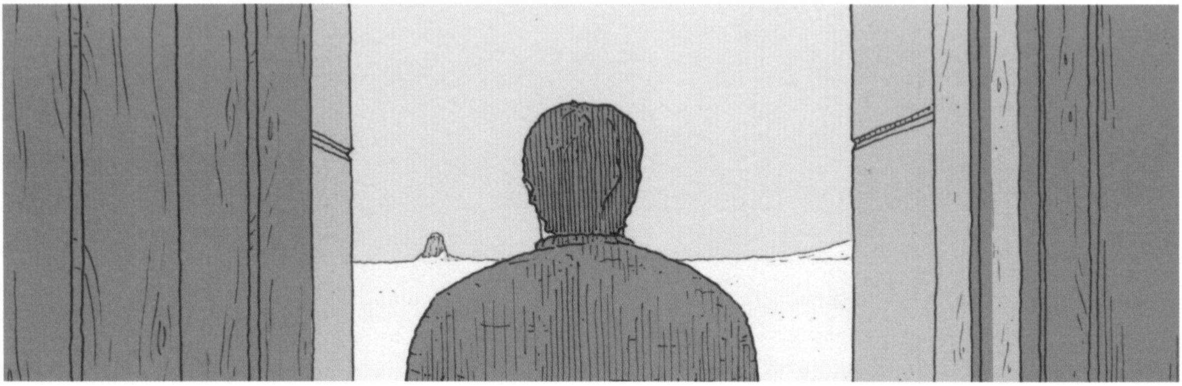

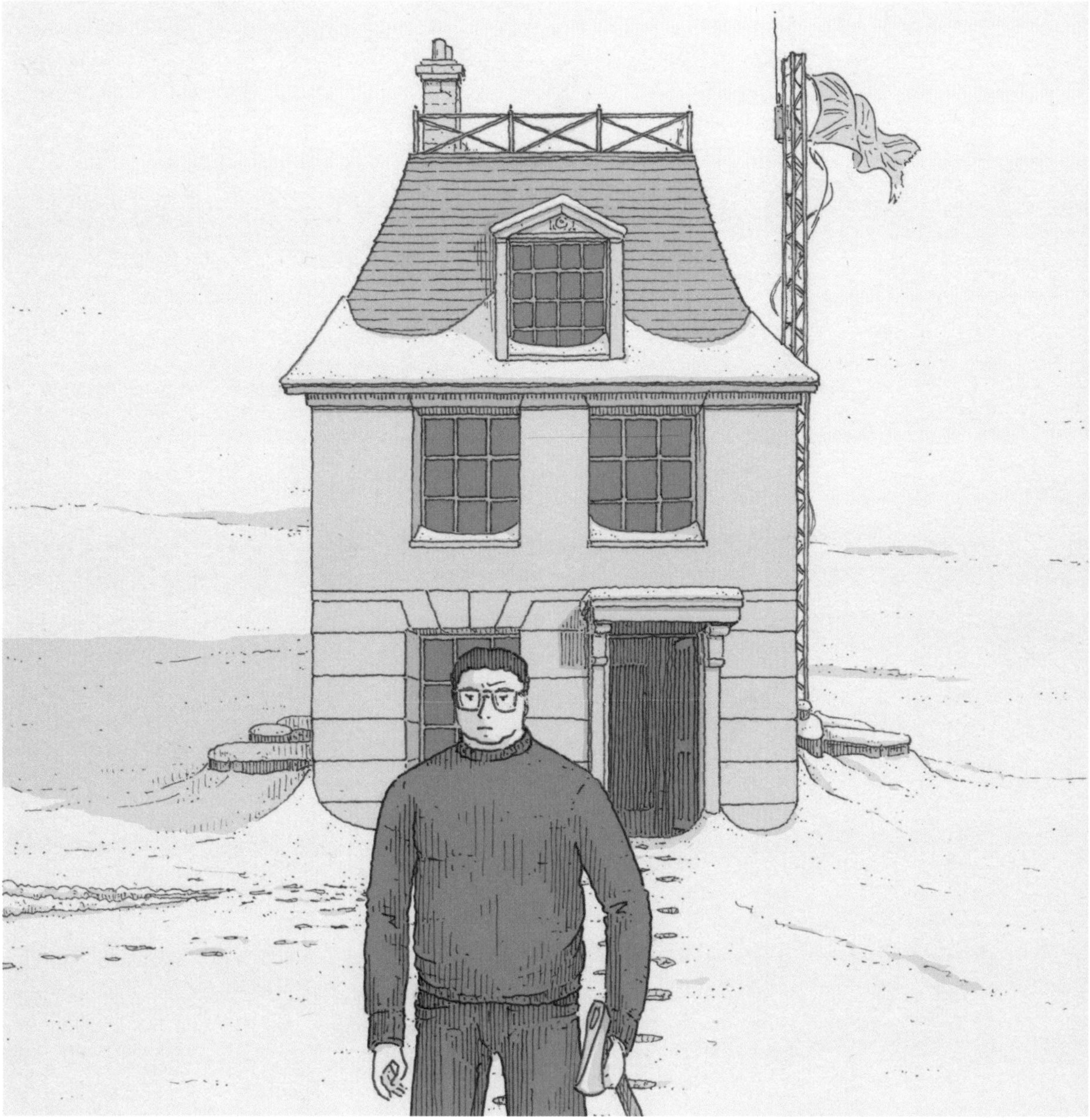

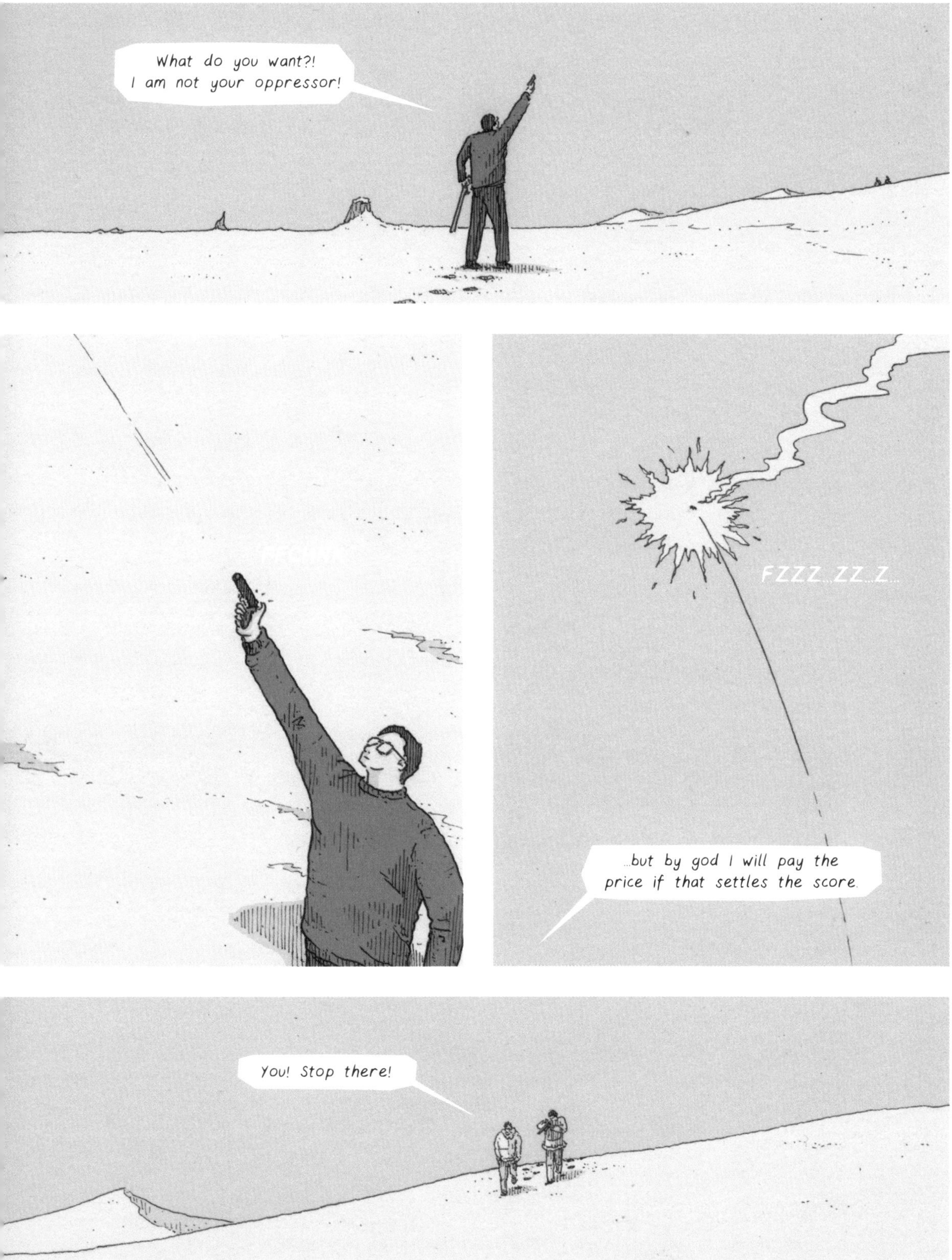
What do you want?! I am not your oppressor!
FZZZ...ZZ...Z...
...but by god I will pay the price if that settles the score.
You! Stop there!

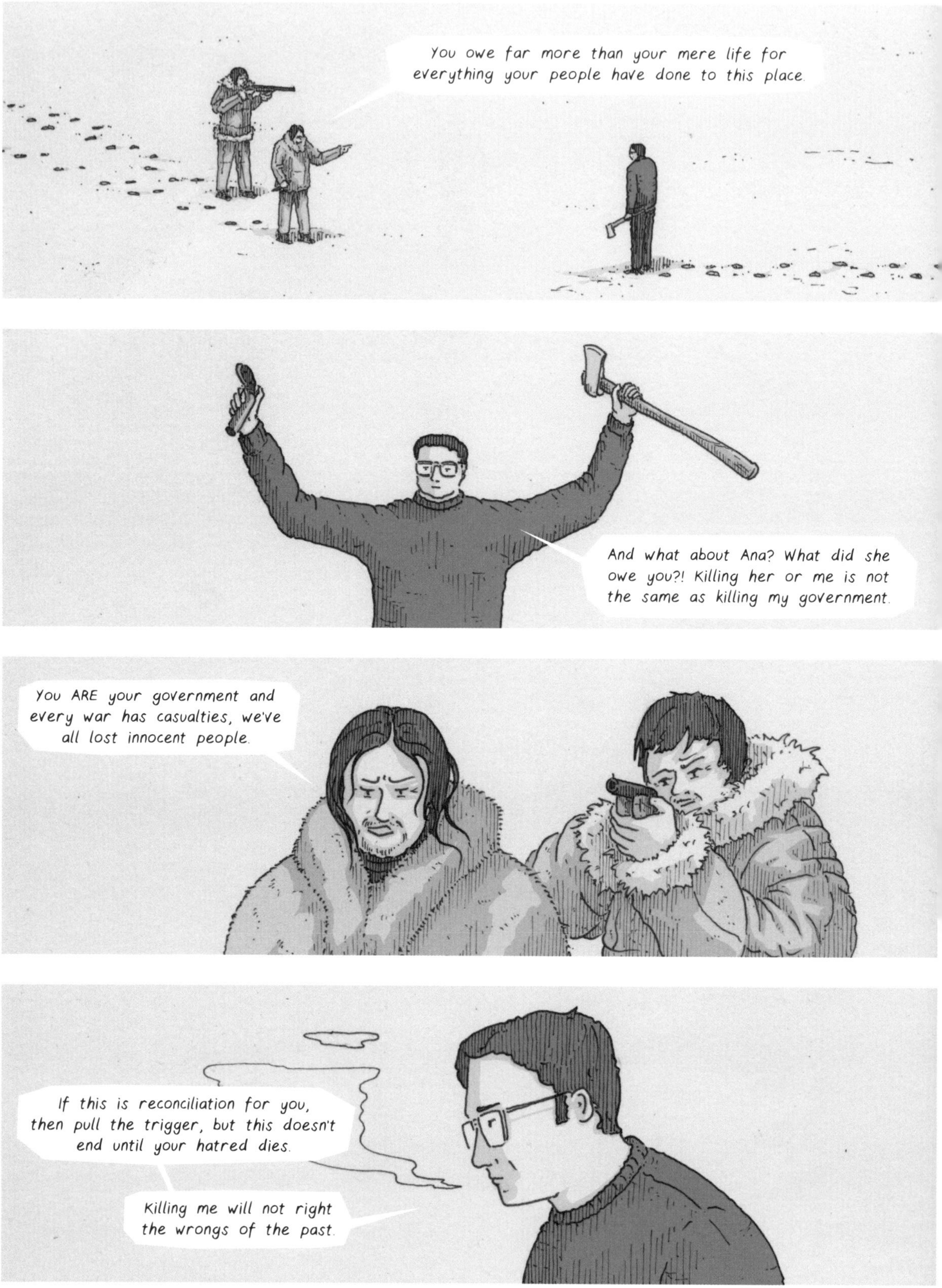
You owe far more than your mere life for everything your people have done to this place.
And what about Ana? What did she owe you?! Killing her or me is not the same as killing my government.
You ARE your government and every war has casualties, we've all lost innocent people.
If this is reconciliation for you, then pull the trigger, but this doesn't end until your hatred dies.
Killing me will not right the wrongs of the past.

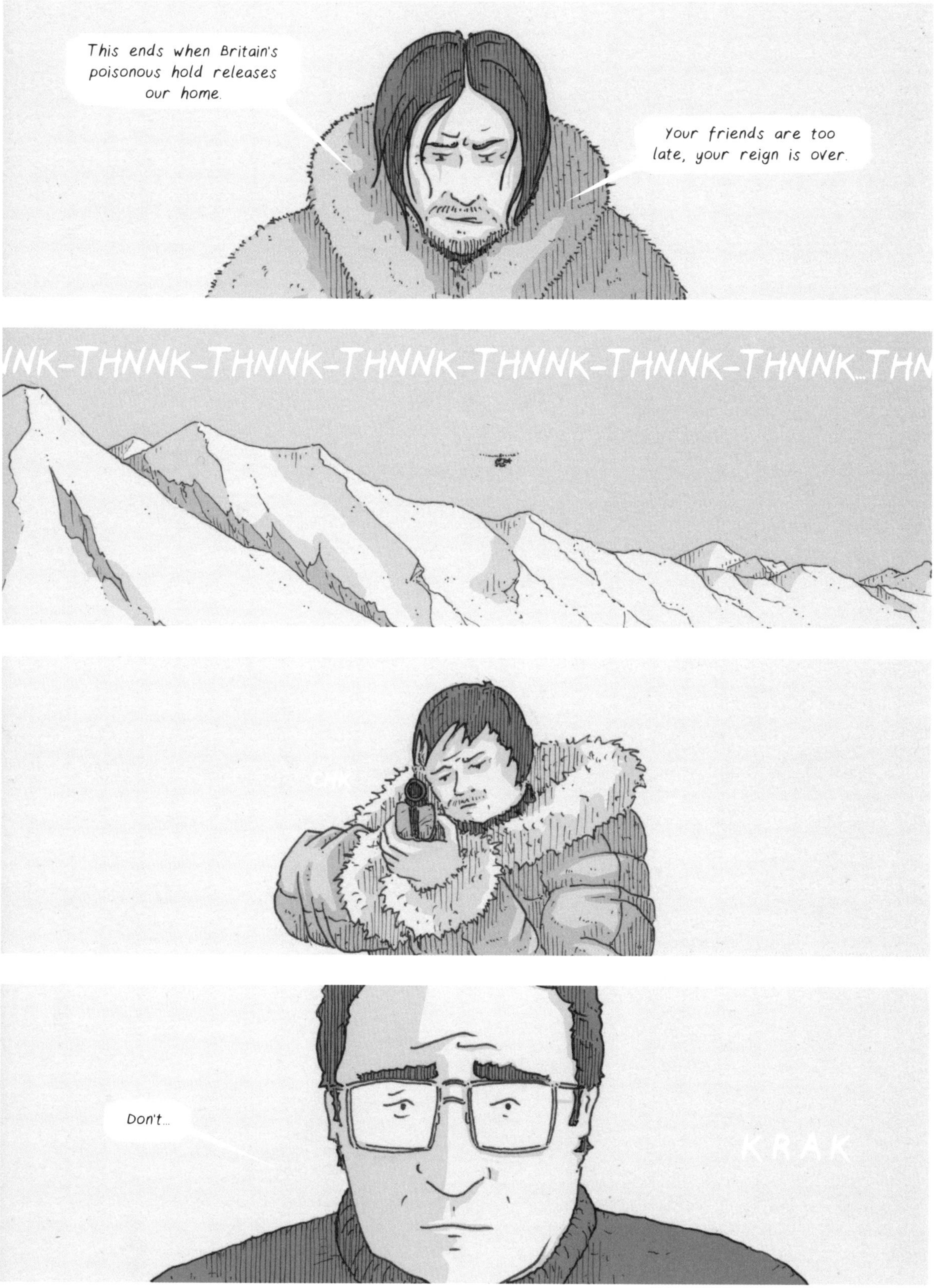
This ends when Britain's poisonous hold releases our home.
Your friends are too late, your reign is over.
NK-THNNK-THNNK-THNNK-THNNK-THNNK-THNNK...THN
Don't...
KRAK

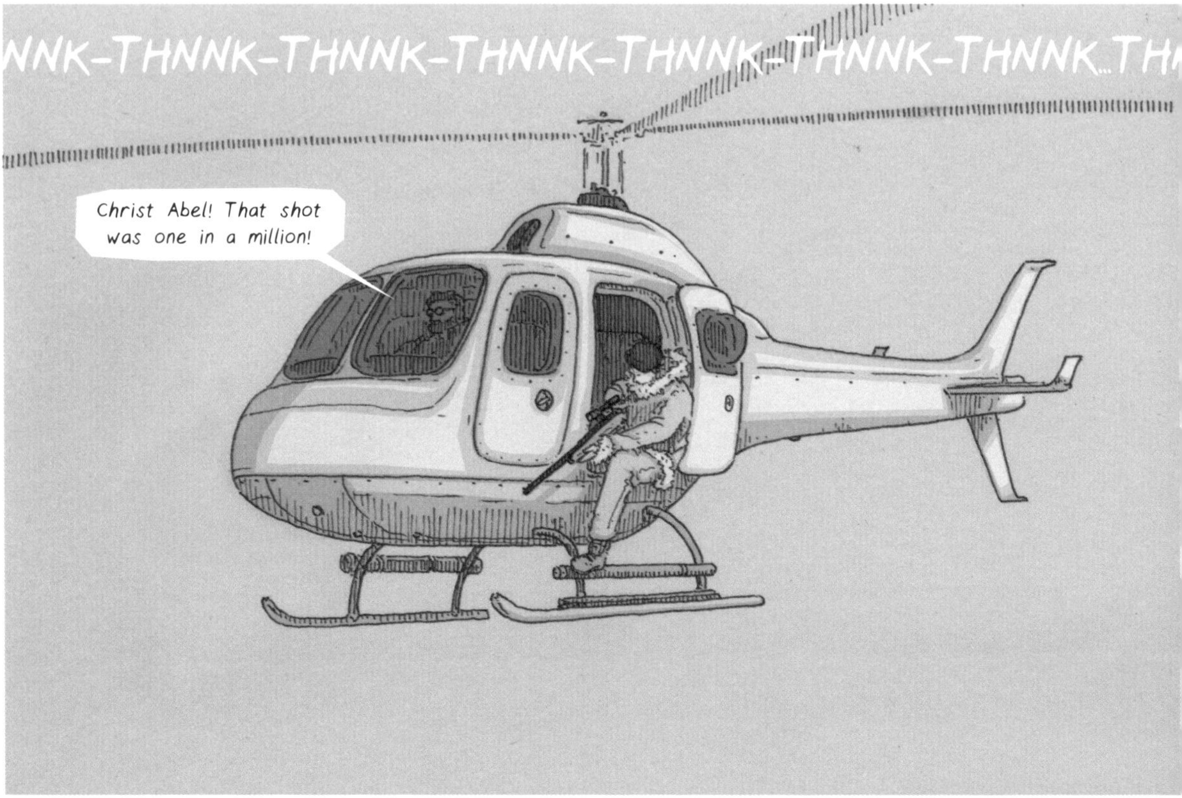
NNK-THNNK-THNNK-THNNK-THNNK-THNNK-THNNK...TH
Christ Abel! That shot was one in a million!

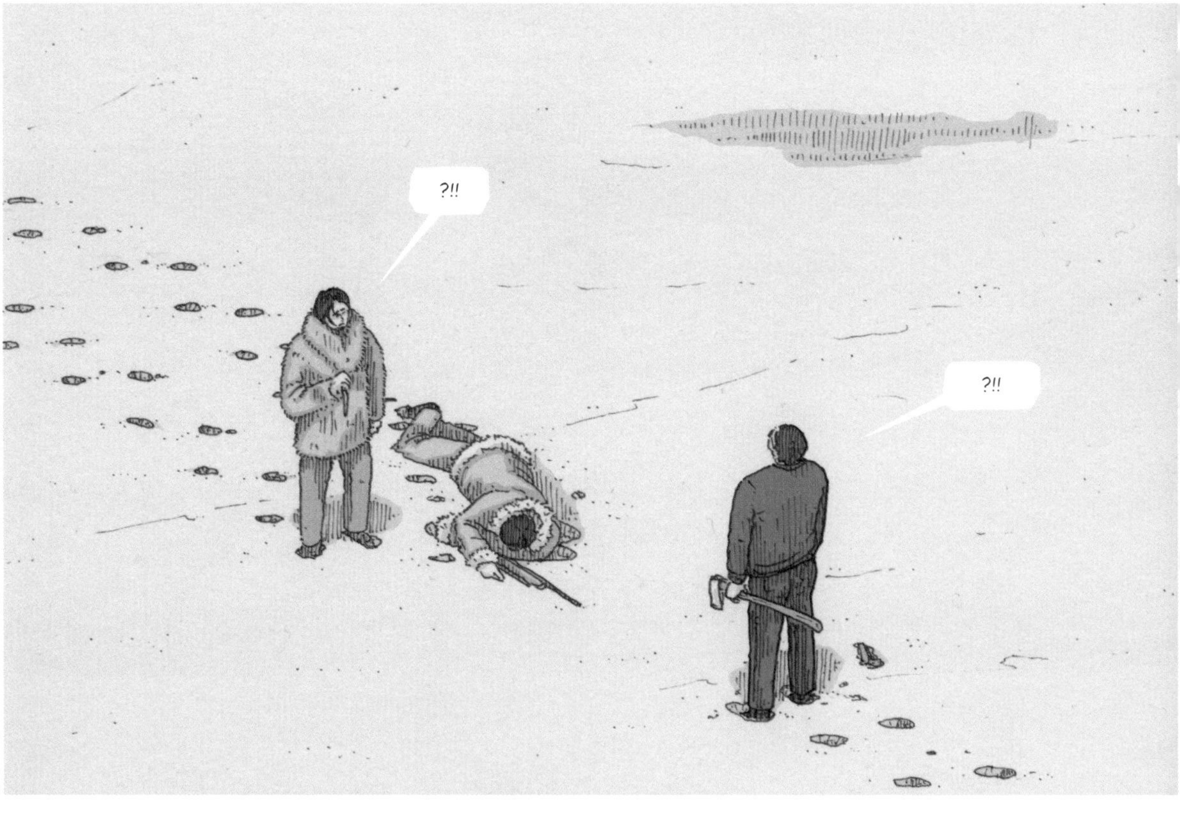
?!!
?!!

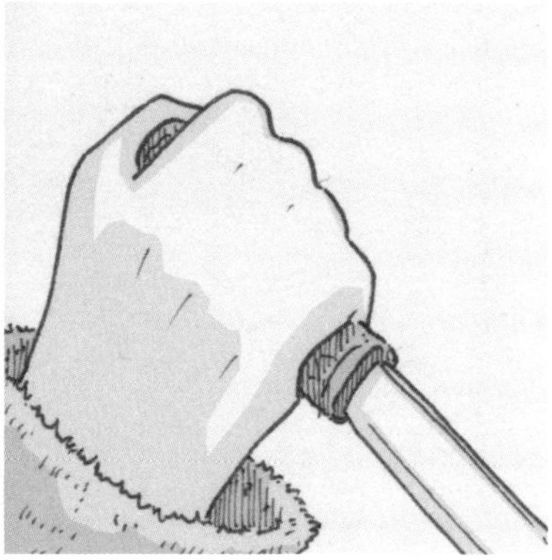

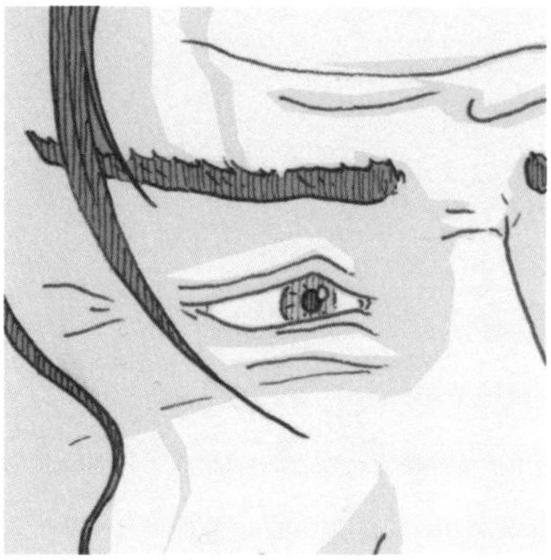

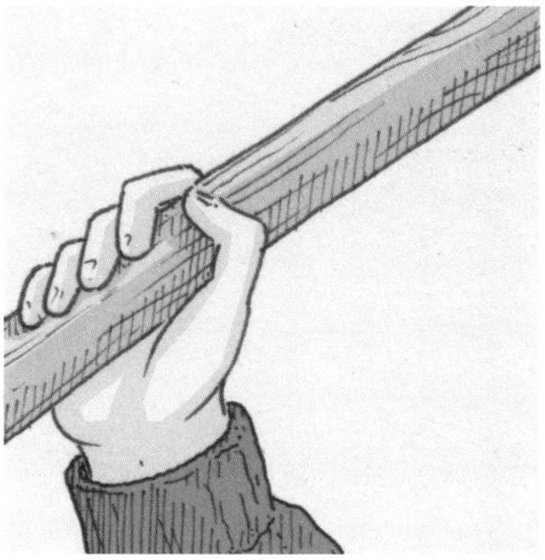

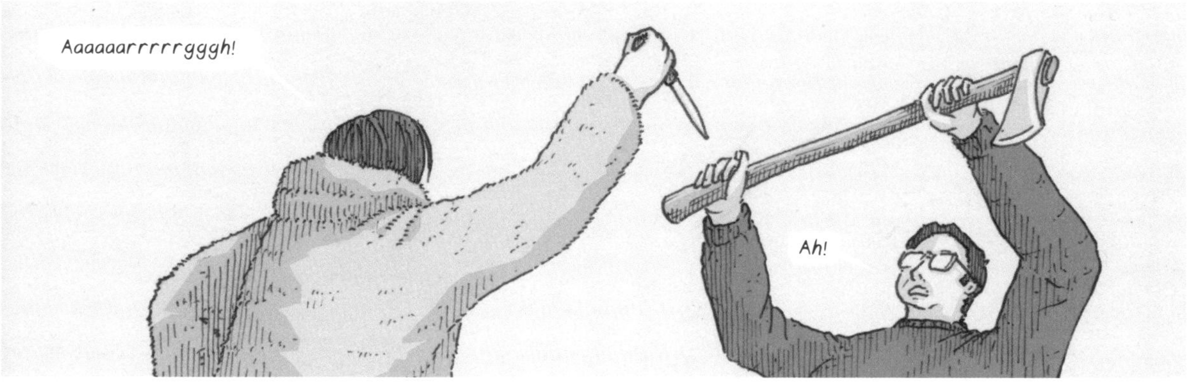
Aaaaaarrrrrgggh!
Ah!

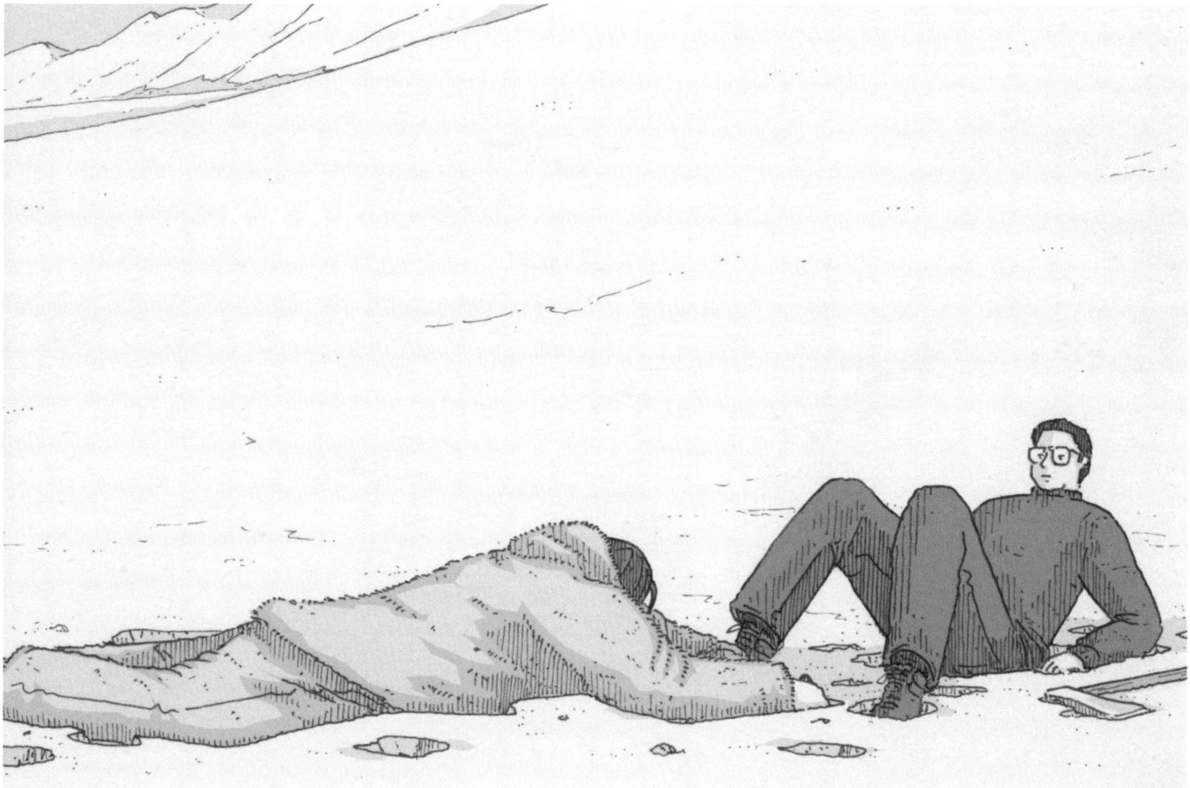

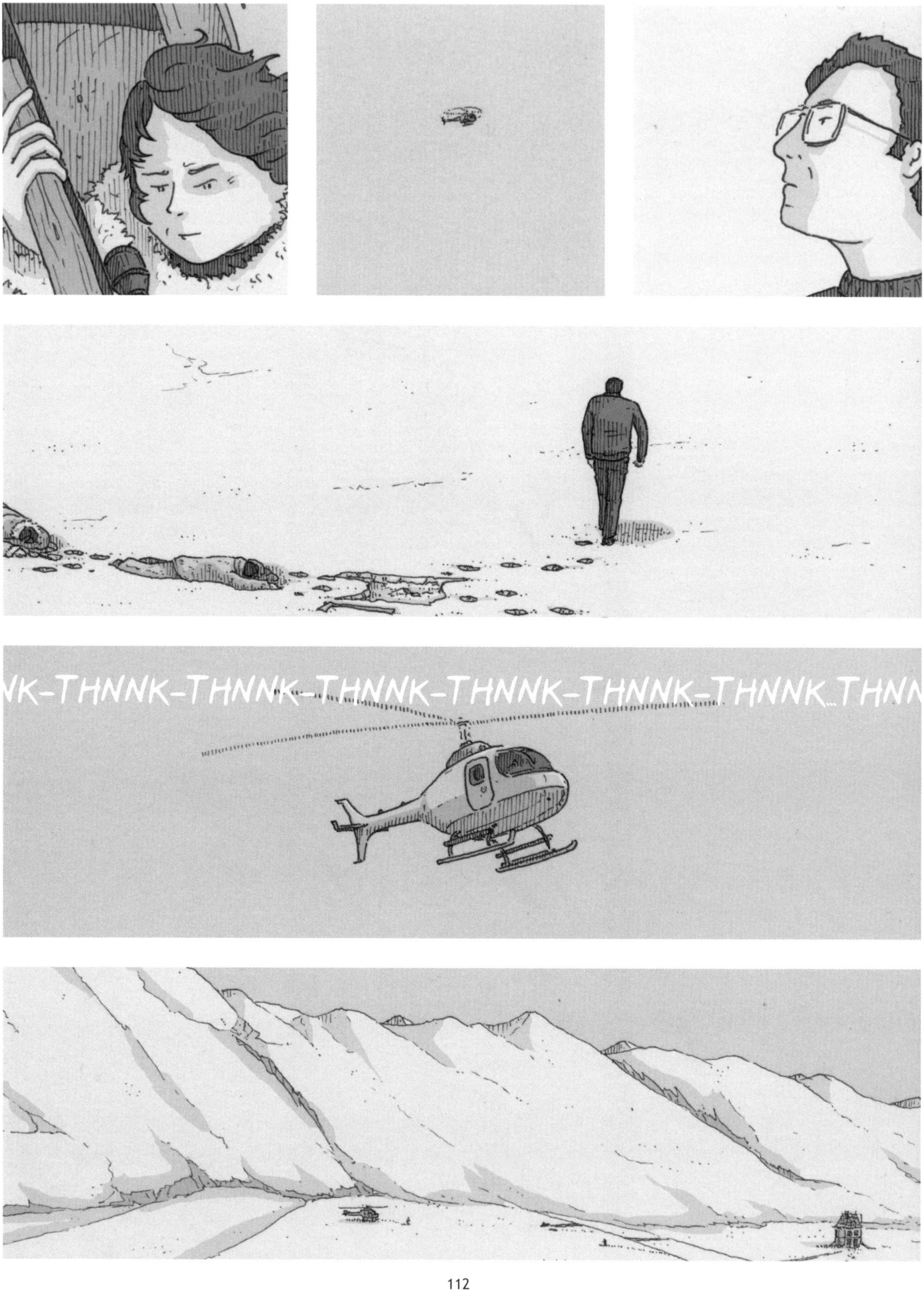
NK-THNNK-THNNK-THNNK-THNNK-THNNK…THNN

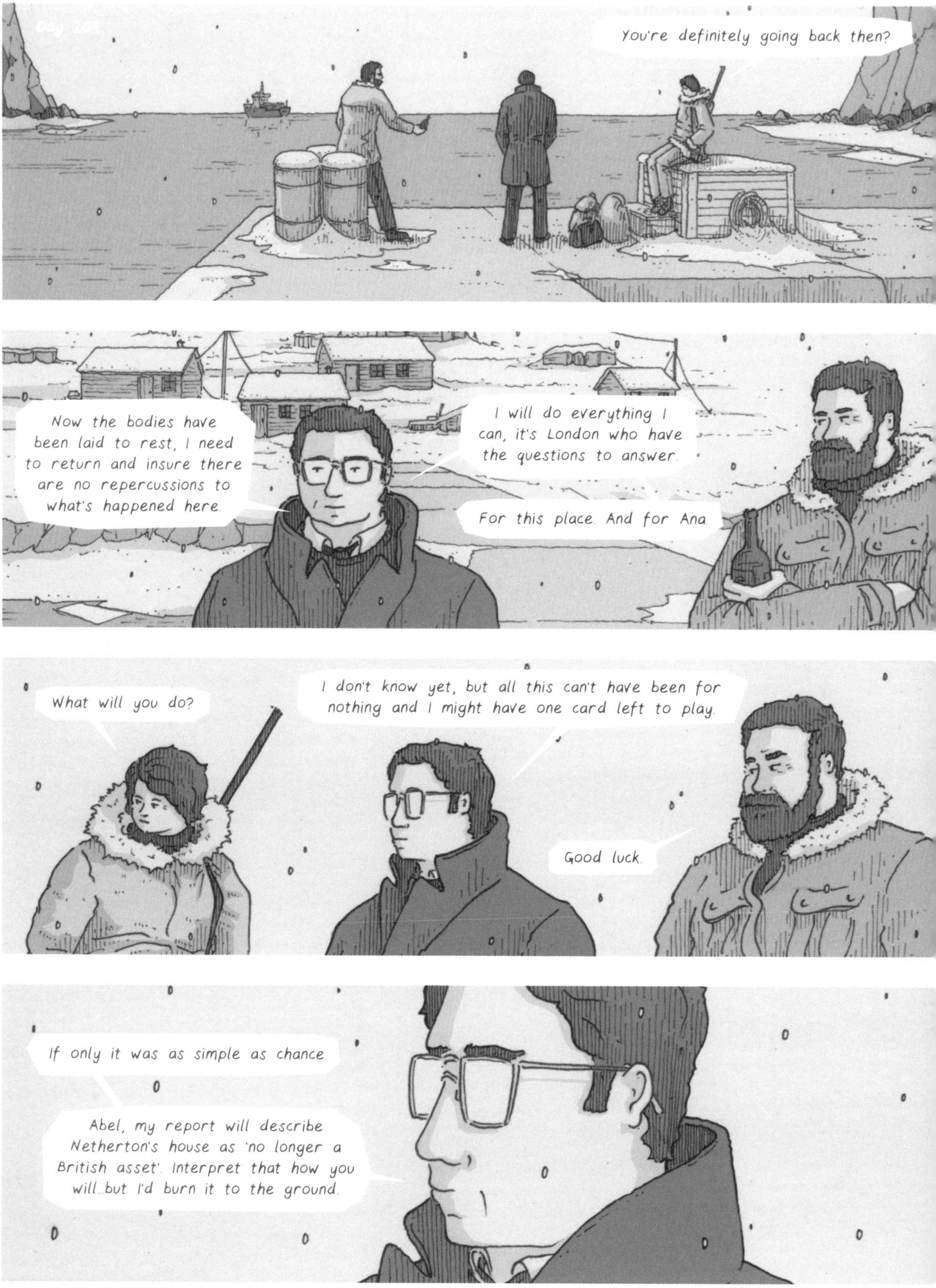

You're definitely going back then?
Now the bodies have been laid to rest, I need to return and insure there are no repercussions to what's happened here.
I will do everything I can, it's London who have the questions to answer.
For this place. And for Ana.
What will you do?
I don't know yet, but all this can't have been for nothing and I might have one card left to play.
Good luck.
If only it was as simple as chance.
Abel, my report will describe Netherton's house as 'no longer a British asset'. Interpret that how you will...but I'd burn it to the ground.

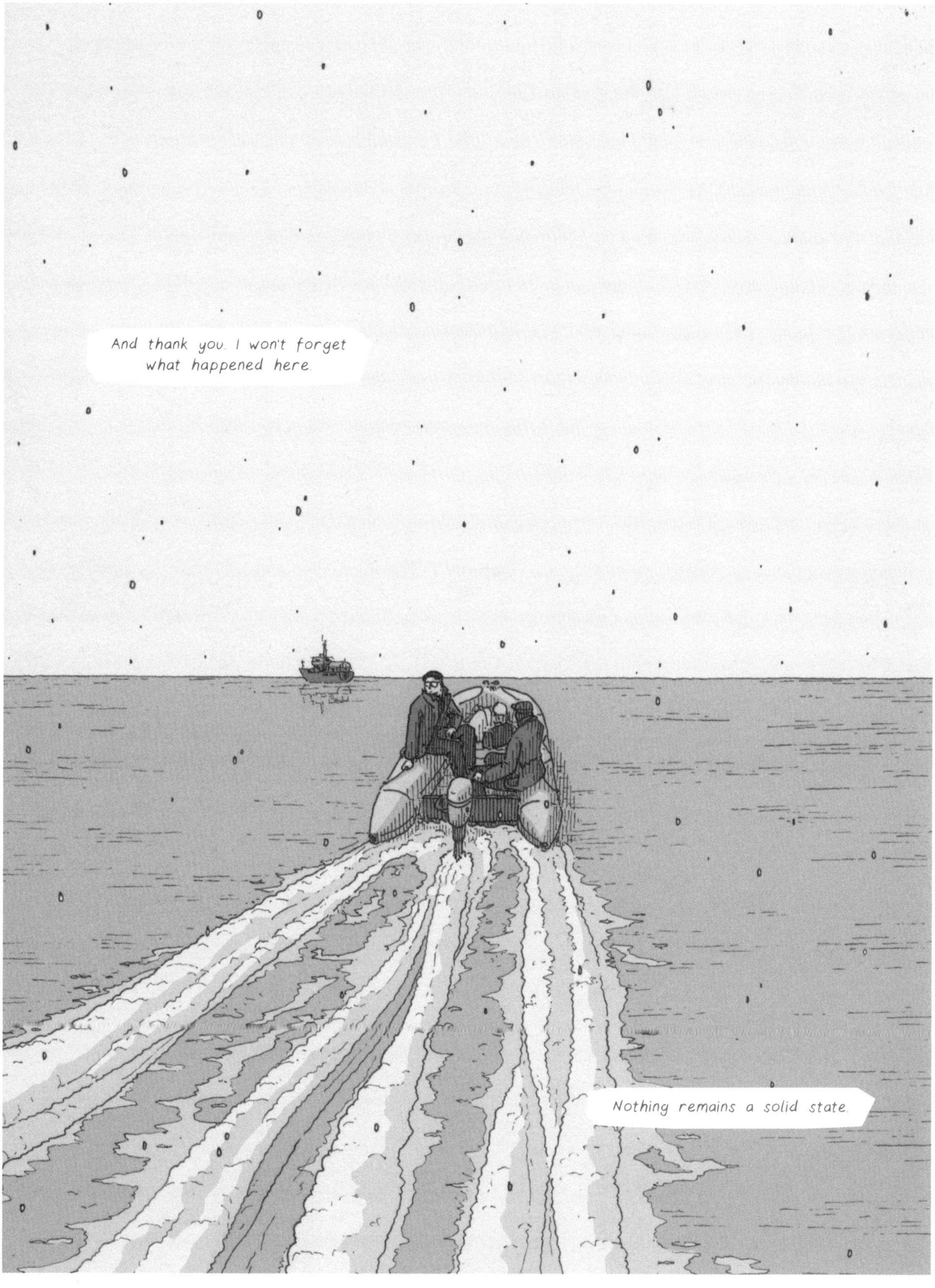
And thank you. I won't forget what happened here.
Nothing remains a solid state.

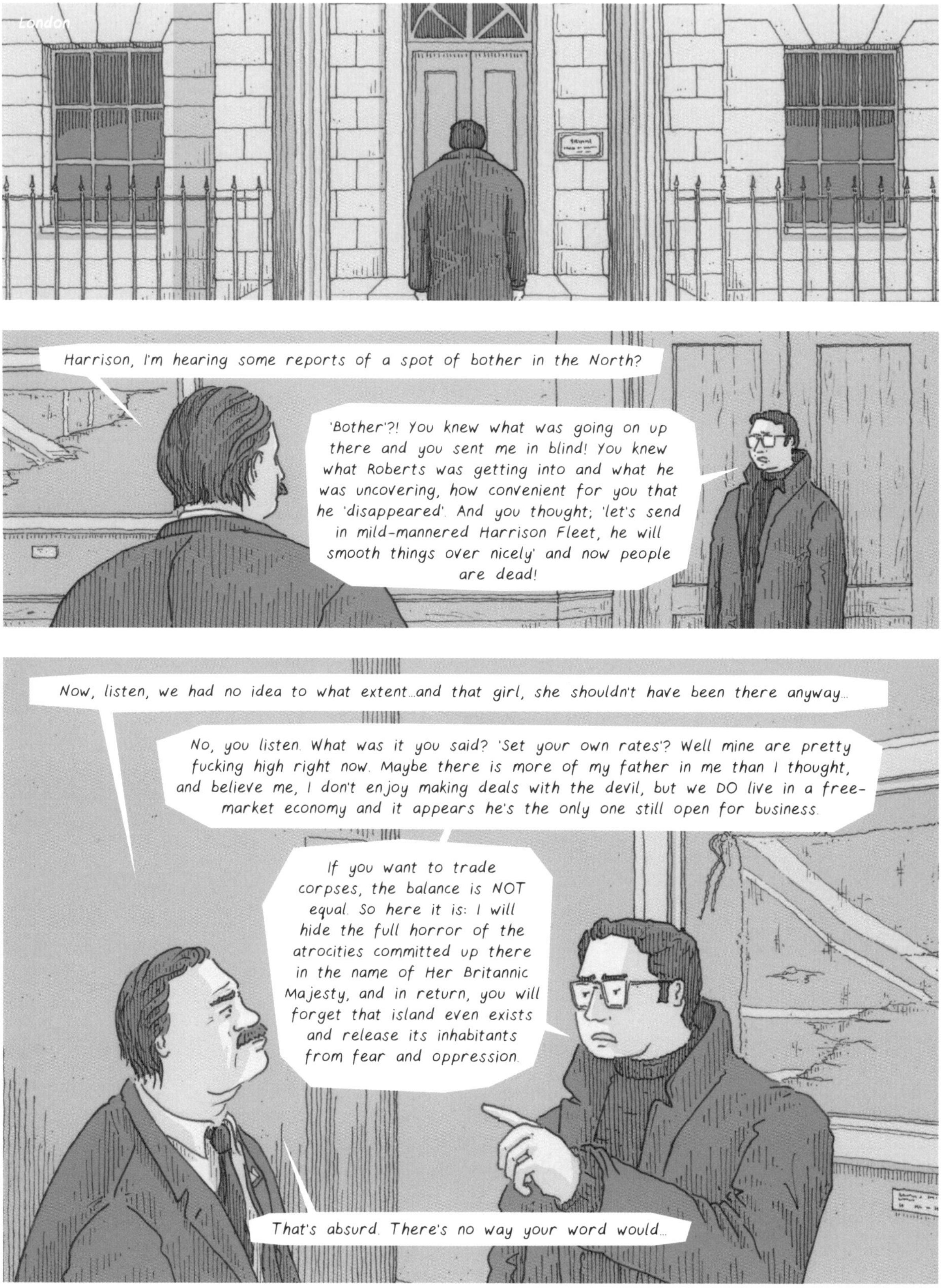
London
Harrison, I'm hearing some reports of a spot of bother in the North?
'Bother'?! You knew what was going on up there and you sent me in blind! You knew what Roberts was getting into and what he was uncovering, how convenient for you that he 'disappeared'. And you thought; 'let's send in mild-mannered Harrison Fleet, he will smooth things over nicely' and now people are dead!
Now, listen, we had no idea to what extent...and that girl, she shouldn't have been there anyway...
No, you listen. What was it you said? 'Set your own rates'? Well mine are pretty fucking high right now. Maybe there is more of my father in me than I thought, and believe me, I don't enjoy making deals with the devil, but we DO live in a free-market economy and it appears he's the only one still open for business.
If you want to trade corpses, the balance is NOT equal. So here it is: I will hide the full horror of the atrocities committed up there in the name of Her Britannic Majesty, and in return, you will forget that island even exists and release its inhabitants from fear and oppression.
That's absurd. There's no way your word would...

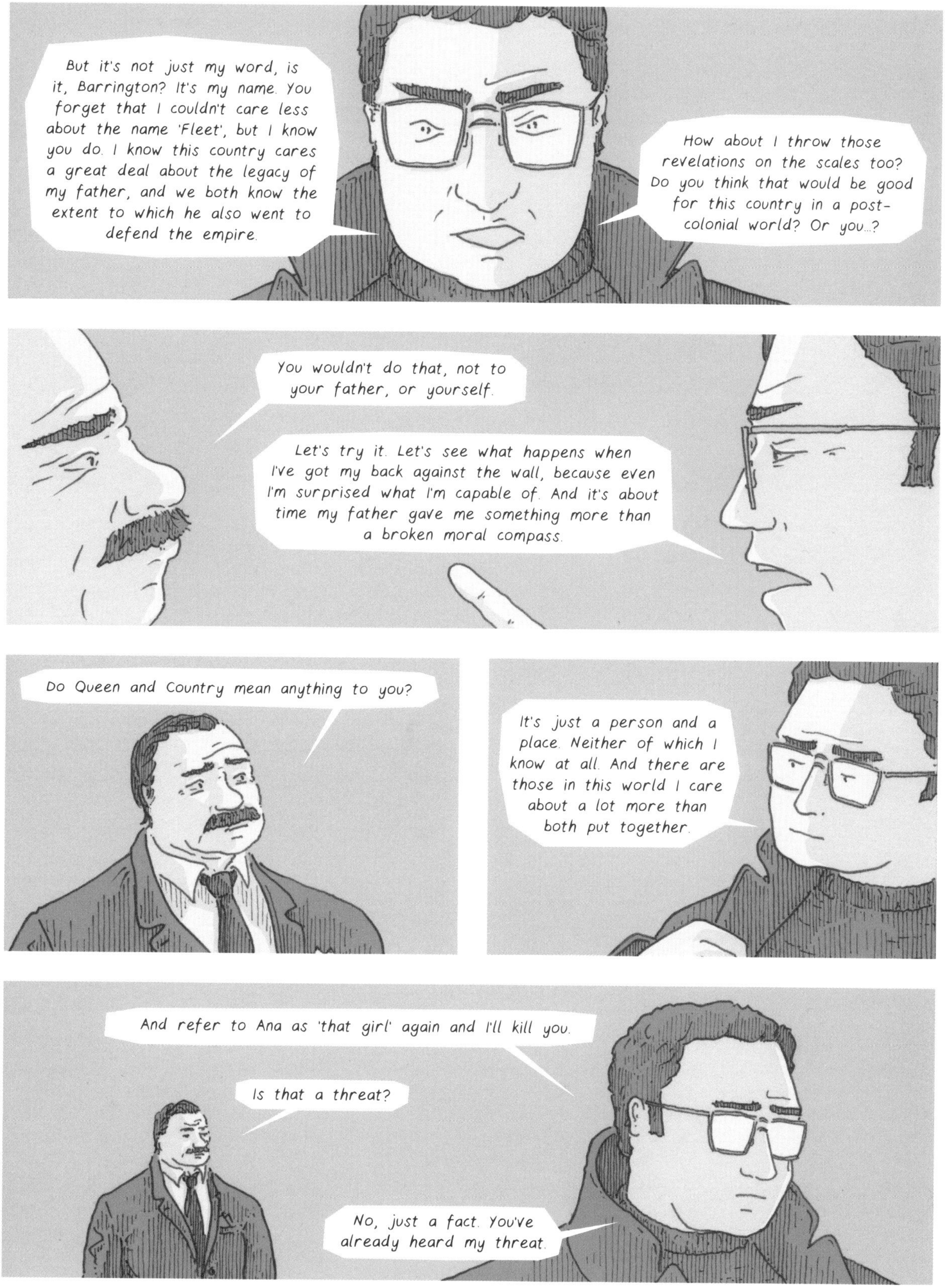
But it's not just my word, is it, Barrington? It's my name. You forget that I couldn't care less about the name 'Fleet', but I know you do. I know this country cares a great deal about the legacy of my father, and we both know the extent to which he also went to defend the empire.
How about I throw those revelations on the scales too? Do you think that would be good for this country in a post-colonial world? Or you...?
You wouldn't do that, not to your father, or yourself.
Let's try it. Let's see what happens when I've got my back against the wall, because even I'm surprised what I'm capable of. And it's about time my father gave me something more than a broken moral compass.
Do Queen and Country mean anything to you?
It's just a person and a place. Neither of which I know at all. And there are those in this world I care about a lot more than both put together.
And refer to Ana as 'that girl' again and I'll kill you.
Is that a threat?
No, just a fact. You've already heard my threat.

EPILOGUE

DESTINATIONS

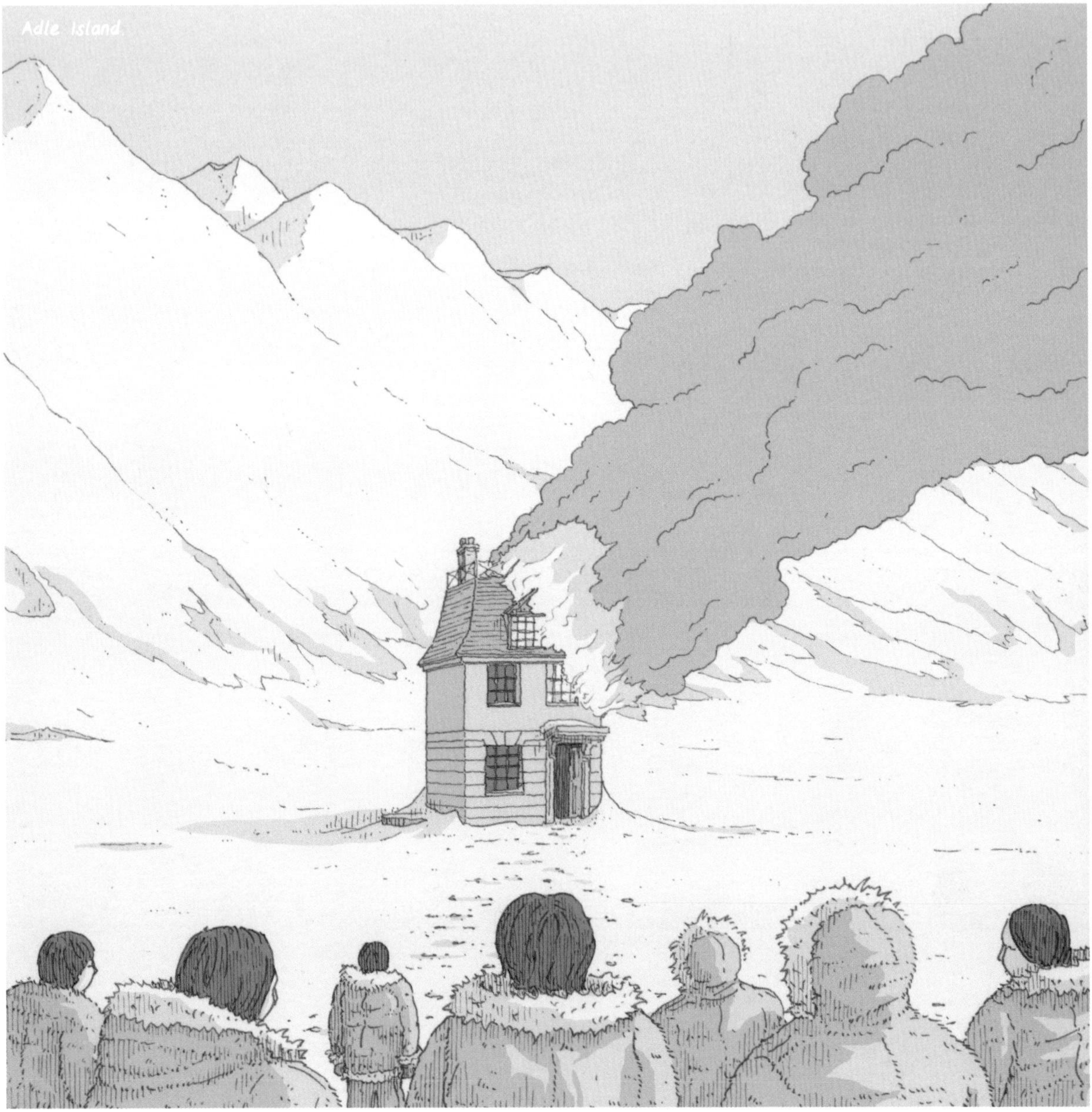
Adle Island.

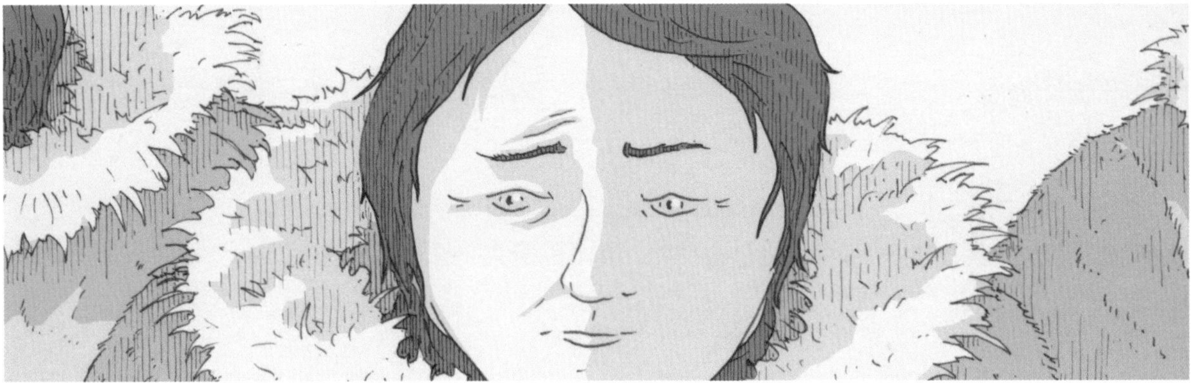

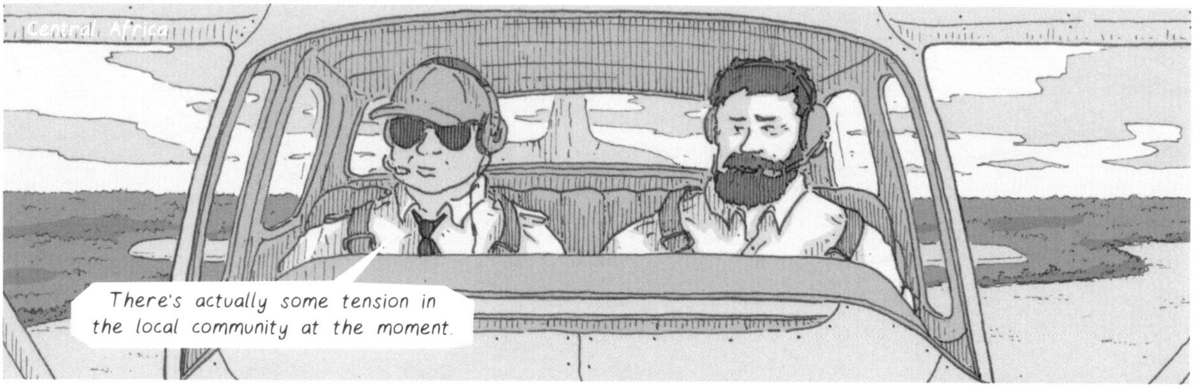
Central Africa
There's actually some tension in the local community at the moment.
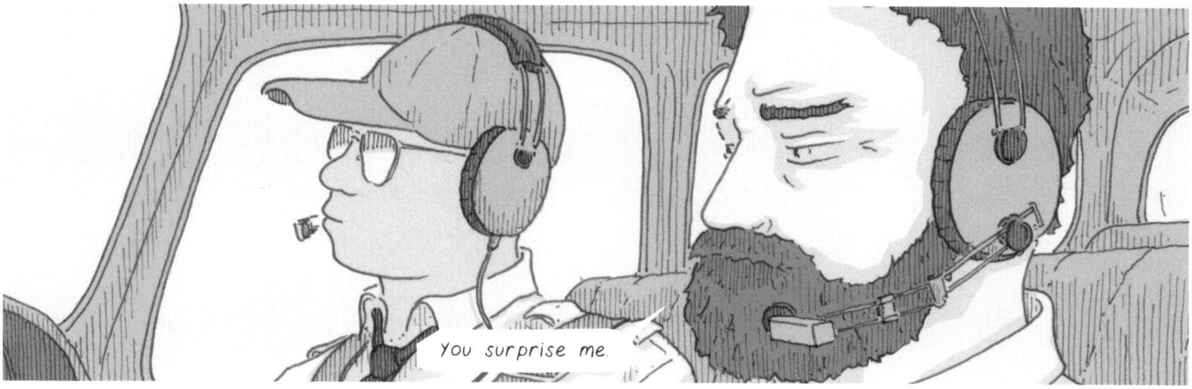
You surprise me.
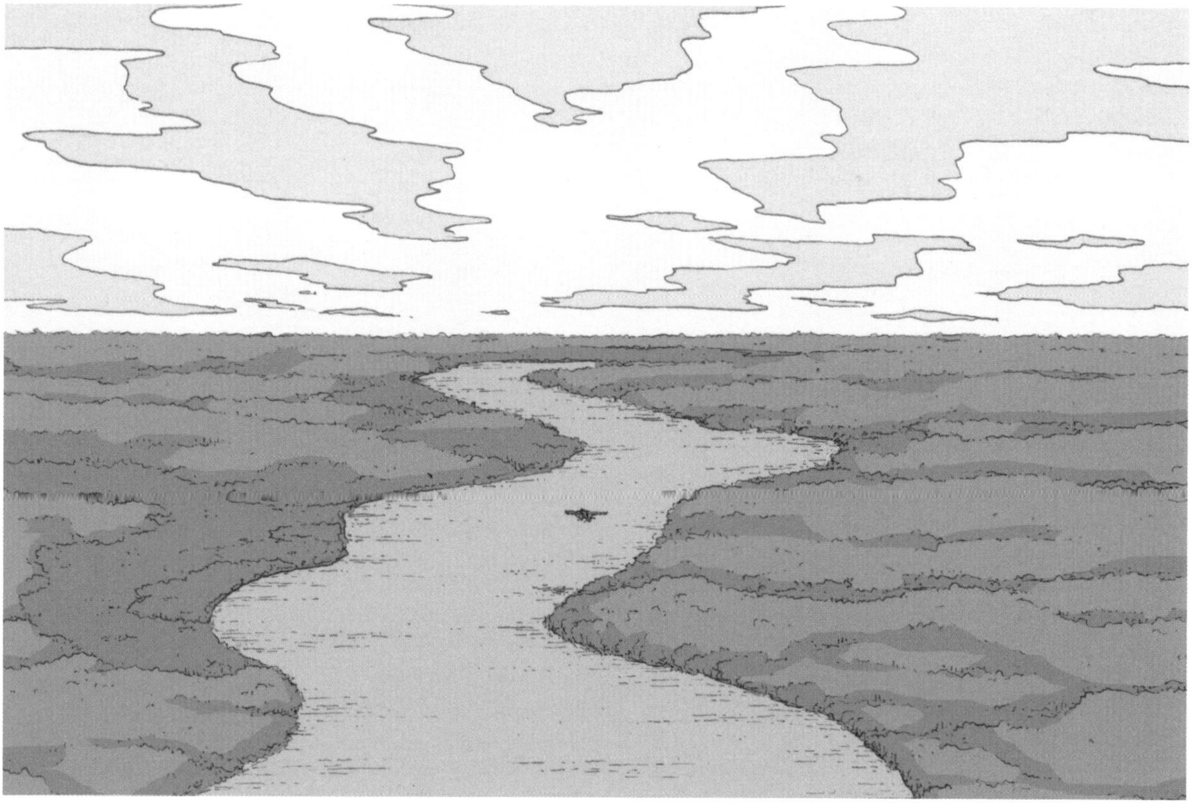

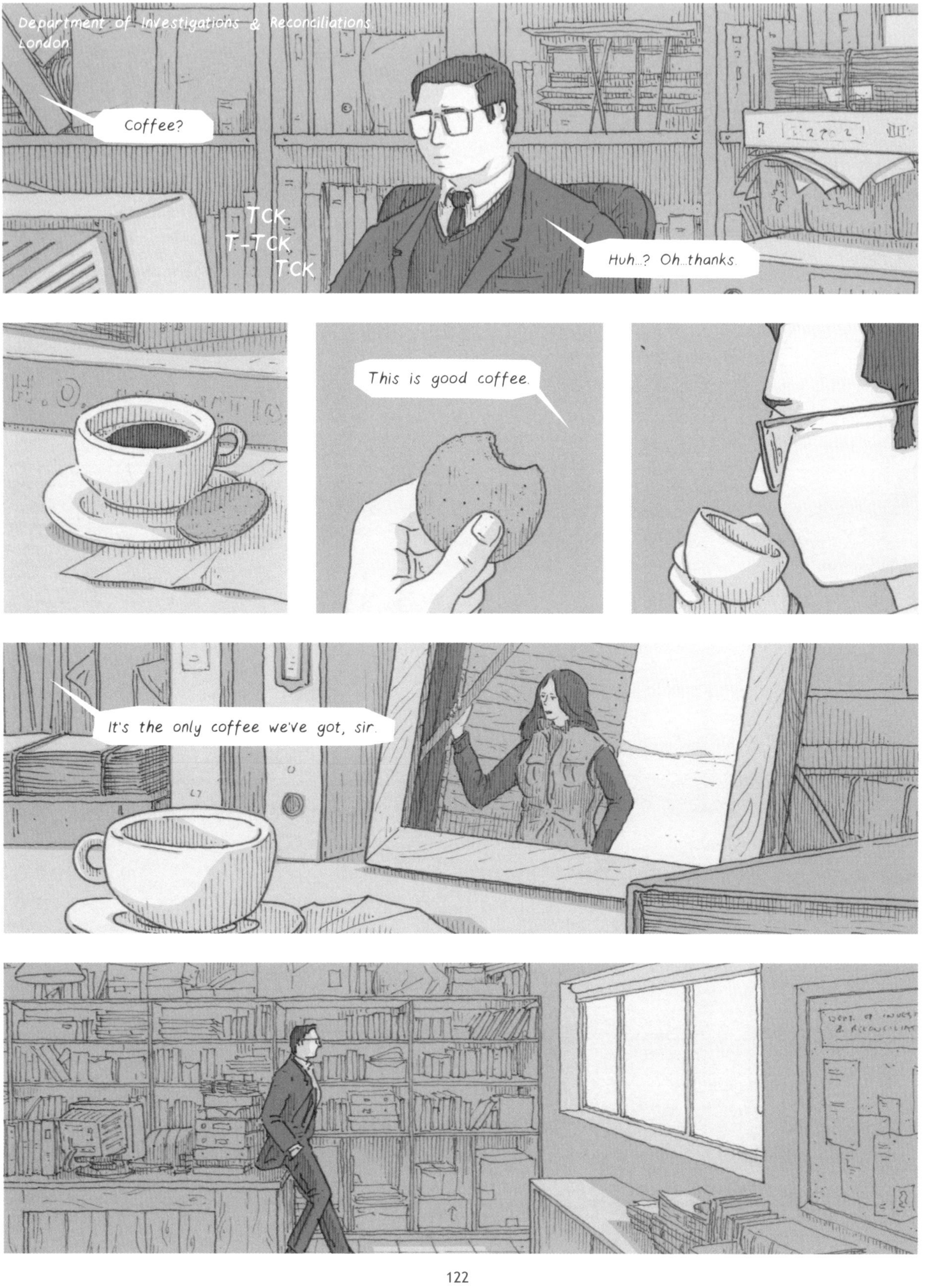
Department of Investigations & Reconciliations.
London.
Coffee?
TCK
T-TCK
TCK
Huh...? Oh...thanks.
This is good coffee.
It's the only coffee we've got, sir.

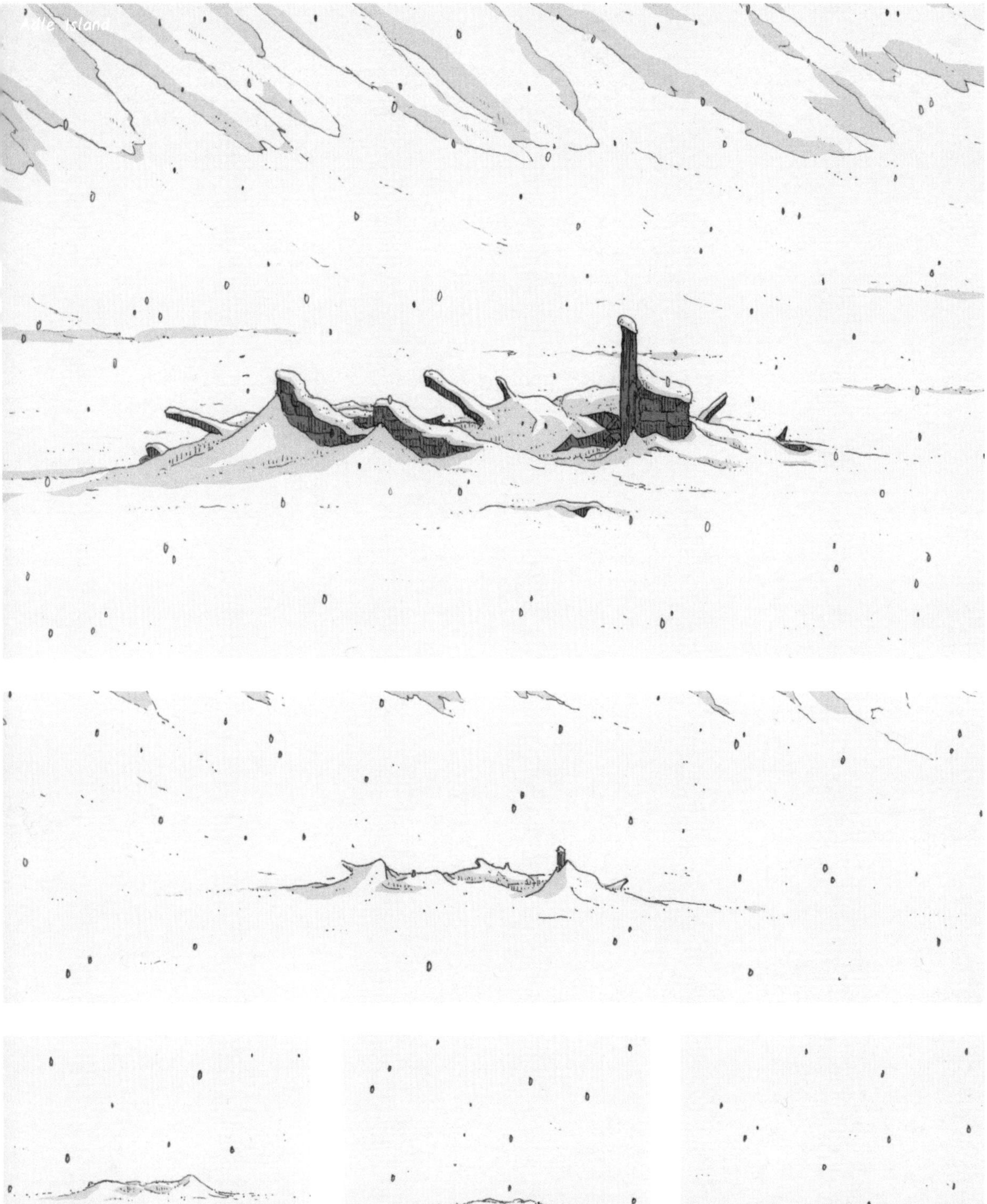
Adle Island

LEGACY

In subsequent years, Britain eventually gifted the island to Canada, due in part to increasing societal pressures and campaigning by Harrison Fleet. However, the deal brokered also included that in exchange for the island, Britain would have favourable, permitted shipping rights in the very likely event of the northwest passage becoming navigable due to global climate change.

In more recent times, Canada's increased activity in the Arctic in pursuit of minerals and other resources has brought the island and its surrounding area into question once again and increasingly, the public eye.

The island's inhabitants officially remain British Citizens, although those who have attempted to exercise their rights as such, and move to Britain, have been stalled by bureaucracy, leaving them currently nationless.

A portrait of Sir Johnathan Fleet was quietly removed from the halls of the Old Royal Naval College in Greenwich. Officially this was for restoration, but there are no plans to reinstate it. Similarly, a statue of Captain Netherton was taken down from a central London square and relocated to the church gardens of the small Oxfordshire village in which he was born.

From there, his crumbling limestone face looks out upon the fields in which he played as a child, taking his first footsteps in the world.

AUTHOR'S NOTE

———————————————

British Ice is set in an imagined British Overseas Territory, inhabited by a fictional indigenous community. There are currently fourteen British Overseas Territories, and they have been described as the 'remnants of empire', existing by virtue of the fact they have something to offer, be that political, economic or scientific.

They have often been locations of controversy; used on one hand as black spots and tax havens, and the sites of conservation and exploration on the other. Over 250,000 British citizens live in these remote outposts and wars have been fought to protect British interests there.

The discovery of mineral wealth in the Canadian Arctic, combined with the increased accessibility due to global climate change, means that remote communities and fragile ecosystems are currently under more pressure than ever before and their future remains uncertain.

———————————————

Despite the occurrence of similar and relevant events, none of what you have read in British Ice ever happened.

AUTHOR'S THANKS

This book exists thanks to the help & patience of:

Lizzy Stewart & Jack McInroy.

With the support of:

*Kate Batchelor, Hannah Berry, Lando,
Anne-Laure Mercier, Ricky Miller, Andy Poyadgi,
Steven Walsh, David White & my family.*

AUTHOR

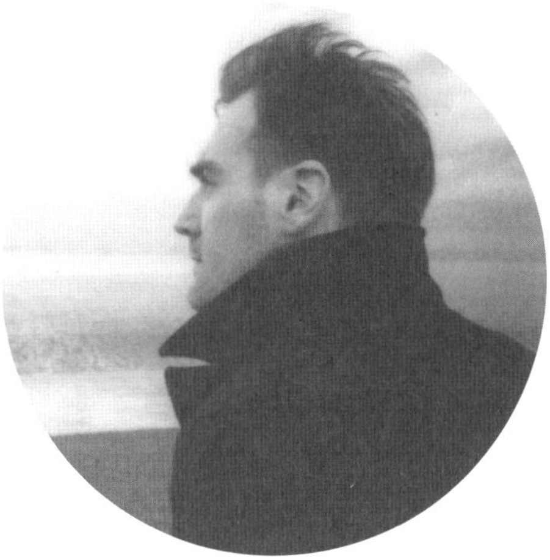

OWEN D. POMERY

Comics creator & architectural illustrator.

*His main interest is in narrative space and he lives
in South London with one eye on the horizon.*

www.owenpomery.com

Author photo by Lizzy Stewart